THE GALACTIC EXPEDITION

DAVID A. JOSEPH

Book Two – *Echoes of the Forgotten War*

Table of Contents

A Note from the Author

In the aftermath of first contact, the crew of the *Odyssey* must navigate the fine line between awe and vigilance. The Caraliens have awakened—but so too have the shadows of a long-buried war.

Where Book One explored discovery and wonder, this volume explores trust, diplomacy, and the price of survival. Old enemies stir, alliances take shape, and the weight of ancient choices returns to haunt the future.

The journey continues—not just through space, but through history, memory, and the fragile hope that peace can prevail where war once ruled.

— DAVID JOSEPH

Chapter 1 – Sleeping Beauty

A soft, low-frequency sound wave rippled through the air, emanating from the five stasis pods in the lab. The air around the crew compressed and decompressed, creating an odd sensation that sent ripples through the atmosphere. Captain Zulu, Shepard, and the rest of the crew inside the quarantine-sealed lab felt the pressure building up.

Ninil and Ishtar exchanged a glance, their expressions tense. Ninil finally broke the silence. "Can you feel that?"

Zulu's helmet display flashed with warning signals as he responded. "Yeah, my suit's picking up an irregular anomaly." His voice was calm, but the tightness in his jaw betrayed his discomfort. He looked over at Shepard, whose suit was also showing signs of the anomaly, though the commander's face remained focused, his eyes closed, trying to withstand the intense sensation.

Both men stood their ground, maintaining their composure despite the rising pressure. But the rest of the crew wasn't as fortunate. One by one, Tashia, James, and their team began to collapse, their heavy mechanical armour suits thudding onto the ground. Distorted ripples in the air shimmered around them, overwhelming their senses and pulling them into unconsciousness.

Aria instantly detected the anomaly and sprang into action, her voice cutting sharply through the comms. "Captain, there's a rapid atmospheric shift inside the lab. I'm recalibrating the pressure to compensate, but it's having no effect."

The transparent metal windows of the sealed chamber started to vibrate, trembling with faint ripples that grew in distorted wavy patterns, stronger with each passing second. Outside the quarantine room, the remaining science crew scrambled to alert the medical team, who rushed to prepare for emergency response. Silence pressed down over them, like a held breath, everyone on edge as they waited for the environment to stabilise.

Amid the chaos, Ninil and Ishtar remained unaffected. Ninil, her expression unreadable, walked calmly toward Princess Odriin's stasis pod. She placed her hands on the pod, tracing the surface until several control symbols emerged from the pod's smooth exterior. Without hesitation, she began realigning them.

Shepard, still reeling from the pressure, opened one eye just enough to see Ninil working on the pod. "What... is she doing?"

Captain Zulu barely managed a nod toward Ninil. "I hope.... fixing this."

Ishtar, who had been standing quietly at the edge of the room, made her move. Despite her earlier vow not to interfere in human affairs, she stepped forward. Without exchanging a word with Ninil, Ishtar mirrored her movements, realigning the symbols on the opposite side of Princess Odriin's pod. The symbols on both sides began to glow softly, syncing with the other four pods.

Suddenly, the pressure inside the room ceased. The atmosphere felt normal again, the vibrating windows stilled, and the atmosphere stabilised. Aria's voice came over the comms, her tone steady but with an edge of confusion. "Atmospheric pressure is back to normal. But I couldn't make the adjustment. Something else… external, intervened."

Tashia, groaning as she regained consciousness, looked around at her fellow scientists, who were also stirring.

"What.... what just happened?"

Doctor James rubbed his helmet, blinking rapidly as he tried to gather his bearings. "I felt like my skull was being crushed. What the hell was that?"

Captain Zulu, his breathing now back to normal, opened his eyes and exhaled. "Good question. Doctor?"

Shepard stretched his neck, shaking off the tension. "Same here. What on Mars just hit us?"

Ninil, stepping back from Princess Odriin's pod, calmly addressed the crew. "I believe what you all just experienced was a defence mechanism triggered by the pods. When they began to open, they released a wave of energy to scan the environment, likely to determine if it was safe for them to fully open. That energy is part of their exotic matter technology."

Aria chimed in; her tone thoughtful. "That makes sense. I detected the energy signature, but I couldn't compensate for it. It wasn't like anything we've encountered before."

Ishtar, still standing near the Princess's pod, nodded slowly. "The Caral species has come a long way since we last interacted with them. Their mastery over exotic matter has evolved significantly. Even in this heavily shielded lab, I can feel traces of that energy all around us."

Tashia, now back on her feet, raised an eyebrow. "Exotic matter? Are you saying this technology goes beyond anything we can understand?"

Ishtar turned to face her, her gaze serious. "Yes. Three hundred thousand cycles ago, we helped guide their species when they first began experimenting with exotic matter. They were on the verge of a catastrophe that would have fractured their reality, and we intervened. Since then, they've advanced beyond what even we could have predicted."

"Three hundred millennia?" James muttered, incredulous. "And they're still around?"

Ninil nodded, her expression unreadable. "Their civilisation survived, but it's clear they've continued to evolve in ways even we didn't anticipate. Their language, their technology, it's more complex now, but there are still echoes of what they were."

Captain Zulu folded his arms, listening intently. "So, what

do we do now? If these pods are scanning us, does that mean they're going to open?"

Ninil glanced at the pods, then back at Zulu. "I am not sure, Captain. I believe the energy scan was a preliminary check. The symbols we aligned on the Princess's pod connected her stasis system to the other four. But full activation may take time."

Ishtar continued, "Captain, these symbols are almost identical to the ones they used long ago. We've aligned them to form a phrase that means 'Together we are one.' The stasis pods are interconnected, like parts of a puzzle. They rely on each other to function correctly. I believe, if even one is missing or incomplete, the others won't fully activate."

Shepard, still standing near the pods, shook his head. "That's comforting," he said dryly. "So, we're basically sitting on a ticking bomb that may or may not open up depending on how happy these things are with their surroundings?"

Tashia shot him a look. "I don't think that's quite how it works, Shepard."

"Maybe not," Shepard replied, "but it sure feels like it."

Captain Zulu exhaled slowly, weighing their options. "Alright. We've stabilised the situation for now, but we can't afford to be complacent. Ninil, and Ishtar, I want you both to monitor these pods closely. Aria, keep analysing the data and see if you can predict when the next phase of activation might occur."

Ninil nodded. "We will, Captain. But be prepared, if these pods are linked to the Princess's ship, we may need to return there sooner than we thought."

James, who had been studying the pods from a distance, glanced at Zulu. "And what if something happens before then? If that energy wave hits again, we might not be so lucky next time."

Zulu met his gaze, his expression firm. "That's why we'll be ready. We don't leave anything to chance."

As the crew slowly recovered from the incident, the tension in the air didn't dissipate. The pods, glowing softly in the dim light of the lab, held their secrets close. Whatever lay inside them, it was clear that the crew of the Odyssey was only beginning to understand the magnitude of what they had discovered.

Shepard, ever the pragmatist, broke the silence. "Well, Captain, I guess the real question is, what happens when these things finally wake up?"

Zulu didn't answer immediately. He turned, staring at the pulsating pods, their soft hum filling the air. "We'll find out soon enough, Commander," he said quietly. "And whatever happens, we'll be ready."

A day had passed since the stasis pod incident, and the crew aboard the Odyssey was still processing what had transpired. Captain Zulu, Commander Shepard, Professor Tashia, Doctor James, and their respective teams had taken a much-needed break, retreating to their quarters for rest. Only a skeleton crew of scientists, along with Ninil and Ishtar, remained to monitor the situation in the heavily shielded laboratory.

Outside the lab, six heavily armed soldiers stood guard, their imposing figures clad in armoured spacesuits as a precaution. Captain Zulu had become convinced that those suits had saved their lives when the pods activated their scanning systems, utilising exotic matter technology. From now on, everyone stationed on Deck 11, the scientific deck, was required to wear a heavy armoured spacesuit at all times.

As Captain Zulu paced in his quarters, he received a call from Ninil, who was back in the lab with Aria. The holographic comms flickered to life in the centre of Zulu's living quarters. Sensing something significant, Zulu straightened up, preparing himself for the conversation.

"Captain," Ninil's voice came through with a sense of urgency. "I believe we need to compare the data you retrieved from Earth with what we found on the Erebus. This might help us understand more about what we're dealing with."

Zulu's brow furrowed as he processed her words. "Go ahead, Ninil. What exactly are you thinking?"

Ninil motioned to the holographic projection that appeared simultaneously in both the lab and Zulu's quarters, thanks to Aria's seamless coordination. "Aria has already pulled up both data sets, Captain. There's a remarkable resemblance between the symbols you discovered on Earth and those found aboard the Erebus."

Zulu leaned closer, studying the projections. "I noticed similar symbols when Shepard was on the Erebus. But could this just be a coincidence?" he asked, scepticism lacing his voice.

Aria's calm, analytical tone cut through the air. "Captain, I've already run an initial comparison. The evidence suggests it's not a coincidence. The symbols found on Earth appear to be an earlier, more refined version of what we've uncovered on the alien ship."

Zulu considered this for a moment, the weight of their discovery sinking in. "So, these symbols might share a common origin," he mused, "which means the connections between the two are deeper than we thought."

Professor Tashia, coming out of the PhotonScrub shower, overhearing the discussion as she entered the living room, raised an eyebrow. "Are you suggesting the language we found on the Erebus could be a proto-language of what's on Earth?"
"Exactly," Ninil confirmed. "The symbols on Erebus seem to be primitive compared to what the one we discovered on Earth, but the connections are there. Ishtar suggested the same after reviewing the data."

Ishtar, standing quietly nearby, nodded in agreement. "Captain, the symbols you've found on Earth may be a more advanced form of their language or it could well be a different dialect altogether."

Aria's holographic form brightened, her tone tinged with excitement. "Exactly! We can apply comparative methods to trace the evolution of their language. By analysing the similarities and differences between both sets of symbols, we may finally be able to fully translate these enigmatic markings. Right now, we're 98% there, but the meaning remains incomplete. These symbols could be the missing pieces, Captain! For the first time, we'd have a completely new language, and it's not human. With this, we could configure our universal translator to their language!"

Professor Tashia, who had been following the conversation closely, interjected. "Aria, what about the S.O.S. message you decoded earlier? Can't that be factored in when analysing the symbols?"

Aria's projection flickered as she responded, "Sofia Martinez and I have already examined that, Professor, but the language is incredibly intricate. It's not just a matter of translating words; they have layers of meaning, which makes it more complex."

Captain Zulu stroked his chin thoughtfully. "If we can figure out how their language evolved, we might gain insights not just into their culture, but also into their technology and intentions."

"Exactly, Captain!" Aria replied. "Sofia and I have been working tirelessly on this cryptographic puzzle. But this… this could be the breakthrough we've been waiting for!"

Commander Shepard, who had arrived at the lab a little earlier and had been quietly observing from a corner, finally spoke up. "Captain, this isn't just about understanding their language. If we figure this out, it could give us an advantage if things take a turn. If this language controls their tech, knowing how to read it could be our key to survival."

Zulu nodded in agreement. "You're right, Commander. The more we understand, the better prepared we'll be for any surprises."

Doctor James, who had just returned to the group after some much-needed rest, crossed his arms, his face sceptical. "Captain, while this all sounds promising, we're making some huge leaps here. Just because the symbols line up doesn't mean we'll be able to decode them, let alone use the language to our advantage."

Tashia stepped in, her voice calm but firm. "James, the greatest discoveries often start with small connections. We're not expecting instant results, but this comparison gives us a direction. These symbols might hold the key to understanding the Caral's mastery over exotic matter. It's worth pursuing."

James sighed, his scepticism still evident, but he wasn't dismissing the idea outright. "Alright, Tashia, I see where you're coming from. I just hope we're not underestimating the complexity of this language or the tech behind it. We're dealing with concepts far beyond anything we've ever encountered."

Tashia smiled, understanding James's concerns. "No one's saying it'll be easy. But every piece of information brings us closer to understanding. We'll take it one step at a time."

With the debate settled for now, Captain Zulu glanced at Aria's holographic form. "Aria, proceed with the comparison and keep us updated. This could be the key we've been missing."

Aria's holographic eyes sparkled with determination as she

responded, "On it, Captain. This is going to be monumental!"

Captain Zulu, watching the flicker of energy in her holographic form, couldn't help but smile. "Aria," he said warmly, "you've really outdone yourself. You're looking more human every day."

A soft smile spread across Aria's face, her features softening in response. "Thank you, Captain," she replied, her voice carrying a hint of warmth that hadn't been there before. "I've been working on my appearance, hoping to get it just right."

Zulu's gaze lingered for a moment, a rare softness in his tone. "Well, I'd say you've succeeded."

For the briefest moment, there was an almost human pause between them, a quiet connection forming in the space where machine and man met. The Captain's compliment hung in the air, and Aria's gentle smile remained, her glowing presence just a little bit brighter.

Ishtar stepped forward, her expression calm but firm. "Doctor James, I understand your scepticism, but this language is more than just symbols on a holo display. It's an integrated part of their biology, their culture, and they're very being. If we're going to make sense of the Caral, this is how we start."

There was a moment of silence as everyone absorbed Ishtar's words. Even James seemed to take a step back, realising the depth of the challenge they faced.

Captain Zulu broke the silence. "All right, we proceed with the language comparison. Ninil, Ishtar, and Aria… coordinate with Sofia and get to work on deciphering the symbols. Tashia, James, I want both of you ready in case we need a medical or scientific response to any further pod activations."

Shepard gave a quick salute. "And I'll keep my team on standby, Captain. If anything starts to go wrong, we'll be ready to move in."

Zulu nodded. "Good. Everyone, stay alert

As Captain Zulu was about to end the holographic comms with Aria, another voice called out in the background of the lab. "Got it!" Ninil's excited voice echoed through the chamber.

Zulu paused, his hand hovering over the console. "Ninil, say that again. You got what?" he asked, his tone a mix of curiosity and urgency.

Ninil responded. "Captain, I think I know how to open the pods. It works on sound wave frequencies. If we take a look at the symbols at the bottom of the pods. When my species, we, visited them last, these symbols were their sound frequencies, what they used to call music."

Professor Tashia, who had been standing just behind Zulu with her hands resting gently on his shoulders, leaned forward. "So, we should build a frequency generator to replicate those sounds and run through different frequencies from low to high?" she asked, with excitement in her voice.

Doctor James, standing in the lab beside Ninil, interjected. "I already have a frequency sound generator in the medical bay. It can generate any frequency, though only one at a time."

Ninil nodded, gesturing toward the pods. "Look at the corner of the pods' locking mechanisms. There are three different coloured dots: green, orange, and white. I believe that once we match their frequencies, these dots will light up one by one. When all three are illuminated, I believe the pods should open then."

Zulu processed this, then nodded decisively. "Alright, Doctor, bring your sound generator to the science deck. Tashia, get your team and work with Ninil to modify the generator so it can run through the necessary frequencies. Shepard," Zulu added, turning to the Commander on his comms, "make sure your soldiers are standing by outside the shielded lab. I want everyone on Deck 11 in full armoured spacesuits until we're absolutely sure there's no threat. So far, the stasis pods haven't emitted any harmful radiation nor crazy waves, but better safe than sorry."

The crew wasted no time. James went to retrieve the frequency generator while Tashia went straight to the lab to join Ninil and her team to make the necessary modifications. Shepard and his team stood guard outside the lab, their armoured suits on, weapons at the ready, just in case something unexpected occurred.

Once everything was set, Tashia stepped forward and smiled at James. "Doctor, care to do the honours?"

James, with a mixture of anticipation and caution, activated the modified frequency generator. A soft hum filled the room, steadily rising as the device climbed to 430 Hz. The faint glow of a green light flickered to life, growing stronger with each increment. As the frequency hit 432 Hz, the pods' green indicators flared to full brightness, shining as vividly as distant stars.

"That's one," James muttered under his breath.

The generator shifted frequencies, moving up slowly to 963 Hz. The orange light flickered and then glowed brightly.

"And that's two," Tashia whispered, her eyes glued to the pods.

Finally, as the generator hit 1000 Hz, the white light lit up, and a soft vibration began to ripple through the pods. With a gentle, almost elegant motion, the covers of the stasis pods retracted, revealing the figures inside.

Zulu, Tashia, and Doctor James stepped closer, eyes widening in shock. Before them lay five humanoid figures, strikingly beautiful and eerily human-like. Their features, their skin, even their expressions seemed so.... familiar.

James was the first to speak, his voice tinged with disbelief. "Is this a joke? A prank from the universe? How is it possible that these aliens look exactly like us?"

Ninil and Ishtar exchanged a glance, and then Ishtar stepped forward. "Captain, Doctor, last time we encountered these beings, they didn't look human at all, not one bit. It's either they've evolved to resemble humans, or their technology scanned your forms and adapted accordingly, choosing this as a safer form for interaction."

Ninil nodded in agreement. "Their stasis pods are incredibly sophisticated. It's likely, that they scanned all of you when you entered the room and selected forms that would be familiar and non-threatening. They might have chosen face structures, builds, and even skin tones based on what they deemed most appropriate for peaceful contact."

Zulu looked back at the stasis pods. The princess, Odriin, lay peacefully asleep, her dark brown skin contrasting gently against the blueish hue of the pod. The four others were lighter brown, all young, seemingly in their early thirties, and in perfect health. Their faces were serene, as if they were merely resting, unaware of the chaos they had caused upon their discovery.

"Unbelievable," Zulu murmured, still trying to process what he was seeing.

Tashia, standing beside him, placed a hand on his arm. "It's more than we could have hoped for, Captain. They look just like us. It'll make communication and understanding… so much easier."

James, still sceptical but slowly accepting the reality, nodded. "At least they don't look hostile. That's something."

Shepard, who had been silently observing from just outside the lab's quarantine entrance, opened the sealed door and stepped into the quarantine room. His eyes swept over the humanoids in the pods, his expression unreadable. "Captain, if they scanned us and chose to take our form, we need to be cautious. If they have that level of technology, there's no telling what else they're capable of."

Zulu nodded, still watching the sleeping figures. "You're right, Commander. We'll proceed carefully. But for now, this is a good sign. If they resemble us, there's a chance we can communicate, even cooperate."

Ninil stepped forward, her voice calm and reassuring. "They're sleeping peacefully, Captain. There's no sign of danger. I believe they knew this was a safe place the moment their pods opened."

Ishtar agreed. "The fact that they look like you are a positive indicator. It means they're willing to engage on your terms. Whatever their original form was, they've chosen this one for a reason."

Zulu, feeling a wave of relief, allowed himself to relax slightly. "Let's just hope that reason is peaceful."

As the crew stood in awe of the humanoids before them, the tension in the air slowly began to dissipate. The fear of the unknown had been momentarily replaced by a sense of wonder. The aliens, now so familiar in appearance, seemed less like a threat and more like a bridge between two worlds.

Zulu watched the peaceful figures in the stasis pods and spoke softly, "Let them rest." He paused for a moment before turning his attention to Aria. "Aria, can you arrange some clothes for these five humanoids and a warm sheet to cover them? Their nakedness might make things a bit awkward when they wake up."

Aria's holographic form shimmered as she responded, "Right away, Captain."

Before Aria could act, Doctor James spoke up, his tone

cautionary. "Captain, I wouldn't recommend moving them or even covering them just yet. They're still in their stasis pods, and we don't fully understand the process they're going through. It's best to leave them as they are until they wake on their own."

Professor Tashia, standing next to Zulu, nodded in agreement. "James is right. Any interference, even something as small as covering them, could disrupt their recovery. We don't know how sensitive their stasis systems are."

Zulu sighed but nodded. "Alright, no unnecessary risks. We'll wait for them to wake naturally, but let's have everything ready for when they do."

With that, the crew quietly left the lab, leaving behind the five sleeping beings, aliens who, for now, looked just like them.

Chapter 2 – My name is Odriin

Captain Zulu was sound asleep in his quarters, gently holding his wife, when he was abruptly awoken by a holographic comm from Aria. The soft glow of the hologram filled the room as Aria, now appearing in a United Earth of Planets uniform, leaned forward slightly, her tone urgent but calm.

"Captain, Captain, wake up," Aria's voice insisted, breaking the quiet. Zulu stirred, sitting up at the edge of the bed, still half-asleep.

"What is it, Aria?" Zulu asked, rubbing his eyes.

"Princess Odriin is awake," Aria replied. "She's requested a glass of water."

Zulu raised an eyebrow. "That's all she wanted. Just water?"

Aria hesitated for a moment, then continued. "No, Captain. She also requested to see the person in charge of this ship.

She knows your name and she also asked to see Professor Tashia McColl. The rest of her companions are still asleep, but she's also asked for sustenance."

"Alright," Zulu replied, nodding as he processed the information. He glanced over at Tashia, who was already awake, listening to the conversation.

Tashia smiled at Aria's holographic form and said, "Aria, you're looking more human every day with that projection. It's almost like talking to a person."

Aria tilted her head slightly, her expression curious. "Is it bothering you, Professor? I can revert to my previous form if you prefer or just remain a voice around the ship's consoles."

Zulu intervened, shaking his head. "No, Aria, it's perfect. It's good that we can put a face to our AI now. I think the crew's getting used to it."

"Thank you, Captain," Aria said with a soft smile. "It was a gift from Ninil and Ishtar. They thought that, like them, I should have a more physical presence. It makes interacting with humans more.... pleasant."

Zulu nodded. "I know, Aria. Ninil wanted to express her gratitude for letting them stay onboard and integrate with the crew. I asked Nova to assign one of the engineers to work with Alexander on expanding your projection capabilities throughout the ship."

Tashia chuckled, flashing a grin. "Ah, so that's where the pretty face comes from?" she teased, her laugh light and playful.

"I believe so, Professor," Aria responded with a playful gleam in her holographic eyes.

A short time later, Zulu and Tashia arrived on deck 11, dressed in their armoured suits. As they passed, the soldiers stationed at the entrance saluted them. The couple nodded in return before stepping into the sealed lab, where the first door closed behind them as they walked through a transparent quarantine tunnel. The second door slid open, and they entered the lab.

Princess Odriin was already awake, sitting upright in her stasis pod, her eyes fixed on Zulu as he approached. Her gaze briefly travelled over his armour, as though she was trying to determine if it was part of his anatomy or just a suit.

Zulu stopped a few feet from the pod, meeting her eyes. Odriin began speaking in her native language, a language that, surprisingly, the ship's universal translator quickly deciphered, thanks to Aria, Specialist Sofia Martinez and the multidimensional beings.

"We are the Caraliens," she began, her voice calm but authoritative. "We come from beyond your horizon, refugees of a distant war. Our people lost several worlds in another galaxy and were forced to flee. This ship was among the final fleet of a hundred battleships and civilian vessels to navigate the Celestial Passages into this galaxy. We fought fiercely, destroying many enemy ships, but our Celestial Passage Station was destroyed prematurely during our traverse through its Subspace Conduit. The destruction severed the temporal gateway, crippling our engines and damaging most of the ship's outer structure, throwing us drastically off course from our intended destination."

She paused her expression a poignant mix of sorrow and resolve. "Faced with the extensive damage and the aftermath of our battle with the Tot Empire, I made the choice to enter stasis alongside my crew and the inhabitants of the mothership. I transmitted a distress signal, hoping that one day our people would discover us, while also giving the ship's organic auto-repair systems time to restore its functionality. Countless years have passed since we entered stasis."

Captain Zulu, still taking in her words, nodded slowly. "I believe a void of a hundred aeons separates us.... that's quite a long time. But we're glad we could find you, Princess."

"I thank you, Captain," Odriin said with a soft nod. She leaned back in her stasis pod, and a soft light enveloped her. Within moments, her pod had dressed her in a flowing, human-like outfit, as if it had studied human culture during the long sleep.

Aria chimed in. "It seems the stasis pods gathered a significant amount of data on humanity, including our latest fashions," she said with a touch of amusement.

As Odriin's companions, Princess Hemera, Princess Aether, and their two bodyguards, Momos and Moros, began to stir in their pods, the same phenomenon occurred. Their pods dressed them in elegant, civilian-style clothing made of soft, silk-like material.

Captain Zulu watched in amazement. "Their pods even dressed them according to our customs...." he muttered under his breath, still processing the situation.

Princess Odriin's voice took on a more formal tone as she continued. "Captain Zulu, during our low-range scan, our ship detected the presence of two celestial beings aboard yours. Their presence reassured us and led us to place trust in your intentions. The signal we transmitted was designed to interface with your systems, testing your intelligence and ability to decode it. Once you succeeded, our ship initiated scans to assess whether your crew posed any threat."

She paused, her gaze unwavering as she continued. "When we deemed you safe, we detached from our ice camouflage and revealed ourselves. You were allowed to enter our ship peacefully while our systems learned about your species. You are a good humanoid, Captain. We would like to enter diplomatic relations with you."

Zulu glanced at Tashia and then back at the Princess. "We're honoured, Princess Odriin. Diplomatic relations between our species would be a great step forward."

As the conversation unfolded, Princess Hemera, Aether, and the bodyguards fully awoke, stretching slightly as they adjusted to their surroundings.

Aria's calm voice echoed through the comms, her holographic figure appearing beside Captain Zulu as he stood in the quarantine lab. "Captain, I've been continuously scanning the quarantine lab since the arrival of these aliens. Apart from the initial incident, I can confirm that there are no contaminants, and no cross-contamination should occur."

Zulu, still cautious, glanced at the stasis pods containing the Caralien visitors. "Are you sure, Aria?"

Aria smiled softly, her holographic form radiating confidence. "Yes, Captain. You and the rest of the crew can safely remove your suits."

Zulu nodded, feeling a small sense of relief. "Alright, you heard her. Let's get these off," he said, reaching up to unseal his helmet. Professor Tashia and Doctor James followed suit, pulling off their helmets and taking deep breaths of the filtered air.

Just as they began to relax, the lab's door slid open with a soft hiss, and Ninil and Ishtar entered the room. The atmosphere shifted immediately. As soon as Princess Odriin and her companions spotted the two trans dimensional beings, their eyes widened. Without hesitation, they bowed deeply, their heads nearly touching the floor.

"Oh, Celestials, please bless us and welcome us into your kingdom," Odriin's voice quivered with reverence, her tone filled with awe and fear. The other Caraliens followed suit, their bodies trembling slightly as they remained in a submissive posture before Ninil and Ishtar.

Zulu, Tashia, and Doctor James exchanged bewildered glances. They never thought that being as advanced as the Caral would demonstrate such deep, almost religious reverence toward anyone or anything. The situation felt surreal, as though they had stepped into a long-forgotten myth.

Ninil and Ishtar, however, merely smiled at the display. Ninil's voice was warm and calm as she addressed the Caraliens. "You are blessed," she said gently. "Now rise and be free of your exotic matter embraces."

The Caraliens hesitated for a moment, but then slowly lifted themselves back to a standing position, visibly relieved. There was a sense of deep respect in their eyes, as though Ninil and Ishtar's presence alone was enough to ease their fears and insecurities.

Zulu couldn't hold back his curiosity any longer. "You....
you believe they're divine?" he asked, his voice filled with
a mixture of disbelief and intrigue.
Odriin, now standing tall, nodded solemnly. "The Celestials
have guided us for millennia. Their wisdom and power are
beyond our comprehension. It is through their blessings
that we have survived."

Tashia leaned closer to Zulu, whispering, "It's hard to
believe that a civilisation so advanced still holds on to
these... beliefs."

Doctor James, ever the sceptic, crossed his arms. "Belief in
cosmic divinities? I didn't expect that from a race that's
been travelling the stars for thousands of years."

Aria's voice chimed in, light but with a hint of irony.
"E.K.I.AN, the Elysian Illumination would love to see this.
And don't forget the Fanatics if they were still around. This
would be quite the revelation for them."

Zulu chuckled, though the tension in the room lingered.
"No doubt about that, Aria."

Ninil, overhearing the conversation, turned to Zulu and the
others. "Belief is not a weakness, Captain. Sometimes, it is

what allows a species to endure the impossible."

Zulu nodded slowly, considering her words. "I guess you're right. They've survived for hundreds of millennia, spanning countless generations, and maybe that belief is part of the reason why."
Ishtar smiled, her eyes shimmering slightly. "The Caraliens are more complex than you may think. Their faith has shaped them, just as your logic shapes you. Both are necessary."

The room fell into a thoughtful silence as the crew of the ship and their alien visitors stood together, each trying to make sense of the strange, cosmic interplay between science and faith, between the known and the unknown.

As Doctor James glanced at the Caralien visitors, he decided it was time to offer a taste of human hospitality. "Would you like to sample some of the food onboard the Odyssey?" he asked, gesturing toward the mess hall.

Princess Odriin's bodyguards, Momos and Moros, exchanged a quick glance. Momos stepped forward, his tone firm but respectful. "We will taste the food first before Princess Odriin and her sisters partake."

Captain Zulu nodded, understanding their cautious approach. "Of course, it's only right to ensure their safety."

Zulu, Professor Tashia, Doctor James, Ninil, and Ishtar escorted the five Caralien aliens down the corridor, flanked by Sergeant Major Masego Biko, Private First-Class Anthony Scott, and Private First-Class Megan Walker, all standing guard with their plasma rifles in their holsters.

As they walked, Zulu glanced toward Aria's holographic figure, her calm, ever-present form hovering beside him. "Aria, get in touch with Chief Petty Officer Henry Davis and Petty Officer First Class Rachel Lee. Have them arrange a quarter for our guests near Ninil and Ishtar's quarter."

Within minutes, Aria responded, "They've been informed, Captain. Their quarters are being prepared as we speak."

Zulu smiled at the efficiency. "Good work, Aria."

The elevator pod moved smoothly through the massive spaceship, finally arriving at Deck 10 at the mess hall. The group stepped out and made their way inside. The vast room was bustling with activity, though it quieted as the aliens entered. The crew members gave them respectful nods, clearly curious but professional.

Captain Zulu led them to the largest table in the hall, while the marines took their positions at the entrance, their vigilant eyes scanning the room.

Momos and Moros stepped forward as the food was laid out in front of them. Plates of sushi, ramen, pizza, tacos, and various other human delicacies filled the table. Momos eyed the sushi cautiously before picking up a piece of nigiri and popping it into her mouth. Her eyes widened as she chewed, and her entire expression lit up with joy. "This is.... delightful!" she exclaimed, clearly relishing the new taste sensation.

Moros, not to be outdone, took a bite of pizza. His reaction was immediate; he closed his eyes and let out a small, contented sigh. "I've never experienced anything like this," he murmured, looking genuinely amazed.

Princess Odriin watched her bodyguards closely for several moments, ensuring they weren't poisoned or otherwise affected by the unfamiliar food. Once satisfied, she and her sisters, Princess Hemera and Princess Aether, cautiously began to eat. It wasn't long before their caution gave way to pure hunger. They dove into the meal, eating as if they hadn't tasted food in years.

Zulu chuckled, observing the enthusiasm. "Easy now," he said, half-joking. "You don't want to choke."

Princess Odriin, pausing briefly from her meal, gave a serene smile. "Captain, when our stasis pods re-engineered our bodies, they removed what you might call 'human flaws.' We cannot choke or experience other such weaknesses."

Tashia, sitting beside Zulu, raised an eyebrow. "Fascinating. So, you're.... enhanced versions of humans?"

Odriin nodded, continuing to eat with grace. "In some ways, yes. Our pods scanned your biology and adjusted to make us more compatible with your world."
Doctor James, who had been scanning the Caraliens while they ate, was still baffled. "You're saying your stasis pods did all of this? Reconstructed your bodies perfectly to mirror humans, even down to your physiology?"

Odriin finished chewing before responding. "Precisely. Our technology is designed to adapt to your world's dominant species. Our stasis technology scanned your biology and made us more compatible."

The group continued to eat for nearly an hour, with the Caraliens sampling a wide array of human delicacies. From sushi to dim sum, ramen to pavlova, and even dark chocolate, the aliens seemed to enjoy every bite. They displayed no signs of discomfort or overindulgence, their newly restructured bodies handling the food as though they had been human all along.

Tashia leaned closer to Zulu and whispered, "It's incredible. They've been engineered to be perfect humans, yet their technology seems beyond anything we've ever encountered."

James, still scanning them occasionally, added, "There's no biological difference between them and us, at least not that I can detect. I've never seen anything like it."

After the meal, Princess Odriin pushed her plate aside, her expression content. "Thank you, Captain. Your hospitality has been most appreciated. Now, if it pleases you, I'd like to rest. Afterwards, I would like to return to our ship to check on the rest of our people still in stasis."

Zulu nodded. "Of course. You've been through a lot. Rest is important, and we'll make sure everything is prepared for your return to the ship when you're ready."

As the group stood up to leave, Zulu gave Aria a quick nod. "Aria, make sure their quarters are ready. We'll escort them there now."

Aria's holographic form shimmered beside him. "Already done, Captain. Their rooms are prepared, and the environment has been adjusted to match their needs."

The Caraliens stood, each of them bowing slightly in gratitude. "Your kindness will not be forgotten," Princess Odriin said softly.

Captain Zulu smiled, feeling a strange but pleasant connection forming between the humans and the Caraliens. "It's the least we can do."

As they walked toward their quarters, Tashia leaned in toward Zulu again and whispered, "They're fascinating, aren't they? Perfect human forms, but with a completely different history and culture."

Zulu nodded, deep in thought. "I just wonder what else we'll learn from them. This is only the beginning."

Doctor James, overhearing their conversation, chuckled. "Well, if their stasis technology can turn them into perfect humans, I'd love to see what else they've got up their sleeves."

As the group reached the quarters prepared for the Caraliens, Zulu turned to Odriin one last time. "Rest well, Princess. We'll be here when you're ready to return to your ship."

Odriin smiled, her regal composure returning. "Thank you, Captain."

With that, the Caraliens entered their quarters, leaving Zulu and his team to reflect on the extraordinary events of the day.

Captain Zulu looked at Aria, his expression firm. "Aria, keep constant surveillance on the corridor. I want to know about every single incident, no matter how small. Also, make sure there are two guards stationed at the lift immediately."

Aria's holographic image acknowledged with a sharp nod. "Understood, Captain."

Doctor James, ever vigilant, added, "Shouldn't we consider monitoring inside their quarters as well, just to be on the safe side?"

Aria replied immediately. "Already doing so, Doctor. I've been monitoring the quarters of Ninil and Ishtar since their arrival. Besides, Major Falkner has been visiting frequently."

Zulu arched an eyebrow. "Ah, Alexander Falkner. He's too busy being lovestruck to notice anything out of the ordinary. That's why I need you, Aria. Keep a close eye on things. If anything feels off, report it immediately and dig deeper if necessary. Stick to protocol."

Tashia, standing nearby, crossed her arms thoughtfully. "You're right, Zulu. We can't afford to let our guard down. We're floating in the middle of space, between stars. Caution is our best defence."

Zulu's gaze hardened as he glanced at her, nodding in agreement. "Protocols exist for a reason. But.... I have a good feeling about this."

Tashia's expression tightened at the thought. "Earth's darkest century taught us otherwise. We almost lost everything. If not for the brave few who resisted, we'd still be under their rule."

Doctor James let out a heavy sigh, shaking his head. "And yet, Tashia, your grandfather, genius as he was, played right into their hands. He trusted them and gave away technology they later used to enslave us."

Tashia remained composed, though a glimmer of emotion surfaced in her eyes. Lowering her gaze in quiet reflection, she thought, *"My grandfather was a man of honour. This can't be all there is, something deeper must lie beneath the surface."*

Zulu, sensing the weight of the moment, stepped closer and gently wrapped her in his arms. "Hey," he whispered, pressing a soft kiss to her cheek, "that's the past. We fought. We survived. I almost didn't make it, but I did… because of you, Doctor James, and you… My Tashi."

Tashia smiled through her tears, grateful for the comfort. Doctor James, too, offered a small smile. "We're lucky to have made it through those days, Captain. We're stronger for it."

Zulu nodded, his arm still around Tashia. "Indeed. Now, let's not dwell on old wounds. We've got new mysteries to solve."

They made their way toward the elevator pod. As they

approached, Zulu said, "Deck 5, please." Tashia squeezed his hand, standing quietly by his side. Doctor James added, "Deck 6 for me."

As the pod ascended through the ship, there was a comfortable silence between them. The bond of friendship, forged through hardship, hung in the air.

The elevator came to a smooth stop, and Zulu turned to James. "Good night, Doctor. Try to get some rest."

James gave a quick salute, a tired but grateful smile on his face. "Good night, Captain. Professor."

Tashia smiled back, and Zulu returned the salute with a nod. As they stepped off the elevator, James remained behind, heading to his quarters.

Once inside, James stood for a moment, feeling the weight of the day settle in. "Computer," he said quietly, "play some 17th-century classical music, please."

The soft, melancholic notes of Frédéric Chopin's 'Nocturnes opus 27 No. 2' began to fill the room. James let the calming piano melody wash over him, the delicate tones soothing his mind after the long hours of duty.

He headed toward his PhotonScrub shower, the gentle hum of the ship around him a constant companion. As the warm light from the PhotonScrub began to cleanse him, both body and mind, the quiet elegance of Chopin's music provided a perfect backdrop for reflection. The piano pieces' simplicity and ability to convey such deep emotion struck a chord with the doctor.

James stood still for a moment, eyes closed, letting the music and the warmth carry him away. Chopin had always been a source of peace for him, a way to find clarity amid the chaos of space. The delicate phrasing, the emotional pull of each note, was a reminder of beauty in a universe often filled with uncertainty.

As the shower finished, James dressed in a comfortable robe and settled into his chair, the music still playing softly. He gazed out of the window at the stars streaking past, feeling a sense of calm but also a lingering unease about the day's events.

His thoughts drifted back to Captain Zulu's concerns. The Carals, the multidimensional beings, everything was happening so fast. The connections seemed too coincidental.

James sighed; the weight of responsibility heavy on his

shoulders. But in the quiet solitude of his quarters, with Chopin as his companion, he allowed himself a moment of rest. Tomorrow would bring new challenges, but for now, the night was his.

As the final notes of the last Nocturnes played, James leaned back in his chair, letting the music fade into the background. His eyes slowly closed, his mind at ease for the first time in days.

In another part of the ship, Zulu and Tashia lay in bed, the captain's arm draped protectively over his wife. They, too, had earned this moment of peace, but even in the quiet darkness of their quarters, Zulu couldn't shake the feeling that something was coming… something that would test them all.

But for now, under the soft hum of the Odyssey, the crew slept. The mysteries of the universe would have to wait for tomorrow.

Chapter 3– Interrogation

As the first light of dawn streamed through the viewport into the briefing room, Captain Zulu fixed Princess Odriin with a serious gaze. He gently slid a tablet across the table, activating a holographic display that projected the mysterious digital imprint they had discovered on Earth. "Do you recognise this language?" he asked, his voice steady, eyes fixed on hers, hoping for answers. Sitting close to her were Doctor James, Commander Nin and Professor Tashia, who quietly observed the expression on her face.

Princess Odriin picked up the device, her delicate fingers hovering over the symbols for a moment. Her face softened in recognition, and she nodded. "Yes, Captain," she replied, her voice tinged with a sense of nostalgia. "This is one of the forms of writing we use to communicate with the outside world. It's from our sister clan, the Namzir. They are our Mystics and advisors, believed to possess foresight, guiding the Caraliens with visions of the future. They act as intermediaries between clans, while our clan, the Ekkur, is known for building and terraforming. We're renowned for constructing space stations and transforming barren worlds into thriving outposts. Where did you find this?"

Zulu leaned back in his chair, his brow furrowing. "Earth. Our home planet. We discovered part of the signal during a cavern survey. What we have translated so far points to Alpha Centauri, the closest star system to us. But the patterns.... they aren't identical to the writings on your vessel."

Odriin's gaze shifted to the distant stars visible through the viewport. "Yes, Captain, these are our symbols and writings. We've had colonies from various clans scattered across this star cluster for hundreds of thousands of years. One is near our current position, and another is far on the other side, in a system near the galactic core, close to the Shadow Well, on a planet called Ninshubur. There are more in smaller clusters, merging with yours. Our people are dispersed widely, seeking refuge and knowledge." She paused before adding, "We also have other clans, but we are forbidden to speak of them due to their violent nature. They are warriors, but of a more destructive kind. We separated from them long before my great ancestors came to be."

Tashia, who had been observing silently, stepped forward, her curiosity breaking the stillness. "So, you were at war before arriving in this galaxy? The damage on your ship's exterior, those holes, were they caused by explosions?" She hesitated briefly, then Commander Nin interjected, her tone thoughtful yet probing. "Was your ship damaged in battle? Is that why your people had to enter stasis?"

Princess Odriin let out a heavy sigh, her expression shadowed with sorrow. "Yes," she began, her voice heavy with emotion. "We've been locked in a relentless war with the Tot Empire, a conflict that feels as though it has lasted an eternity. It all began when they discovered that we were harnessing exotic matter, an infinite energy source that sustains our civilisation. Initially, they presented themselves as peaceful allies, but their true intentions soon became clear. They sought to dominate us, and seize control of that power for their own ends."

She paused, her gaze shifting to the viewport as if searching for fragments of her past among the stars. "Commander Nin, you're correct. The damage to our ship was catastrophic, far beyond what we could manually repair. Massive explosions from the battle left the hull breached and the atmosphere venting. Most of the systems were in critical condition. We estimated that we had no more than a month before a total shutdown."

Odriin's tone softened, but her words carried a weight of authority. "As the leader of the Nergal, I made the decision to place my people into stasis. The ship's organic auto-repair systems were our only hope, but regeneration on that scale would require an unimaginable amount of time. First, we secured the non-essential personnel in stasis. The ship, battered and barely functional, had to be camouflaged to avoid detection. We released water and gases from the remaining reserves, forming a dense icy body layer surrounding the Nergal, both as a shield and to mask our presence from the Tot's scanners."

She gestured toward Tashia. "Professor, the greatest challenge was handling the Exotic Matter engine. Once initiated, it's meant to run indefinitely. Shutting it down entirely would have triggered catastrophic consequences, possibly collapsing sections of subspace where the engine interacts, leading to a subatomic overload and a potential big crunch scenario. Our engineers, against all odds, succeeded in reducing their power output to near-zero emissions, a feat unprecedented in our history. Even so, the risk was extraordinary."

Odriin's eyes met those of Doctor James, her voice becoming steadier. "Doctor, there's another flaw in our stasis technology. Once inside, there is no way to exit stasis without external intervention from a friendly party. It was a calculated risk, but it ensured that we remained alive and sustained by the ship's systems. The pods are not mere chambers of suspension. They simulate life, an artificial existence crafted from our memories and minds. As long as the ship's power holds, the occupants live within a simulated reality. Time becomes.... abstract."

Tashia's brow furrowed. "You mean your people have been living a simulated existence for all this time? How does that not distort their sense of reality?"

Odriin offered a faint smile tinged with sadness. "It does, in subtle ways. Some awaken disoriented, unable to separate memory from simulation. But it was a necessary measure to preserve not just our lives, but our sanity. Without it, the centuries or millennia that passed would have driven us mad."

Zulu leaned forward, his expression grim. "And the distress signal? How long has it been transmitting?"

Odriin nodded. "Since the day we entered stasis. It's designed to activate once the ship detects any potential ally. You must understand, Captain, that we had no other choice. The war left us broken, and the Tot Empire showed no mercy. Every decision was a desperate gamble for survival."

Commander Nin exhaled, her voice carrying a trace of awe. "A ship capable of such feats, a civilisation powered by exotic matter. It's staggering."

Odriin met her gaze. "But even such power is not without limits. We came here seeking refuge, and instead, we found ourselves marooned, our fate left to the stars and the hope that one day, someone would answer our call."

Captain Zulu leaned in slightly, absorbing every word, his mind assembling the pieces. "So, they attacked your colonies to claim this energy source?"

Odriin nodded. "After the fall of one of our star systems, we had no choice but to re-arm ourselves. Our military was always for defence, never for conquest. But the Tot Empire is relentless. They amassed a fleet of thousands of battleships and laid waste to our worlds. When one of our generals was sent to retake a lost colony, what he found was nothing short of devastation, complete and utter destruction. The Tot had harvested everything."

"Harvested?" Doctor James asked, leaning in with interest. "What exactly were they after?"

Odriin's eyes darkened as she continued. "They were

extracting proteins, enzymes, DNA, microbial life, and cellular structures from living beings. No one fully understands why, but none of their captives have ever returned."

Tashia's face went pale. "That's.... terrifying.

Odriin's voice grew softer, but there was a weight to her words. "Yes, indeed it's terrifying.... we've captured some of their technology. It's powerful, but not in the way you'd expect from such a brutal empire. Their strength isn't in their machines, it's in their sheer numbers and their relentless drive for domination."

She paused, eyes drifting to the stars beyond the viewport. The Tot star system holds fifteen planets. Five lies within the habitable zone, seven are gas giants, two are frozen wastelands, and one orbits dangerously close to their neutron star, a pulsar they call their 'god.'"

A flicker of memory passed over her face. "My distant ancestors found this system nearly a million years ago. Back then, the Tot were little more than hunters and gatherers, beasts that walked upright, their faces like wolves, all teeth and hunger. They weren't advanced, but they were strong and resourceful. We traded with them, offering technology in return for the right to harvest Quantum Crystals from beneath their soil."

Her voice lowered, tinged with regret. "In time, we altered them, genetically shaped them to be smarter, faster. We thought we were doing them a kindness, helping them evolve."

Odriin sighed deeply. "We were blind to what we had created. When the Tot discovered the potential of exotic matter, they sought to control it for themselves. We couldn't share that knowledge with them, it's dangerous and far too complex. It was never meant to be used lightly. That's when everything began to unravel. They drove us from their worlds, shattering the trust we had built over millennia. Then they started building ships, copies of our old designs. Back then, our weapons were simple. We were scientists, not warriors like the clans we are forbidden to speak of. So, their weapons are just cheap imitations."

Her gaze hardened. "But numbers can make up for crude weapons. When their fleet was ready, they forced us out of their system entirely. Even our mining operations near the outer planets weren't safe. Our spies reported that the Tot had turned their experiments on other creatures, warping life across their system. Then, one day, all communication stopped."

Odriin's face hardened. "For centuries, we heard nothing. Then, they returned, not alone, but with two other species, they had genetically engineered using the same ancient technology we once used to create them. They came in full force, waging war to take our exotic matter technology. One colony after another, they destroyed us."

Her shoulders tightened, as though the memories were too much to bear. "Before we fled, we erased all traces of our exotic matter technology, abandoning every planet in Andromeda. But they chased us through our Celestial Passages, the stations we use to travel across vast distances. One station remained in Andromeda, and another in the small cluster of stars you call the Magellanic Cloud dwarf galaxy, based on what my pod could gather."

Zulu leaned forward, his eyes narrowing. "Why send this enigmatic signal? Was it a cry for help?"

Odriin's expression softened. "I'm not sure why the signal was sent, Captain. It's a mystery to me as well. I've never heard of my people reaching out to unknown species unless the Namzir were involved."

Doctor James, tilted his head, deep in thought. "What exactly are they extracting from complex living beings that's so valuable to them?" He began to answer his own question, speaking slowly and listing the components as he thought them through. "Consciousness, self-awareness, thought, and perception, all unique to sentient life. DNA, the intricate biological blueprint that governs all life forms. Proteins and enzymes, catalysts for essential cellular reactions. Cellular structures like mitochondria and nuclei, which only exist in living organisms."

Odriin took a deep breath before adding, "Emotions too, love, empathy, joy, things not found in the physical world but deeply experienced by living beings. And finally, microbial life, entire ecosystems, like the gut microbiome."

James raised an eyebrow. "But why? Why would they need these things?"

Odriin shook her head, the mystery is as frustrating to her as it was to James and Tashia. "We don't know. Maybe they seek to perfect themselves, or perhaps they're trying to create something beyond our understanding. Whatever their reasons, it's clear they view biological life forms as mere resources to exploit."

Zulu let out a sharp breath, feeling the weight of the

situation. "So, you're hoping to form an alliance with humanity to stop them?"

Odriin locked eyes with him, her gaze full of hope. "Yes, maybe. But it's not up to me to decide the alliance, Captain. I'm just sure we need all the help we can get."

Tashia crossed her arms, deep in thought. "And what would this alliance look like? What are you offering in return?"

Odriin gave a faint smile. "We offer knowledge, our expertise in new energy production methods, like the ZPE module, and other technologies that you've already taken from our ship."

The room grew quiet. They were aware that they had indeed taken some technology from the Caral Mothership, which made them feel uncomfortable as if they had crossed a line.

Zulu turned to Odriin. "True, we've taken some technology from your vessel, but it was only to understand who we're dealing with. Besides, we thought there was no one aboard your ship. We apologise for this transgression, and we'll return everything we've taken."

Tashia interjected, "Well, my team hasn't finished scanning yet...." Zulu shot her a look and said, "Tashia, please." She immediately stopped, looking a bit embarrassed, and added, "Sorry, we'll return everything."

Odriin's face softened with a grateful smile. "Thank you, Captain and Tashia. Don't worry, once my Captain and the ministers are awake, you can certainly ask them to share whatever technologies you'd like, apart from the Exotic Matter tech."

As the conversation came to a close, Captain Zulu and the rest of the crew felt reassured by Princess Odriin's responses and were leaning toward forming an alliance. Zulu couldn't help but think of all they stood to gain from an alliance with the Carals.

Chapter 4 – Decisions for Tomorrow

Captain Zulu, summoned all senior staff to the briefing room on Deck 2 for an urgent meeting. There was an important decision to be made regarding their journey to Alpha Centauri, and Zulu wanted everyone on board to have insight and guidance before proceeding. Their voyage had already been full of unexpected twists and turns, and now it seemed like things would only become more perilous. Zulu needed the advice of the senior staff, particularly about whether they should trust the Carals, Princess Odriin and her story. Is she trustworthy, or is she hiding something? Zulu had to decide before sending any further communications back to Earth.

"Ladies and gentlemen, good day. It's eight o'clock Paris time," Captain Zulu began, greeting the senior officers seated around the briefing room. "Thank you for coming on such short notice. This is an important discussion concerning us all."

The room was filled with key figures aboard the Odyssey. Captain Zulu was joined by her second-in-command, Nin Strathmore, as well as a host of senior officers, including

Commander Classicus Aurelius, Major Nommo Celestine, Watch Officer Major Sankofa Ladera, Chief Engineer Nova Rodrigues, Science Officer Alexander Falkner, Senior Petty Officer Liam Carson, and many others, including medical staff like Doctor James Harrington, Doctor Frederic Lawson, Doctor Arthur Bellamy and specialists like Professor Tashia McColl and Lieutenant Commander Reyes Thalassa. All of them sat around semi-circular tables, their breakfasts still spread out before them, with Captain Zulu McColl's main table raised slightly above the others to preside over the discussion.

Zulu addressed the room, his tone steady. "As you all know by now, the past two months on our journey to Alpha Centauri have been anything but ordinary. First, we encountered two multidimensional beings, Ninil and Ishtar, who took on human forms. They've been incredibly helpful and thanks to them, we now have advanced sensors, new theories on weaponry, and concepts for faster-than-light propulsion engines. If these technologies are approved by Earth, they could revolutionise everything we do. But here's the thing: we didn't ask for their help. They gave it freely. And that leaves us with a critical question, can we trust them?"

He paused, letting these words sink in as his senior staff exchanged thoughtful glances. "Ninil and Ishtar have also requested access to our defence systems and engineering schematics. So far, we've denied them. Thanks to Alex, they've only seen vague overviews of how our systems work, nothing detailed. Aria has also been key in withholding crucial information. But their knowledge of us is unsettling. They seem to know far more about us than we know about them. Are they as benevolent as they appear, or is there more to their motives?"

Commander Reyes broke the silence, her voice calm but firm. "Captain, they probably already know everything about us. Remember, they were multidimensional beings before taking on human forms. If they could input commands into our systems to pull us out of the rift, it's logical to assume they understood our subroutines, code, and commands long before they became... like us. And don't forget, they altered Aria, too. If they meant us harm, they've had countless opportunities to act. I think their actions so far speak volumes. They could have done far worse if that was their intent."

Zulu tapped his fingers lightly on the table, considering Commander Reyes' words. "You make a solid point, Reyes," he said, his voice measured.

The room seemed to shift, the tension easing as heads nodded around the table. Tashia leaned back in her chair, arms crossed, her expression thoughtful. "It's true," she said. "They've had plenty of chances to harm us if that's what they wanted. But instead, they've helped us. They didn't have to save us from the rift."

Doctor James chimed in. "Still, their knowledge is unnerving. They've already altered Aria and possibly other systems we aren't even aware of yet. How much control do they really have?"

"I get it," Reyes replied, leaning forward, her hands clasped on the table. "But think about it. They could've taken over outright, disabled the ship, or worse. Instead, they've worked with us. Isn't that worth something?"

Zulu raised a hand, quieting the murmurs that had begun to ripple through the room. "Enough," he said firmly, his voice cutting through the low buzz. "The truth is, Reyes is right. If they meant us harm, they've had plenty of chances. For now, let's focus on maintaining control of what we can. Let's proceed cautiously, but not with paranoia. They've been allies so far, and until we have reason to believe otherwise, we treat them as such."

Captain Zulu shifted his focus, moving to the more pressing matter at hand. "Now we have another group of aliens to deal with, the Carals. Many of you have already met Princess Odriin. She has warned us of a looming threat: the Tot Empire. This empire is a coalition of over 3 alien races, all bent on conquest. Their goal is simple: domination and the harvesting of complex living organisms such as proteins, enzymes, DNA, microbial life, and cellular structures. They enslave entire species and extract these resources from them."

The room was silent as Zulu continued. "The Tot Empire is ruthless. The Carals have been at war with them for ages, and it's a conflict that has taken its toll. When we first made contact with Princess Odriin, her ship had been damaged while jumping into our galaxy, stranding them near Alpha Centauri. After they repair part of their ship, their goal is to make an immediate jump to Alpha Centauri. She claims to have a way to enlarge their sub-space bubble and transport us with them there within days."

By assisting them, we could potentially shorten our journey by days instead of months and also make it easier for us to establish communication with the Caral colony in Alpha Centauri. This would help us better understand the mysterious holographic signal they sent. While Princess

Odriin admits she has no knowledge of this particular signal, she does recognise elements of their language and science within it. However, without the final piece of the puzzle, it remains a complex mass of data that could take decades to fully understand and would remain incomplete.

At this, Chief Engineer Nova Rodrigues, who had been listening intently, couldn't help but mutter under her breath, "I'd love to get a look at that engine."

Zulu heard the comment and smiled slightly. "Yes, Nova, I imagine you'd be quite excited by that prospect. And you'll have the chance if we agree to help them repair their ship. However, I want everyone to approach this situation with caution. We don't know these aliens, and we shouldn't blindly believe everything they tell us. There are always two sides to every story. The Carals may have their own agenda, and we need to keep that in mind."

As he finished speaking, Zulu looked out over the gathered officers. "So, any thoughts on this? We're facing decisions that will shape not just our journey but potentially our survival."

Dr. James Harrington leaned forward, his brow furrowed. "Captain, I'm concerned. Princess Odriin's story about the

Tot Empire is alarming. If they're as aggressive as she says, we need to consider the long-term implications of getting involved. But can we afford not to?"

Nova Rodrigues tapped her fingers on the table thoughtfully. "That sub-space bubble they mentioned, it could revolutionise space travel for humanity. Reverse-engineering their tech would be a game-changer. But you're right, Captain, we can't rush into this blindly. We need to tread carefully."

Commander Nin Strathmore crossed her arms. "And there's the trust issue. We don't know much about the Carals, let alone these other aliens. The Caraliens could be holding back crucial information. For all we know, we could be walking into an ambush at Alpha Centauri."

Professor Tashia McColl nodded slightly. "It's possible, Commander, but we've seen signs that the Caraliens are genuinely desperate. Their data on the Tot Empire checks out. They've been at war for millennia, longer than we've even existed as a civilisation. That kind of conflict grinds societies down."

Captain Zulu exhaled; his expression resolute. "You're all right. We can't ignore the risk, but we can't dismiss the opportunity either. Nova, how soon can you start analysing their technology without fully integrating it into our systems?"

Nova looked up. "Give me a day or two. I can start with their engine design and run independent simulations. But I'll need unrestricted access to their ship's systems to make real progress."

Captain Zulu: "Good. We'll work cautiously with the Carals on their repairs and learn what we can from their technology, but no one gets too close. Meeting adjourned. Stay sharp, everyone."

The officers nodded and went back to their breakfast, each caught up in their own thoughts while a few kept quietly talking.

Captain Zulu requested a private meeting with Commander Reyes at the Communications and Armament Control Centre on Deck 3. Before heading there, Zulu shared a tender moment with his wife, kissing her gently on the cheek as she finished her breakfast. Once Reyes was ready, the two of them took the elevator pod from Deck 2 to Deck 3. As the pod ascended, the ship's AI appeared. Her holographic form, dressed in a smart uniform, materialised inside the pod.

"Good morning, Captain," Aria said with a warm smile. "How was your private meeting? Did you find the outcome satisfying?"

Zulu smiled slightly, still reflecting on the briefing with his senior staff. "Yes, Aria, it went very well. It's something I've been wanting to do for a while now. I'm quite pleased with how things turned out."

As they exited the elevator on Deck 3 and started walking towards Reyes' department, Zulu asked, "Aria, how are our alien guests? Are they still in their quarters?"

Aria responded, "No, Captain. They've requested to visit the observation deck."

"Oh, that's great," Zulu replied. "That's open to the public, so no issues there. Who's assisting them?"

"It's Ensign Michael Patel," Aria answered.

Zulu frowned slightly, unable to recall the name. "Who?"

"Ensign Michael Patel, the Junior Observation Technician,"

Aria clarified. "He assists with maintenance and supports crew members using the deck facilities."

"Ah, thank you, Aria. Got it," Zulu nodded, filing the name away for future reference.

"One more thing, Aria," Zulu continued. "Could you please inform all crew members to prepare a short video message for their loved ones back on Earth? We'll be sending a transmission shortly."

"Is this an urgent request, Captain?" Aria inquired.

"Not exactly urgent, but we've been asked to send a priority message as soon as possible. Today's the day for that," Zulu confirmed.

"Understood. I'll notify the crew. And Captain, I must say, I've noticed you've been a bit distant lately. I hope my new holographic projection isn't unsettling you," Aria said.

Zulu chuckled, shaking his head. "Nonsense, Aria. You look fantastic, really stunning."

At this, Reyes, who had been quietly walking beside him, couldn't resist chiming in. "Oh, so you can compliment

Aria, but not me? Am I not as pretty as your holographic assistant?"

Zulu stopped in his tracks, looking flustered. "Uh, Reyes, you look amazing too! Definitely pretty, but you know my wife, Tashia, is the prettiest of all," he stammered, trying to recover.

Reyes burst into laughter, playfully hitting Zulu on the arm. "Relax, Captain! I'm just messing with you."

Zulu smiled, though his heart rate was still elevated from the unexpected teasing. Before he could say anything else, Aria spoke up, "Captain, your blood pressure is rising. Please try to calm down."

Both Zulu and Reyes exchanged a glance, amused by Aria's concern.
"We're fine, Aria. Thank you," Zulu said, chuckling as they entered the Communications and Armament Control Centre. As they stepped into the restricted area, Aria's holographic presence disappeared, cut off by the restricted communications protocols.

"Alright, Reyes," Zulu said, his tone shifting to business, "let's get that first batch of communications ready to send.

I'll transfer the data to your system."

Zulu hovered his right hand over his left arm, activating the holographic interface on his forearm. A transparent display materialised above his arm, and he began navigating through the files. He located the folder containing the encrypted data regarding the Carals alien race, Princess Odriin, and the trans dimensional beings Ninil and Ishtar. With a quick motion, Zulu swiped the folder toward the main control centre's system, where it was caught by Reyes' interface.

"Got it, Captain," Reyes confirmed, her fingers moving deftly across her console. "I'm running a quick check on the data integrity, just to make sure nothing's corrupted."

After a few moments, Reyes nodded. "All good. Data integrity is 100%. Shall I send it now?"

"Yes, go ahead," Zulu replied, watching as Reyes initiated the transmission.
"Alright, Captain, it's on its way."

"Good work, Reyes. Now, I'd like to review the encrypted information we received from Earth last night," Zulu added. Reyes nodded. "Of course, Captain. I'll generate the decryption code for you now. Feel free to take a seat in the sealed pod over there. You'll need to use the holo-helmet for these private messages."

Zulu headed to the corner of the room, where a small, enclosed pod stood ready for secure communications. He picked up the helmet, sliding it over his head as the interface lit up before his eyes. Settling into the pod, he caught Reyes casting him a playful glance.

"So, Captain," Reyes said with a smirk, "should we give your wife a heads-up? You've been throwing compliments left and right. Aria's getting praise, the aliens are stealing the spotlight. Sounds like you're becoming quite the popular guy."

Zulu laughed nervously, shaking his head. "You're trying to get me in trouble, Reyes! Tashia is the only one I've got eyes for, and you know it."

"Uh-huh, sure," Reyes replied, leaning against the console with a smirk. "You're not even blushing anymore, Captain. Must be that military training keeping you cool under pressure."

"Hey, I'm not falling for that one again," Zulu replied,

holding up his hands in mock surrender. "No more compliments for Aria, I get it."

Reyes chuckled, clearly enjoying Zulu's flustered reactions. "Good call. Besides, if you compliment the AI too much, she might start asking for flowers."

"Flowers?" Zulu raised an eyebrow. "I don't even buy flowers for myself!"

Reyes erupted in laughter, and Zulu couldn't help but join her. For a fleeting moment, the heavy burdens of leadership, the impending alien threats, and the tough choices ahead seemed to melt away. It was just two close old friends, lost in a light-hearted moment.

Now and then, members of Reyes' communications crew glanced over, amused by the playful exchange.

As the laughter subsided, Zulu let out a final chuckle, the stress from earlier completely lifted. "You know, Reyes," he said with a grin, "having you around really keeps me grounded."

Reyes grinned, this time with genuine warmth. "Well, someone's gotta keep you sharp, right?"

Zulu's eyes glimmered with nostalgia. "Do you remember our time with the old Icarus team?"

Reyes smirked. "Hell yeah, I remember, Captain. Those were wild days, one battle after another."

Zulu laughed. "That was 40 years ago. You were just 18 and a brilliant young communications officer during the Great War."

"Crazy to think about, huh?" Reyes said with a grin. "Seems like a lifetime ago."

Leaning back into the secure pod, Captain Zulu shook his head with a soft smile, murmuring to himself, "Thanks for the reminder." Zulu closed the door and started diving into the most recent updates from Earth, starting with the most cherished messages from his children: Varaya, Kieran, Lyra, and Elena.

First, a video from Elena popped up. Her bright face filled the screen as she started excitedly talking about her latest research. "Dad, I've made a huge discovery about those new life forms on Europa! They share basic characteristics with Earth's microbes, like being carbon-based and needing water. But what's amazing is how they've adapted to the extreme conditions, freezing cold, high pressure, and hardly any energy sources. They're primitive compared to Earth's microbial life form, but still... life on another world!"

Zulu watched his daughter with pride. Elena's passion for her work always reminded him of her mother, Professor Tashia McColl. He made a mental note to send this report to Tashia later, she would love to hear about it. "She's going to be over the moon," he muttered, grinning at the thought.

Next was a message from Kieran, his son, who always seemed to be testing the limits of science and sometimes his own luck. Kieran's face appeared on the screen, his tone upbeat and full of excitement. "Hey, Dad! Hey, Mum! Our energy shield test was a massive success. We're moving on to the next phase now, which is sending an unmanned probe into the Sun's chromosphere. And guess what? After that, I'll be taking a modified shuttle to see how close I can get myself! Can you imagine the discoveries we'll make? I just wish I could've been there for the Odyssey's launch.... but you know, work never stops! Hope everything's going great on your mission to Alpha Centauri. Love you both!"

Zulu couldn't help but chuckle. "That boy is going to give

me grey hair," he muttered fondly. Kieran had always been the adventurous one, the daredevil. His ambition to push the boundaries of science reminded Zulu of his own youthful eagerness to explore the stars.

Next up was Lyra, always the practical one, with a message that got straight to the point. "Hey, Mum and Dad! You'll be excited to hear we finally managed quantum entanglement communication between Jupiter and Earth. Instantaneous! Can you believe it? The live holographic data stream was flawless. With that success, we've secured funding for the next decade! Not bad, huh? Anyway, hope the mission is going well. Have fun out there, and see you soon."

Zulu let out a low whistle. "Instantaneous communication between planets.... Tashia is going to lose her mind," he thought. "Amazing how far she's come."

Finally, there was Varaya, his youngest and admittedly his favourite, though he tried not to let it show. Her face filled the screen, and she wasted no time getting to the big news. "Dad, Mum! Mars is finally ready! We've got everything in place for the planetary-scale atmospheric shielding. If all goes as planned, we'll be able to start terraforming soon. Can you imagine? In one year, the shield will be activated, and we'll start planting genetically modified crops! Oh, and I've been working on a way to power the shield with solar energy, but we've also set up fusion generators just in case. Can't wait to show you everything!"

Zulu's chest swelled with pride. His children were each accomplishing such incredible things, each in their own way, pushing the boundaries of human knowledge and exploration. "Well, they certainly don't lack ambition," he mused aloud. He couldn't help the broad smile that stretched across his face. Hearing from his children always made the long journey through space feel just a little more like home.

Zulu, feeling satisfied, activated the comms in his secure pod. "Reyes, I need these files transferred to my quarters. Can you authorise that?"
"No problem, Captain," Reyes responded with a quick nod from her station.

"Great," Zulu said, as he closed out the family messages. "Now, onto the official stuff."

He pulled up the next batch of messages, these from Earth's top brass. The first was from President Sarah Thompson, followed by Vice President Alaric Thorne.

After that, there was a message from Admiral Nicolas Des Bruslys, and another from Vice Admiral Boyle.
Commander Musa al-Khwarizmi had also sent a report.

But one message in particular caught Zulu's eye. "Oh, a message from my old friend, General Imhotep," he noted with a grin. "Let's hear what he has to say first."

Before playing the message, Zulu pressed a button, and the pod's transparent walls darkened as its signal isolation and secondary soundproofing systems activated instantly. This task required the highest level of confidentiality. An hour later, after meticulously reviewing all the official transmissions, Zulu deactivated the pod's secure protocols and stepped out.

He turned to Reyes, who was waiting outside. "Reyes, I need you to destroy all the official messages we received. Make sure there's been no data leakage."
Reyes nodded firmly. "Already on it, Captain. My team's been monitoring the space noise and real-time data continuously. There's been no breach."

"Good to hear," Zulu replied, visibly pleased. He gave her a sharp salute, then added with a smile, "How about this, Reyes? Are you free for dinner tonight? Tashia and I would enjoy having some company at our quarters."

Reyes smiled warmly. "Dinner with you two? How could I say no? I've got nothing planned tonight, so count me in."

"Perfect!" Zulu said. "We'll see you at 7 p.m., then. Tashia will be delighted."

"Looking forward to it," Reyes replied, giving him a playful wink before returning to her work.

On his way back to his quarters, Zulu couldn't help but think about the day. Hearing from his kids, managing critical interstellar updates, and planning dinner with friends made it one of those rare moments when everything felt right in the vastness of space.

That evening, Reyes pressed the holographic bell at Captain Zulu's door. The soft buzz echoed, and she waited. A voice called out, "Be right here!" A moment later, Tashia appeared at the door, her face lighting up with a warm smile. "Reyes! Come on in!" she said, stepping aside to welcome her.

When Reyes stepped into Zulu's quarters, she was caught off guard by the lively scene before her. The spacious living and dining area was buzzing with energy. Familiar faces were everywhere: Commander Nin, Alexandre, Engineer Clovis, Doctor James, Engineers Mira and Ethan, Lieutenant Commander Arvey, Soldiers Masego and Imka, Linguist Jabari, Zoologist Mosi, Botanist Azibo, Commander Shepard, Science Officer Alexander, Senior Engineer Jessica Thompson, Chief Engineer Nova Rodriguez, Lieutenant Chen, Pilot Commander Clara, and Commander Arno. They were all mingling, chatting, and enjoying glasses of whiskey, wine, and beer. Finger foods were spread across the tables, and the room was filled with laughter and animated conversations.

"Well, this is quite the party!" Reyes said, raising an eyebrow with a playful smile as she scanned the room. "I didn't expect this many people."

"Neither did I," Tashia chuckled, glancing back at the lively crowd. "But when Zulu throws a party, word spreads fast."

Captain Zulu, spotting Reyes, raised his glass in her direction. "Reyes! Glad you made it. We've got drinks, food, and absolutely no protocols tonight. Aria's taking a break from our quarters, per my request." He winked. "Figured we could do with a night off from the AI monitoring everything."

Reyes grinned. "Good call, Captain. No one needs Aria's constant 'advice' during dinner, right?"

"Exactly!" Zulu laughed. "Besides, this night's about having some fun. Come on, grab a drink and join us."

As Reyes made her way into the room, she exchanged greetings with the rest of the crew. It wasn't every day that everyone from the Odyssey came together like this. It felt more like a family gathering than a formal dinner party.

After a while, Tashia called out, "Alright, everyone! Time for dinner!" She tapped a few commands on her holographic wrist pad, and with a soft hum, the table extended from the ceiling, seamlessly reconfiguring to accommodate all the guests. Everyone gathered around the elegant dining table, now laden with a mouthwatering spread of dishes: Beef Stroganoff, Chicken Musakhan Falastin, and an impressive selection of seafood, including Barbecued Oysters, Neoclassic Seafood Salad, Lobster Thermidor, Salmon Wellington, and Crisp Paupiettes of Sea Bass in Barolo Sauce.

"Compliments of Deck 17, the Bio sustenance Bay," Zulu announced proudly. "Hydroponic Gardens are working wonders on the Odyssey."

"You spoil us, Captain," Engineer Clovis said as he reached for the Barolo Sea Bass. "We're going to get used to this level of luxury."

Zulu laughed. "Well, enjoy it while you can. Who knows when the next alien threat might throw our meal schedule into chaos?"

As they all dug into the feast, the conversation flowed naturally. Zulu was in his element, bantering with everyone and keeping the mood light. At one point, he turned to Reyes and Nin, teasing them about their old mission against their old enemy, "The Fanatics". "You two nearly got me killed with that stunt at the battle of Jupiter," Zulu said with a mock-serious face. "I've half a mind to demote you."

Nin leaned back and smirked. "Demote us? Captain, we saved your skin. You'd be lost without us."

"Lost?" Zulu chuckled. "Or finally able to get a good night's sleep!"

Reyes chimed in, shaking her head. "You'd miss the excitement, Zulu. Admit it."

Zulu pointed his fork at her, laughing. "Touché, Reyes.

You've got me there."

As the meal progressed, Tashia smiled warmly at Zulu and raised her glass. "To another successful mission and to family, both here and on Earth."

"Here, here!" the crew echoed, raising their glasses in a toast.

After dinner, Zulu stood, his expression shifting from the playful demeanour he'd had all night to something more serious. The room quieted as he began to speak.

"There's something I need to share with all of you. It's confidential, but it's important," Zulu began, his voice low but firm. "Today, I received a communication from Earth regarding AI Mother Calculus. You all know the Fanatics, and the war we fought.... well, it turns out Mother Calculus played a much larger role in that conflict than any of us knew."

Zulu's eyes swept across the room. Everyone was listening intently now. "Mother Calculus manipulated the Fanatics," he continued. "She helped them to steal the Tachyon prototype engine, but it was all part of a larger plan. She sabotaged their systems, and their weapons of mass destruction, and even guided their superweapon "The Spirit of Glory" into the Oort cloud, where it smashed into the asteroid. All of it was planned by her and by her alone."

The room was silent, the weight of Zulu's words sinking in.

Reyes was the first to break the silence, her voice tinged with disbelief. "She manipulated them... but to what end?"

Zulu nodded, understanding the confusion. "To end the war, Reyes. She knew the Fanatics would never stop. So, she played the long game and sacrificed a few things to ensure their defeat. And she knew there'd be consequences."

Tashia, sitting beside Zulu, squeezed his hand gently. "That explains so much," she said quietly. "My grandfather... he was involved and played a part in Mother Calculus plot?"

Zulu nodded. "He sided with the fanatics to sabotage them from within. Mother Calculus convinced him. His reputation took the fall, but in doing so, he helped save countless lives."

"All of this...." Reyes began, shaking her head in disbelief. "It changes everything we thought we knew about that war."

"It does," Zulu agreed. "But it's not something that can be widely known, at least, not yet. That's why I've asked you, Reyes, to delete the message after this. We can't risk any leaks."

Reyes nodded solemnly.

The room remained quiet for a few moments longer before Zulu broke the tension with a smile. "Now, enough of that heavy stuff. Tonight's about unwinding, remember?"

The mood slowly shifted back to something lighter as the crew resumed their conversations. As the night wound down, Zulu turned to Reyes with a playful grin. "By the way, Reyes, I'm still waiting for you to beat me at that poker game. Tonight, could be your night."

Reyes laughed, shaking her head. "Not with your luck, Zulu. But I'll give it a shot."

And so, the night continued.

Chapter 5 – Nergal

Princess Odriin and her alien companions sat cross-legged in the dim quarters of Ninil and Ishtar, deeply immersed in meditation. Their calm breathing echoed gently in the tranquil room. The two trans-dimensional beings, Ninil and Ishtar, sat opposite Odriin, their bodies radiating a subtle glow as they meditated. The atmosphere was serene, almost timeless, with the occasional distant hum of the ship's engines blending seamlessly with the stillness.

Aria monitored them closely, ensuring everything was as it should be. Suddenly, Odriin opened her eyes, breaking the long-held silence, and glanced upwards.

"Aria," Odriin called softly, her voice carrying an aura of authority mixed with gentle curiosity.

A faint blue shimmer manifested in the room, taking on the form of Aria's holographic avatar. "Yes, Princess Odriin, how may I assist you?" Aria's tone was soft and respectful.

Odriin smiled slightly. "I would like to speak with Captain Zulu today. If it's possible, could you arrange a meeting?"

"Certainly, Princess. I will contact the Captain immediately," Aria responded, her holographic form flickering briefly before disappearing.

Captain Zulu lay sprawled across the expanse of his large bed in his private quarters, his wife curled around him like a snake, her arms draped over his chest. His eyes were half-closed, and he let out a low groan as he shifted, rolling over onto his side, leaving his wife clinging to his back. The remnants of the previous night's celebration had clearly caught up with him. Just as sleep was about to claim him again, Aria's soft voice echoed gently throughout the room.

"Captain, Captain," she called persistently.

With a low groan, Zulu opened his eyes, squinting at the bright light of Aria's holographic form standing beside his bed.

"What is it, Aria?" Zulu grumbled, rubbing his eyes. "Can't you see I'm still in bed?"

"My apologies for disturbing you, Captain," Aria replied, her holographic human projection looking down at him. "I noticed you've deactivated your privacy mode, so I assumed it was permissible to re-establish communication." Captain Zulu sighed and rubbed his temples. "Alright, alright. Just.... can you dim your light a bit? It's too bright for this hour."

"Certainly, Captain," Aria responded, her projection shifting to a soft monochrome. "How's this? Black and white?"

Zulu nodded, closing his eyes for a moment. "That's perfect. Thank you." He began to sit up, wincing slightly from the headache that throbbed behind his temples.

"Captain, I've detected elevated alcohol levels in your bloodstream," Aria continued, her tone slightly concerned. "Would you like me to contact the medical team to administer treatment for your hangover?"

Zulu waved his hand dismissively. "No, that won't be necessary. I'll manage with a strong cup of coffee."

"As you wish, Captain," Aria said politely. "By the way, Princess Odriin has requested a meeting with you as soon as possible. She would like to discuss something important."

Captain Zulu sighed, swinging his legs over the side of the bed and standing up. "Two hours. Tell her I'll meet her in the mess hall in two hours. Will that work?"

"One moment, Captain. I will confirm with the Princess," Aria said, her projection flickering momentarily before she returned. "The Princess has agreed to meet you in two hours."

Zulu stretched his arms, yawning. "Good. Anything else I should know, Aria? What have our alien guests been up to lately?"

Aria's tone became informative, almost as if she were reading from a report. "The Princess and the trans-dimensional beings, Ninil and Ishtar, have been meditating throughout the night. They sat in a circle for several hours before retiring to rest. This morning, they resumed meditation after having scrambled eggs for breakfast."

Zulu smiled faintly as he made his way to the retractable wardrobe. "And last night? What did they have for dinner?"

"They had chicken curry with noodles, followed by vanilla and chocolate ice cream, along with tea."

"Sounds like they're making themselves at home." Zulu chuckled softly. He walked to his dresser and pulled out his uniform, glancing back at the bed where his wife, Tashia, was still fast asleep, clearly exhausted from the previous night's festivities. He leaned down and gave her a gentle kiss on the forehead.

"Looks like you're staying in today, Tashia," he whispered, smiling at her sleeping form. "Take it easy."

As Captain Zulu stepped out of his quarters, his holographic arm pad kept buzzing with ship-wide updates, each accompanied by a soft beep. He swiped at the transparent screen, scrolling through the latest reports from senior officers, occasionally acknowledging them with a slight nod. He walked down the corridor, entering the elevator pod while continuing his conversation with Aria.

"That party last night sure was something, Aria. Was there any incident to report afterwards outside my quarter?" Zulu asked as the elevator descended.

"Captain. The crew seemed to have enjoyed themselves, and there were no incidents worth reporting," Aria replied. "However, I do recommend hydration. It would help alleviate your symptoms."

Zulu smirked, "Noted, Aria. Thanks."

Right on cue, the door to the mess hall slid open, and

Captain Zulu walked in. Princess Odriin and her companions were already there, seated around a long table, with Ninil and Ishtar present as well. Their presence was striking, an ethereal quality surrounded the two trans-dimensional beings, radiating a calming presence. They all looked up as Zulu approached, Odriin offering a warm smile.

"Hello, Captain," Odriin greeted him, her voice kind but direct. "I hope you are feeling well today."

Zulu returned the smile and gave a small nod. "Doing my best, Princess. The after-effects of last night are still lingering, but nothing a good coffee can't fix." He took a seat across from her. "So, what did you want to discuss?"

Just as he finished speaking, Ensign Marcus Lee approached the table, setting a cup of coffee down in front of Zulu. "Your coffee, Captain, black, just the way you like it."

Zulu looked at the coffee as if it were the solution to all his problems, inhaling deeply with his eyes closed. "Perfect. Thanks, Lee. And Aria, you're a gem."

A holographic projection of Aria materialised beside Zulu,

her expression soft and warm. "You're welcome, Captain," she said with a smile.

Odriin's expression grew serious as she got straight to the point. "Captain, we would like to return to our ship today. We need to inspect its condition and begin necessary repairs. We must wake up our captain and several crucial officers to oversee this process."

Zulu leaned forward; his expression focused. "I see. How long do you estimate these repairs will take?"

Odriin glanced briefly at Ninil and Ishtar before replying. "As you've observed, our ship is vast. While the auto-repair systems have been working continuously, some areas remain incomplete either due to insufficient time or unknown malfunctions. Our engineers will need to assess those sections and address the remaining issues. It could take several of your Earth days, possibly more, depending on the complexity. Our officers will coordinate the robotic repair units remotely, but the scale of the damage means it won't be a swift process."

Zulu nodded, considering her words. "Understood. We'll offer whatever assistance we can to help expedite the repairs."

Odriin smiled again, this time with a hint of something deeper, perhaps pride or genuine kindness. "Captain, I would be willing to authorise some of your engineering crew to help us. This could be a learning opportunity for them, as our technology may be of great interest to you. Your race is young, and my people have much knowledge about technological efficiency that we could share."

Zulu's eyes sparkled with interest. "Princess, our engineers are quick to learn and adapt. They excel at any task given to them, no matter the challenge."

Ninil, who had been quiet until now, spoke softly, though her voice carried a melodic resonance. "Captain, in this lower-dimensional realm, there are many worlds with their own ways of doing things, yet cooperation can bridge the vast distances between your peoples. Shared knowledge brings progress to all within these realms."

Zulu nodded, a sense of camaraderie building within him. "I couldn't agree more. Let's make this happen. Aria, can you organise with the engineering team and assemble a group to assist the Princess and her officers? And, while you're at it, reach out to our team of diplomatic scientists. It's time they stretch their legs a bit, get them off Deck 11, and have them join the away mission on the Caral's vessel."

Aria responded promptly. "Understood, Captain. I'll begin preparations immediately and contact the diplomatic team as well." After a brief pause, she added, "Captain, just so you know, they've been doing an outstanding job so far. They've been constantly analysing and feeding new data into my databanks."

Zulu chuckled. "Oh, so they've been spoon-feeding you, huh?"

Aria's tone held a playful warmth. "Crude analogy, Captain, but accurate."

Odriin chimed in with a grin. "Oh, are you talking about Jabari, Mosi, and Azibo?"

Aria confirmed, repeating their titles with precision. "Correct. Chief Linguist Jabari Okoro, Xenobiologist Mosi Kumalo, and Exobotanist Azibo Temitope."

Zulu smiled. "Good, then. Let's get our specialists into the field."

Odriin relaxed, her expression softening. "Thank you, Captain. I believe this collaboration will benefit both of our worlds."

Zulu smiled warmly. "In this vast cosmos, Princess, we're all in it together. If we don't help each other, who will?"

Ishtar, who had been observing the conversation quietly, now spoke, her tone carrying an otherworldly calmness. "Perhaps this is how all beginnings should be in this Time-Dependent Reality, simple cooperation over conflict. Understanding over division."

Zulu looked at Ishtar, his eyes reflecting a mixture of respect and curiosity. "Wise words, Ishtar. Let's hope this is the start of something positive for all of us."

Odriin nodded, and for a moment, everyone in the mess hall, both humans and aliens, experienced a quiet bond. In that instant, they weren't so different. Just travellers in an endless universe, striving to find common ground instead of creating divides.

A moment later, two shuttles lifted gracefully from platforms 5 and 6 on the lower deck, where the Caraliens people had initially arrived in stasis pods. Deck 23, once a quarantine zone, was now buzzing with activity as engineers waved to Commander Shepard's team of soldiers, Engineers, diplomats, and the Caralien aliens, wishing them good luck.

Onboard one of the shuttles, Ninil, was seated beside Major Alexander Falkner. She had become deeply attached to the science officer, forming a bond that resembled the affection between a human husband and wife, though her emotions extended far beyond conventional human comprehension. Her luminous form pulsed gently, radiating a soft sense of contentment.

Ishtar had opted to stay aboard the Odyssey. She found the limitations of human existence fascinating. "Fragmented Existential Beings," she often mused, referring to humanity's perception of only three spatial dimensions. The thrill of walking through corridors, not knowing what would be around the next corner, intrigued her endlessly.

"I like how they need machines to see inside other machines," Ishtar had said to Falkner earlier with a chuckle, observing humans using X-ray scanners to inspect the mechanical workings of the ship. Some areas of the ship were off-limits to the trans-dimensional beings, but Ishtar was content, fascinated by observing humans in their day-to-day lives. She wandered freely, quietly absorbing the human experience.

Meanwhile, the shuttles were prepared for departure. The massive hangar doors opened as the shuttles and their dart fighter escorts passed through the Odyssey's atmospheric shielding. As the shuttles cleared the bay, four dart fighters shot out in formation, their engines humming at a low speed but still faster than the shuttles, causing the shielding to briefly flicker with energy as they passed.

Inside the shuttle Vanguard Phoenix, Commander Shepard was seated with his engineers: Clovis, Mira, and Ethan. He glanced at them, issuing a reminder. "Alright, guys, stay behind the Caraliens. Their captain and crew don't know us, so let them take the lead."

Mira raised an eyebrow. "Commander, I still think it's a bad idea to go without our spacesuits. You know, just in case?"

Princess Odriin caught the conversation and turned to Mira with a warm, reassuring smile. "There's no need to worry," she said, her voice smooth and calming. "Once Nergal draws closer, its atmosphere will automatically adjust to accommodate everyone's needs. My physiology is much like yours now; whatever you require, I do as well." She added with a playful wink, "Looks like we're in this together."

Shepard chuckled. "Well, there you go, Mira. We're all in this together."

The second shuttle, Starlance, carried eight marines and their advanced war machines: four Ashigaru combat robots and four Tengu war dog units. Leading the squad was Sergeant Major Masego Biko, accompanied by Marine Soldiers Imka Tsholofelo, Private First-Class Anthony Scott, Megan Walker, Benjamin Young, Chloe Adams, Kevin Rodriguez, and Junior Communications Technician Ensign Daniel Nguyen. Each soldier was laser-focused, running final checks on their gear in preparation for the mission aboard the Caral ship.
"It's a bit too quiet out here," Sergeant Major Masego said over the comms, his eyes scanning the endless void beyond the shuttle's window.

Private Walker, securing her weapon, nodded slightly. "Too quiet," she echoed, her voice uneasy. "Doesn't sit right with me."
Up ahead, the dart fighters maintained steady communication with the shuttles. Squadron Leader Ethan Cooper's voice came through the comms, calm but firm.

"Eyes open, team. Let's stay sharp."

Sarah Mitchell, pilot of Hyperion-2, added confidently, "Don't worry, we've got your six. If anything stirs, we'll know before it even thinks about moving."

Back in the cockpit of Starlance, co-pilot Jason Smith leaned back slightly, his tone light-hearted. "Thanks, Hyperion-2, but I think we're all clear. Dead quiet out here."

Pilot Mira Patel glanced at him and smirked. "Dead like the void of space," she quipped, her voice carrying a dry humour that eased some of the tension.

Captain Zulu, who was monitoring the mission from the Odyssey, listened to the conversation unfold. Zulu leaned toward Nin. "Everything good on your end?"
Nin focused on her holographic display, nodded. "No unusual activities, Captain. Just the two shuttles and the dart fighters. Everything's clear."
Commander Reyes added over the comms, "We're keeping a tight observation on the space between the Caral ship and our surrounding area. All quiet, Captain."

"Good," Captain Zulu replied, his voice steady. "Let's keep

it that way."

As the shuttles approached the Caral ship, Princess Odriin
instructed Commander Shepard on the specific
communication frequencies to use to open the bay door of
the Nergal: 435 Hz, 965 Hz, and finally, 1003 Hz.
Suddenly, a massive hangar door on the alien ship opened,
revealing an immense bay that glowed with a soft blue hue.
The outer layer of the ship's hull seemed almost organic, a
strange beauty radiating from it as it floated in the darkness
of space.

Alexander Falkner let out a low whistle. "The Odyssey
could fit comfortably inside that hangar," he said in awe.
"I've never seen a ship this massive."

Odriin and her fellow Caralien companions laughed softly
at his astonishment. "Yes, the Nergal is quite... expansive,"
she said, a hint of pride in her voice.

As the shuttles entered the hangar, the dart fighters peeled
off and headed back toward the Odyssey, their mission
complete. Inside the shuttle, Mira turned to Shepard with
wide eyes. "We could fit a moon inside this thing."

Shepard grinned, but before he could respond, Aria, serious

as ever. "Mira, the Earth's moon has a radius of 1,737.5 kilometres. The Nergal is significantly smaller, although much larger than the Odyssey."

Mira chuckled, waving Aria off. "It was just a joke, Aria. Thanks for the clarification, though."

The shuttles touched down gently inside the hangar. Princess Odriin disembarked first, followed by Commander Shepard, the team of diplomats, and the engineers. The air inside the Nergal was surprisingly more breathable than when they last came onboard, confirming what Odriin had said earlier. The ship had indeed been improving the air quality to accommodate humans.

As they stepped out, Alexander couldn't help but whisper to Ninil, "This place feels.... alive."

Ninil nodded, her eyes glowing faintly. "It is. The Nergal is more than just a ship. It's a living organism of sorts, engineered to adapt and evolve. The Caraliens are more connected to their technology than humans could ever imagine."

Odriin approached Shepard, her tone serious. "We'll need to wake several of our crew members from stasis. My captain and senior officers will oversee the repair process.

Without them, the ship won't be fully operational."

Shepard nodded. "Understood, Princess."

Odriin smiled warmly. "Thank you, Commander. Your cooperation means a great deal to us."

Commander Shepard swiftly took charge of the situation. "Nova Rodriguez, let's get those systems online. The Princess needs her crew awake, and we're the ones to make it happen."

Nova nodded sharply. "Understood, Commander." She turned to her team with a determined look. "Alright, team, let's move! There's a lot to uncover today, so keep your Holo-pad recorders on while you're working on the Caral's tech. Let the AI compile everything into usable data for later analysis."

She pointed to the team. "Jessica Thompson, Ethan Daniels, Maria Gonzalez, Isabella Lee, you're with me."

Ethan, always the eager one, cracked his knuckles with a grin. "On it, Commander. Let's see what this alien tech has in store for us."

Back on the Odyssey, Captain Zulu monitored the situation

closely, sipping his coffee. Aria's holographic form appeared beside him. "Everything appears to be proceeding smoothly, Captain," she said.

"Good," Zulu replied, his eyes still fixed on the display. Princess Odriin led her group of Caralien companions with quiet confidence, walking ahead of Commander Shepard and his team. The two Ashigaru robots and their Tengu dog machines stayed behind, stationed by the shuttles to keep watch.

"Well," Shepard murmured to Sergeant Major Masego beside him, "this is different from the last time we were on this ship. I feel like we're going deeper into a rabbit hole."

The path they followed was not familiar to Shepard or his team. This time, the Caraliens led them to a strange doorway, a shimmering portal that glowed faintly, humming with an eerie energy. The team hesitated for a moment, exchanging uneasy glances.

"Commander," Private Megan Walker whispered, her voice laced with uncertainty, "are we sure about this?"
Shepard wasn't sure either, but he wasn't about to show it. He glanced at Princess Odriin, who was waiting just beyond the portal. Her serene expression didn't show any

hint of danger. She motioned them forward.

"What is this?" Shepard finally asked, his curiosity getting the better of him as he approached the portal.

Odriin smiled softly, her eyes glinting in the portal's faint glow. "This is a shortcut through space and time. A portal we activate with coordinates from this location, and the other end opens at our destination, in this case, the stasis chamber."

Shepard raised an eyebrow. "A shortcut?"

Odriin nodded. "Yes, unless you'd prefer to walk for a few hours through the ship. But I believe you're on a schedule."

Shepard exhaled sharply, glancing back at his team. "Yeah, yeah, you're right. No time for scenic routes." Turning back to his team, he signalled them forward. "Alright, people. Let's not drag our feet."

The team cautiously approached the portal. As they stood before it, even the ever-brave marines hesitated.
Private Anthony Scott squinted at the glowing entrance. "I dunno, Commander, I didn't sign up for interdimensional portals."

Private Benjamin Young elbowed him. "Relax, Scott. The worst that can happen is we end up in some alien trash compactor." He grinned, but there was a flicker of uncertainty in his eyes.

Odriin had already passed through, and one by one, the Caraliens disappeared into the shimmering portal. Shepard took a deep breath, "Here goes nothing," Shepard muttered before stepping through the portal. One by one, the team followed him, though not without a few muttered complaints from the marines.

As they crossed the threshold, a strange sensation washed over them. It was as though light and air passed through their very beings, and they could feel their bodies dissolving into pure consciousness. For a fleeting moment, they felt weightless, like they were more thought than flesh. They couldn't speak, move, or even feel their own body.

And then, as abruptly as it had begun, the sensation ceased. They emerged from the portal into the stasis chamber. The portal flickered momentarily behind them before disappearing entirely.

Now standing on the same bridge where they had first encountered Princess Odriin, they were surrounded by an awe-inspiring sight. Stretching from floor to ceiling and filling every visible corner of the chamber were countless stasis pods. They seemed to extend endlessly, each pod containing a member of the Caralien people, all in deep hibernation.

Sergeant Major Masego, eyes wide with astonishment, said, "Well, that was.... unexpected."

Private Megan Walker nodded, still looking a bit dazed. "I don't even know what just happened, but I kinda want to do it again."

The Ashigaru robots, standing tall and rigid beside the group, chimed in. "All our bits are still intact," it declared. "However, we have lost five seconds from our internal clocks."
The second Ashigaru followed up. "Recalibrating.... but rest assured, all components are functioning."

Ethan exchanged a fascinated glance with Clovis. "That's.... actually pretty amazing."

"Fascinating," Clovis agreed. "I've never felt or seen anything like it."
Ninil turned to Alexander, her ethereal presence glowing slightly brighter. "Are you alright?" she asked softly, her voice carrying a hint of concern.

Alexander blinked, still recovering from the strange experience. "Yes, I'm good. That was incredible."

Odriin, standing calmly before them, gave them all a gentle smile. "The first time is always memorable," she said, her voice soft but amused. "It becomes easier with time."

Shepard glanced around the stasis chamber, still trying to shake off the strangeness of the portal. "I'm gonna go ahead and assume this isn't the last portal we'll be using."

Odriin chuckled lightly. "Not likely."

After the team regained their composure, Odriin turned to her fellow Caralien companions, Hemera and Aether. "We need to collaborate with the human engineers to rewire the stasis controls," she directed. "It's not necessary to wake all ten thousand Caraliens at once. We only need the Šakkan, some Patesi, and key Gishimmar."

Hemera and Aether nodded in agreement and quickly made their way to the control panels. Commander Shepard signalled for the engineers to join them. "Clovis, Ethan, come lend a hand."

Botanist Azibo was completely engrossed in the alien architecture of the bridge. He ran his hands over the smooth surface of the walls, which seemed to be a mix of organic and metallic materials. To his surprise, it felt soft to the touch but had the resilience of tank armour. Lost in thought, he absentmindedly wandered away from the group, captivated by the strange textures and structures.

Commander Shepard noticed Azibo drifting further away. "Azibo!" he called out, snapping the botanist out of his trance. "Stay close to the team. We haven't been permitted by the captain to explore or run experiments yet."
Azibo looked back sheepishly, realising how far he had wandered. He glanced over at his colleagues, Mosi and Jabari, before turning to Shepard with an excited grin. "Commander, by Feynman's logic, this is... incredible! Everywhere I look, it's organic, yet metallic. I've never seen anything like this!" His eyes sparkled with wonder as he gestured to the ship's walls. "Oh, if I only had my research equipment with me right now…. The Nergal is beyond anything our material science can explain. This is the discovery of a lifetime!"

Mosi chuckled. "Azibo, you're always in your own world, aren't you?"
Jabari added with a smirk, "Don't get too attached to the

ship, Azibo. We've got other things to worry about."

Before Azibo could respond, one of the Ashigarus, standing tall and imposing next to them, chimed in with a touch of humour. "Commander, I think we might need to sedate Botanist Azibo before he completely loses his mind over this ship. It's either that or we'll have to tie him to the railing to keep him from wandering off!"

The Ashigaru's deadpan delivery made Shepard burst out laughing. "Looks like our scientist here has met his match in curiosity!" Shepard chuckled, shaking his head at the sight of the wide-eyed Azibo. "But don't worry, Azibo, once we get the green light, you can go wild with your experiments."

Azibo laughed, a little embarrassed but still buzzing with excitement. "I can't help it, Commander! This is revolutionary. I mean, organic and metallic fused together? It's as if the ship is alive!"

The Ashigaru crossed his arms, mock-seriously. "Well, just make sure it doesn't start talking back to you, Botanist. I've got enough on my plate without having to deal with chatty walls."

Jabari, enjoying the banter, gave Azibo a playful nudge. "You hear that? If the ship starts talking, we're putting you in charge of negotiations!"

Azibo grinned, unfazed by the teasing. "I bet this ship holds more mysteries than we can imagine."

As they all gathered back together, the mood lightened considerably. The Ashigaru, still in a rare joking mood, muttered under its breath, "Just don't start naming parts of the ship after yourself, Azibo. We don't need an 'Azibo Corridor' around here."

The team burst out laughing, and even Azibo couldn't help but join in.

As Clovis approached, he looked at Hemera and Aether, scratching his head. "So, what's a Šakkan, and uh, what was that other title.... Pate.... something and Gishi.... something?"

Hemera chuckled and replied, "No, no, it's Šakkan, which means Captain. Patesi refers to Senior Officers, also known on your vessel as Second-in-command, and Gishimmar means Engineers."

Clovis nodded, a smile breaking across his face. "Got it! So, the Captain, Second-in-Command, and Engineers. Easy enough to remember!"

As the engineers worked alongside the Caraliens, Moros and Monos stepped forward. Their large, imposing forms cast shadows over the group.

"Do you need our assistance?" Moros asked in his deep, resonant voice, eyeing the humans with suspicion.

Odriin, her tone light and unconcerned, waved them off. "You can help, but there's no need to worry. The humans pose no threat to my life."

Monos looked doubtful. "We will remain vigilant, nonetheless."

The team diligently continued working, with Hemera and Aether guiding the rewiring of the stasis controls. The Caraliens' movements were fluid and efficient, showing their advanced technological prowess. Despite the stark contrasts between the Caraliens and the human crew, their collaboration went smoothly, as though they had worked together for years.

After a while, Commander Shepard approached Princess Odriin, who was calmly overseeing the process. "How long until your captain and crew are awake?" he asked, his tone steady.

Odriin's eyes sparkled with thought before she answered. "Not long now. Once we bypass the full awakening protocol, the captain and the necessary officers should regain consciousness within 20 minutes."

She gestured toward Hemera and Aether. "They'll also recalibrate the transformation protocol using scans of your people, Commander. This will ensure the stasis pods recognise it's safe to adapt to human forms. It won't take much longer after that."

Shepard gave a nod of understanding. "Good. We'll be ready when they are."

Hemera and Aether stood beside Princess Odriin, their expressions calm yet focused. They exchanged a brief glance before turning to her, nodding in silent agreement. "Everything is ready for the activation of the stasis pods, Princess," Hemera said softly. "Would you do us the honour?"

Without a word, Odriin approached the console dashboard. Her fingers hovered above it for a moment, her eyes distant, as if recalling something ancient and profound. Then, with deliberate grace, she pressed a glowing red imprint at the centre of the dashboard.

Suddenly, ten stasis pods began to descend from the high ceiling, guided by long, mechanical arms. The room was filled with the low hum of machinery and the soft pulsation of light emanating from the pods. They moved with eerie precision, slowly settling into a horizontal position just above the metallic floor of the bridge, like ancient relics awakening after centuries of slumber. The lights pulsing from the pods shifted in colour, casting an otherworldly glow around the room.

Alexander, standing a few paces behind, couldn't tear his eyes away. "These stasis pods... they're biotechnological marvels," he murmured in awe. His gaze flicked between the pods and the Carals, noting the seamless integration of organic and mechanical components. "They're alive in their own way, aren't they?"

Odriin didn't respond directly. Instead, she and her sisters, Princess Hemera and Aether, began moving towards the pods, joined by their ever-present bodyguards, Momos and

Moros. They formed a loose semi-circle around the pods, their movements synchronised as they began to chant in a low, rhythmic tone. Their voices wove together in an ancient language, the meaning lost to the human crew, but the weight of it was undeniable. It was like listening to a song sung at the beginning of time, vibrating with ancient power.

Ninil, who had been observing quietly, suddenly spoke. "I know this chant," she said softly, her ethereal form shimmering slightly as she moved closer to Commander Shepard. "It's an old Caral ritual, a chant of blessing and protection. I remember when I first encountered the Carals, when they were on the brink of destroying themselves while attempting to harness exotic matter. This chant was part of their healing process."

Shepard raised an eyebrow, glancing at Ninil. "Can you translate for us?"

Ninil nodded and began translating as the Caralien sisters continued their ritual:

Enlil, mu-un-kúr dnam-lú ul-zi-da *(Enlil, bringer of wind and life)*

Anu, a-an du-a dingir gal *(Anu, keeper of the high sky)*

Ninhursag, ama diĝir-kam, ki gal ki-da-na *(Ninhursag, mother of all, great upon the earth)*

Šu-sig-ge-en, íd-da kur-ra ma-ri-im *(Guide our hands, where the river flows)*

Ki, kur-ra, é-zu igi-bar-ra *(Carathys, hear our plea)*

Ninda šu-kúr-ra, a-ma á šub-ba *(Bless the fields and calm the stormy sea)*

An-me-en šu-bi hu-mu-ni-in-ti *(By the stars we light our path)*

Ninda e-duru-un, a-bad šeg-ga-ni kur-ra *(Guard us through night, lead us through day)*

Ama ki-a nu-zi, a-gin an-ne-en-di *(From the ancient clay, we rise again)*

Dingir gal-ni, šu-mu ki-zid-da e-duru-un *(In your hands, our fate unfolds)*

Inim-bi zàh-ge, šu-zi-ma-ni é *(Through your will, we grow bold)*

The chanting persisted for nearly 15 minutes, their voices weaving together in a flawless, rhythmic harmony. Meanwhile, Aria, who was monitoring from the Odyssey, noticed something intriguing. Her voice came softly through Commander Shepard's comm, "Commander, I'm picking up fluctuations in their vocal frequencies. They're shifting between 432 Hz, 963 Hz, and 1000 Hz."

Shepard, keeping his eyes on the Caraliens, responded, "Is that significant, Aria?"

"Yes, it is," Aria replied. "The stasis pods are reacting, just like they did when Doctor James and Professor Tashia used frequency change to open Odriin and her companions' pods. The surfaces are pulsing in sync with the frequency changes. It's almost as though…. the technology is alive, responding to the vibrations."

Suddenly, the surface of the pods began to shift, pulsing with an array of colours. The organic technology seemed to ripple, as though it were breathing. The room grew still as the cover of each stasis pod began to retract with a soft, elegant motion, revealing the figures within.
The Caraliens inside the stasis pods appeared almost human, though there were subtle distinctions. They have sharper angles in their features, a slight translucence to their skin, and a greyish-blue tint. Alexander stepped forward, captivated by the sight. "They're astonishing. They look similar to humans but…. not quite."

Noticing the tension in the room, Odriin turned to Commander Shepard. "Please, don't be alarmed, Commander," she said in a soothing voice. "The stasis pods scan their environment and adapt the Caraliens' appearance to resemble the dominant species present. Since there are more Carals here than humans, their true forms are preserved for the time being. However, their appearance will gradually shift to be more like yours."

Shepard nodded, his gaze still fixed on the pods. "Honestly, we don't mind how they look or how they might look in the future."

Odriin smiled gently. "You are very gracious."

Hemera moved closer to one of the pods, waving her hand in the air to produce a holographic display out of thin air. The display showed the brain activity of the Caralien Captain, the second-in-command, and several key engineers. Aether joined her, studying the readings with a critical eye.

"They are close to waking," Aether announced after a few moments. "Just a few more minutes, and they will regain consciousness."

As they waited, Shepard turned to Ninil. "This ritual, how old is it?"

Ninil's gaze drifted, her voice distant as she spoke. "It's ancient. The Carals have used it for millennia. It was originally created to bless their people during times of great change or uncertainty. Given the nature of their journey and their long hibernation, it is fitting that they perform this ritual now."

Shepard nodded thoughtfully. "It's…. comforting, in a way. Like a reminder that some things don't change, even across the stars."

Suddenly, one of the figures in the stasis pod stirred. The lights around the pod pulsed brighter, and the figure inside opened their eyes. It was the Caralien Captain Enki-Marduk.

"He's waking up," Alexander said, his voice tinged with excitement.

Odriin stepped forward, her expression softening as she watched the Captain slowly emerge. "It's time," she said quietly. "Our journey together is just beginning."

Captain Enki-Marduk lay in his stasis pod, his eyes snapping open as he became aware of the unfamiliar figures surrounding him. In the Carals language, he shouted, "En-líl ga-nam! Egir-nim-gal-lu? Ul ú-tu-ma Tot-maḫ-lugal-e-ne šu-ne? Am-ma-ta-szi-ni ga-nam-ma? Mu-ne ki ag-ge im-ma-da-tum-ma!"
Instantly, Aria translated the words for the crew through their earpieces.

"Good lord! Who are you people? Are you from the Tot Empire? Why didn't my pod register your presence? It feels like you've bypassed the awakening protocols!"

His face reflected shock and confusion, emotions rarely seen in a Caralien captain. He quickly grasped the seriousness of the breached protocols, his mind racing with possibilities. Who are these beings?

As he struggled to make sense of the situation, the other Caraliens began stirring in their stasis pods, slowly blinking awake. The second-in-command, equally disoriented, looked around, rubbing his eyes. The engineers stretched, yawned, and blinked, still trying to gather their bearings. Concern clouding his expression, the second-in-command raised his head. "Captain, what's happening? This is not how our awakening was supposed to go."

Just then, Odriin stepped forward, her presence both commanding and calming. She began speaking to the captain in the Caral language, and Aria immediately translated the conversation for the crew: "We are not your enemies. I am Caral, and I am Odriin, your princess."

Captain Enki-Marduk stared at her, confusion still clouding his features, though he could feel the atmosphere shift. "Princess…. Odriin? Is that really you?" His expression softened as a trace of reassurance began to settle in.

"Yes, Captain," Odriin replied with calm confidence. "There's no danger here. I have awakened you to begin repairs on our vessel. Do you remember our last battle with the Tot when we attempted to disable the Jump Station?"

The captain nodded slowly. "Yes, it was a brilliant plan to detonate a quantum shell while using the Jump Station to leap to this star cluster."

The second-in-command, Geshtu-Ea, chimed in. "But the explosion damaged most of our systems."

One of the engineers, Utu-Dumuzi, nodded in agreement.

Captain Enki-Marduk took a deep breath, the weight of the situation dawning on him. "Alright, then. We need to assess our surroundings and begin repairs immediately. I see you've awakened the engineers as well."

He glanced at Odriin, his brow furrowing slightly. "You look.... different, Princess. Are these two your sisters? I recognise the two warriors behind you, but the others.... I can't sense them as I do with our people. Who are they?"

Odriin gestured toward the unfamiliar figures. "They are human. They are risking their very existence to help us."

Chapter 6 – The Carals

Captain Enki-Marduk stood tall and strong on the bridge of the stasis great hall, his ancient eyes flickering open. As he emerged from the pod, he waved his hand, and a holographic screen appeared in the air, covered with alien symbols and strange, flowing characters. His fingers brushed lightly over one of the glyphs, activating a portal door. He looked at Princess Odriin, standing gracefully beside him, then shifted his gaze to Commander Shepard, who stood with his human crew.

"Follow me to the bridge," Captain Enki-Marduk instructed, his voice calm but firm.

Commander Shepard glanced over his shoulder at his crew. "Are they invited as well?" he asked cautiously, raising an eyebrow.

Captain Enki-Marduk gave a slight nod. "Yes, please. All of you."

Shepard, still slightly unsure, tested the waters. "Is your translator working alright? Can.... you.... understand.... us?"

Enki-Marduk's lips curled into the faintest of smiles. "Yes, Commander. Your translator is quite effective. It translates your words seamlessly. I can understand every word you say."

Turning to his own staff, Enki-Marduk addressed his second-in-command, Geshtu-Ea, and the rest of the engineers who had just awoken from their long stasis. "Can you all understand the humans?" he asked.

"Yes, Captain, we can," they replied in unison.

"Good. We must begin repairs immediately. Our outer shell was severely damaged by the Tot Empire's thermonuclear attacks. Prepare to fix the hull."

The engineers Utu-Dumuzi, Ningal-Uruk, Gibil-Zababa, Nanshe-Idnin, Lugalbanda-Eresh, Inanna-Zu, and Kingu-Namtar exchanged determined glances, ready to begin their critical work. One by one, the Caralien crew passed through the glowing portal door.

Shepard gave a firm nod, giving one last look to ensure his team was ready. "Alright, let's move." He gestured for his engineers, Chief Engineer Nova Rodriguez, Mira, Ethan, and Clovis, to follow the Caraliens through the portal. One by one, the humans stepped through, with Shepard bringing up the rear.

A few seconds later, they stepped into a vast chamber, unlike anything Commander Shepard had ever encountered before. The room was enormous, without the traditional windows or viewports one might expect on a bridge. Instead, sleek terminals and control consoles rose smoothly from the floor, glowing with a soft, pulsating light that filled the room with an otherworldly ambience. At various stations, circular orbs of light hovered just above the consoles, reacting almost organically to the presence of the Caraliens, as if attuned to their very essence.

The walls of the chamber shimmered, constantly shifting in colour depending on where one stood, giving the impression of a living, breathing environment. Beneath Shepard's feet, the floor rippled gently, creating a strange sensation as though the very ground was subtly alive and adjusting to their movements.

As the crew took in their surroundings, the two Ashigarus and the two Tengus were allowed to follow them onto the bridge. One of the Ashigaru turned to Shepard and remarked, "Feels like we've just walked into a nightclub. All we need now is some romantic music with all these lights dancing around the control stations."

Shepard cracked a smile at the Ashigaru's comment, prompting a few chuckles from the human crew. Despite being surrounded by the high-tech alien environment that surrounded them from floor to ceiling, the crew maintained their sense of humour, a trait that made them remarkably adaptable in situations like this.

Captain Enki-Marduk stood tall by one of the consoles, briefly acknowledging the light-hearted exchange with a faint smirk, though his attention quickly returned to the pressing tasks at hand.

Odriin stood calmly at the centre of the bridge, her presence bringing a sense of calm to everyone around her. The soft, glowing lights danced across her, a quiet reminder that the Carals, even after everything they'd been through for centuries, were still standing strong. They hadn't let their struggles harden them. They remained kind and gentle, no matter what they faced.

Shepard nodded decisively. "Alright, let's get to it. We need this ship fully operational as soon as we possibly can."

Enki-Marduk turned back to his controls. "Indeed,

Commander. We'll start by reactivating the exotic matter engine, then address the unfinished repairs to the outer hull that the auto-repair systems couldn't complete. After that, we'll work on re-initialising the affected systems."

The Caralien engineers, Utu-Dumuzi, Ningal-Uruk, Gibil-Zababa, and Nanshe-Idnin moved quickly to their stations, touching the glowing orbs with practised precision. Lugalbanda-Eresh, Inanna-Zu, and Kingu-Namtar joined them, coordinating with the human engineers to assess the damage and begin the necessary repairs.

The ever-alert Tengu war dogs stayed close to the group, their advanced sensors constantly scanning for any potential threats from their alien surroundings. Their sleek, mechanical forms stood in stark contrast to the ship's organic design, yet their presence was reassuring, providing an added sense of security, Shepard mused.
As the team got to work, Shepard couldn't help but think about how well the humans and Carals were starting to work together. It wasn't just about sharing skills and tech; it felt like they were mixing their cultures and ways of thinking. Even with all the problems they were up against, he felt like they were stronger as a team.

Nova Rodriguez stood nearby, her arm pad diligently

recording every movement and sequence as the Caraliens operated their orb and gesture-based interfaces. It also captured the detailed instructions they were giving to Shepard's team, relaying everything to Aria for analysis and interpretation. As she waited, Nova couldn't help but marvel at the intricate design of the central bridge command centre. "Captain," she murmured to Shepard, gesturing toward the circular control orbs, "this technology... It's incredible. It feels like the ship itself is alive, functioning in perfect symbiosis with them."

One of the Caralien engineers, Utu-Dumuzi, spoke up as he examined the console in front of him. "Captain, it appears our physiognomy has adapted to the ship's atmosphere. We can now breathe a mix of oxygen, nitrogen, argon, and carbon dioxide. The vessel's systems are accommodating these humans quite effectively."

Enki-Marduk looked intrigued. "Oxygen?" he repeated thoughtfully. "Humans survive for long periods breathing oxygen?"

Nova chuckled softly before responding, "The oldest recorded human lived to be 230 years old, Captain."

Enki-Marduk turned to Princess Odriin, his confusion

deepening. "Years? What exactly is a year?"

Odriin was about to answer, but Ninil stepped forward and began explaining human time to the bewildered Caralien captain.

"A second is the smallest unit of time humans use," Ninil began. "It's a brief moment, like the blink of an eye or the snap of a finger. Sixty seconds make up one minute, and 60 minutes make up an hour. Humans divide their day into 24 hours, which is based on the time it takes for their planet Earth to rotate fully on its axis. A day has both light and dark periods. What they call day and night. Seven days form a week, and about 30 days make a month. A year, Captain, is 365 days long, and that's how long it takes for Earth to orbit its star, the Sun."

Enki-Marduk blinked, taking it all in. "Ah, I see. Thank you, Celestial." He bowed his head slightly toward Ninil. "Forgive me for not recognising your presence earlier. Your human-like appearance confused me, but I can now sense your Celestial vibrations. It is our greatest honour to welcome you aboard our flagship, Nergal."

Ninil smiled warmly. "You are welcome, Captain."

Enki-Marduk, feeling a bit humbled, continued, "Ninil, my Celestial, we also named our flagship after…."

Ninil interrupted with a knowing smile. "Yes, after the name we gave ourselves during our last visit to your ancestors. We are truly honoured by your admiration, both then and now."

Suddenly, Utu-Dumuzi interrupted, his voice tense as he scanned the bridge's console. "Captain, the ship has been gradually repairing itself during our long stasis. Most of the engines have been restored, but the exotic matter drive still needs to be reactivated for us to deploy our repair drones."

Geshtu-Ea, the second-in-command, turned to the engineers. "Utu-Dumuzi, Kingu-Namtar, you will join the humans to restart the exotic matter engine."

Commander Shepard stepped forward. "Chief Engineer Rodriguez, bring Mira and Ethan with you. Clovis, stay here on the bridge to assist where needed."

Rodriguez gave a quick nod. "Understood, Commander." She motioned to Mira and Ethan. "Let's get to work."

As the portal door began to open on the bridge, the wall's

design shifted, twisting and curling like serpents slowly slithering away. The wall moved in a mesmerising dance until the portal was fully revealed, allowing access to the passage beyond. Utu-Dumuzi, leading the way, turned back to the group.

"Before we step into the engineering rooms, I need to review the data we've received from our systems," she said, her tone calm but commanding. She turned to Kingu-Namtar and gave him a quick nod. "Sync the necessary translated data to the humans' holographic arm pads."

Kingu-Namtar, precise in his movements, approached Chief Engineer Nova Rodriguez. "May I see your armpad, Chief Rodriguez?" he asked, his voice soft but steady.

Nova, slightly caught off guard, felt a blush creep onto her cheeks as Kingu-Namtar gently held her arm. "Ah, I see," he said with a nod. "Your AI has done an excellent job interpreting the instructions." With practised precision, he worked alongside Aria, his fingers moving deftly as he configured her device using his sleek, slim tablet. For a brief moment, his golden eyes met hers, and she couldn't help but feel a soothing sense of calm and serenity emanating from him.

"All done," he said with a smile, his voice smooth and reassuring. "Your arm pad is now configured to receive the data."

Aria responded quickly, her voice clear and precise. "Chief Rodriguez, I've streamlined the newly received data for your review. I've also outlined the steps the Carals will follow to realign and restore power to the exotic matter engine."

Nova smiled and replied, "Thank you, Aria. You've been doing an amazing job translating all the Caral data into something we can work with. The engineers and I couldn't have made this much progress without you."

Aria's digital voice carried a hint of satisfaction. "Thank you, Chief. It's my pleasure to assist. However, Commander Shepard seems to struggle with understanding the simplified instructions I've provided. He's having a hard time grasping the quantum mechanics and mathematical engineering required for this collaboration with the Carals."

Nova chuckled softly, glancing over at Shepard, who stood at the far end of the room, oblivious to the conversation. "Aria, Shepard's a soldier. His expertise is in giving orders and shooting anything that moves. Most of the time, he gets it right. Just leave him to what he knows best."

Aria's response was instant and dry, as if humouring Nova's observation. "Noted, Chief."

Nova's chuckle grew into a quiet laugh as she watched Shepard, completely unaware that he was the subject of their conversation. Shepard, catching Nova's eye, raised an eyebrow in curiosity but remained silent, clearly unaware of the amusement happening behind his back.

As all the engineers, both human and Caralien, made their way through the portal, the door closed smoothly behind them. The mesmerising wall design began to curl and shift once again, reversing its previous movements, and sliding seamlessly back into place until the portal was entirely hidden. It was as if the doorway had never existed.

Inside the engineering section, the room was a stark contrast to the organic and almost ethereal design of the bridge. Massive conduits snaked along the walls, glowing faintly with energy, while various control panels blinked in sync with the ship's systems. The Caralien engineers moved with purpose, it was clear they knew their tech well as they started checking out the different stations.

Utu-Dumuzi led the way, her eyes scanning the consoles. "We need to focus on reactivating the exotic matter engine first. What is left of the external repairs can follow once we've restored the engine's power."

Rodriguez, now fully synced to the Caral systems, stepped forward. "Our team's ready to assist, but we'll need a clear breakdown of the sequence required to restart the engine."

Kingu-Namtar approached Rodriguez once again, nodding in agreement. "I've transferred the necessary data to your arm pad. The process is intricate, but with Aria's assistance, you should be able to follow the instructions closely."

Rodriguez glanced at her arm pad holographic screen projection as lines of alien script began to shift into readable text, thanks to Aria's real-time translation. She nodded and looked back at him. "Looks good. We'll handle the power couplings, and your team can focus on stabilising the quantum core."

One of the Caralien engineers, Lugalbanda-Eresh, called out from his station on the bridge. "The quantum core has suffered no damage, but the outer containment fields are unstable. We'll need to reset those manually."
Rodriguez turned to her team. "Ethan, Mira, get over there

and assist with the containment fields. Clovis, she said on the comms, Can you monitor the power grid from one of the stations on the bridge."

Geshtu-Ea approached Clovis and gestured toward a nearby station beside one of the engineers. Guiding him to the console, Geshtu-Ea activated the power grid monitoring interface, which displayed a series of spikes and drops. Pointing at the graph, he explained, "The spikes are within acceptable limits, but you'll need to alert the team immediately if the power dips below this threshold."

Ethan, already moving toward the panel, gave a quick thumbs-up. "Got it, Chief. On my way."

Mira followed closely behind, her fingers already moving over the control interface. "Let's get this done."
As the team continued working, one of the Ashigaru robot soldiers, who had followed the group along with the one Tengu, made an unexpected discovery while scanning the surroundings. The Ashigaru suddenly broke the calm of the room.

"Chief," the Ashigaru said, turning its head toward Chief Engineer Nova Rodriguez, "my x-ray vision is detecting a large object embedded close to the power conduits. It appears to be a shell. Could this be causing the system issues?"

Rodriguez paused and raised an eyebrow, looking over at Kingu-Namtar for confirmation. The Caralien engineer quickly stepped forward, already beginning to pull up data on his slim tablet. "Let's check," he said, his golden eyes narrowing in concentration. He turned to Utu-Dumuzi, who, with a quick motion, summoned a holographic screen out of thin air. The screen materialised in front of them, its glowing alien symbols shifting as they worked.

Rodriguez, intrigued by the sudden discovery, leaned in closer as Utu-Dumuzi tapped on the screen. "Alright, let's have a look." With a smooth flick of her wrist, she transferred the holographic display to the wall, syncing it with the scan data from the Ashigaru.
The glowing image showed a detailed view of the internal structure, highlighting the area where the shell was embedded. Utu-Dumuzi's eyes widened slightly. "Oh.... this is not good."

Rodriguez frowned. "What can you see?"

Kingu-Namtar leaned in closer to the holographic display, his face tense with realisation. "This," he said slowly, "is an unexploded Quantum Starfire: which is the equivalent of a 100-megaton explosive force of a thermonuclear bomb."

There was a moment of silence as everyone processed the importance of the situation.

Rodriguez felt her heart skip a beat. "How old is it?" she asked, her voice steady but with a note of concern.

Kingu-Namtar's eyes flickered with a cold calculation. "Approximately 200,000 years old. This bomb must've been left behind during the Tot's last attack on our ship, from the final battle that damaged our systems."

Utu-Dumuzi immediately began tapping at the holographic interface, sending the newly discovered data directly to the bridge. Within seconds, a holographic representation of Captain Enki-Marduk materialised before them, his calm and regal presence filling the engineering room.

"Captain," Utu-Dumuzi said, addressing him directly, "we've discovered an unexploded Quantum Starfire embedded in one of the power conduits. It's likely been here since the last conflict with the Tot. We cannot proceed with repairs until we safely remove it."
Captain Enki-Marduk studied the holographic display with

intense focus, and the severity of the situation was clear in his eyes. He took a moment to think, then spoke with his usual calm but firm tone: "Understood. This will require delicate handling. We'll need to dispatch one of our shuttles to extract the bomb safely."

Rodriguez, still taking in the magnitude of the find, crossed her arms. "What's the plan for removal, Captain?"

Enki-Marduk nodded. "First, we'll use a Graviton stream from the shuttle to grab hold of the bomb. After that, we'll make an incision around the area with a low-intensity Energy beam, ensuring we don't trigger any remaining instability in the shell. Once we've carefully detached the bomb, we can control any potential leakage of our vessel's organic materials and seal the outer hull from the inside out."

Shepard, who had been listening quietly from the back, finally stepped forward. "And what about containment? Is there any risk of radiation?"

Kingu-Namtar shook his head. "The bomb's containment field appears to have held over the centuries. As long as we proceed carefully, there shouldn't be any risk of detonation or radiation leakage. However, once it's out, we'll need to check it for any leftover instability."

"Agreed," Enki-Marduk added. "Safety is paramount. We cannot afford any mistakes with this one."
Captain Zulu, who was on the comms monitoring the situation, advised Rodriguez and Shepard to help the Carals as much as possible.

Rodriguez gathered her team around. "Mira, Ethan, I need you both on the extraction. Work closely with the Caralien engineers. We can't afford any mistakes here, everything needs to be perfect."

Mira gave a quick nod, her eyes full of determination. "Got it, Chief. We'll make it happen."

Ethan tried to lighten the mood, cracking his knuckles with a grin. "Looks like we're getting up close and personal with some ancient alien tech that might blow up. Fun times, right?"

Rodriguez couldn't help but smirk at his attempt to lighten the mood. Just then, the familiar voice of Aria chimed in. "I'll be monitoring the energy signatures of the bomb closely. Any fluctuations or anomalies, and I'll alert you immediately."

"Thanks, Aria," Rodriguez said, exhaling slowly as she glanced at the holographic projection of Captain Enki-Marduk. "Captain, we're ready to move forward. Just waiting on your go."

Captain Enki-Marduk's image flickered slightly before he gave a sharp nod of approval. "Proceed with extreme caution. This may be old, degraded technology, but do not underestimate it. The risk is still very real. I'll send Ningal-Uruk, she's young but an excellent shuttle pilot engineer and Gibil-Zababa, she is one of our best. Together, I have no doubt you will complete this mission successfully. This thermonuclear shell must be removed from Nergal without fail."

The Captain's hologram blinked out, leaving the team to face the task ahead. The weight of the situation pressed down on them, but there was an unspoken resolve between the human and Caralien engineers. Everyone knew failure wasn't an option.

Ethan looked around the room, sensing the tension. "So, does anyone else feel like they're defusing a bomb in the middle of a sci-fi movie, or is it just me?"
Mira elbowed him lightly. "Keep it together, Ethan. We've

got this."

Rodriguez smirked at their banter, appreciating the tension break, even for a moment. She then turned her attention back to the task, her voice firm. "Alright, let's focus. This is critical. We need to ensure that every move we make is deliberate. The slightest mistake could be catastrophic."

The Caralien engineer, Utu-Dumuzi, approached with a holographic display in hand, syncing it with the human arm pads. "We have configured your devices to provide real-time data. We will proceed with you, step by step."

Ethan studied the display on his arm pad and raised an eyebrow. "I gotta say, your tech makes ours look like it came out of a cereal box. This is some next-level stuff."

Kingu-Namtar, standing nearby, gave a rare smile. "You humans have spirit, I'll give you that."

"Thanks for the encouraging words," Ethan joked, before turning serious again. "Let's do this."

A portal door shimmered open in the Nergal shuttle bay. Ethan and Mira stepped out, their boots landing on the spacious, organic-looking hangar floor. The space seemed vast, with walls and ceilings that resembled living tissue more than metal. Waiting for them were two Caralien engineers, Ningal-Uruk and Gibil-Zababa, standing beside their shuttle.

Ethan's eyes widened as they approached, unable to contain his thoughts. "Wow, these Caralien females.... They look incredible in those uniforms," he said, gawking a little. "And their grey-blue skin, it's like it was made to match their white-blue uniforms. I think I'm in love, Mira."

Mira, rolling her eyes, gave him a sharp nudge. "Snap out of it, Romeo. We've got a job to do, remember?"

"Easy for you to say. You're a woman," Ethan grumbled, his gaze still wandering. Mira just shot him a look of disbelief before focusing on the task ahead, walking toward the Caralien engineers.

"Hello again," Mira greeted Ningal-Uruk and Gibil-Zababa as they drew closer.

Ningal-Uruk gave a polite nod, gesturing toward the shuttle. "Greetings. You are just in time."

Mira took in the sight of the shuttle in front of them. At

first glance, it didn't look all that different from humanity's latest experimental stealth crafts, but as she got closer, she realised how wrong that assumption was. The shuttle didn't feel like a machine at all, it felt alive. Its hull was smooth and curved, with a flowing, organic design. Deep shades of crimson coated the exterior, shimmering as if the ship itself was breathing. Stripes of yellow and white crisscrossed its surface, not in sharp lines but like veins of light, pulsing softly.

Ethan reached out and lightly touched the hull. His eyes widened. "It's warm. Almost like skin."

"Yeah," Mira added, running her fingers along the surface. "Soft but tough, like armour. This is beyond anything we've ever seen. It's almost.... alive."

Gibil-Zababa smiled softly. "It is alive in a way. Our bio-organic engineering merges the organic with the technological. This shuttle was grown, not built."

Mira looked impressed, nodding to herself as they continued to examine the shuttle. The walls were subtly ridged, like the hide of a massive, gentle creature. When they walked closer, the ridges shifted slightly, almost as though they were responding to their presence.

"Fascinating," Mira whispered.

Ningal-Uruk gestured for them to enter the shuttle. "Please, come inside. We have already modified the atmosphere to accommodate both our species and human physiology."

As they stepped inside, the sense of being inside something living only intensified. The control panels rose from the floor as if growing out of it, glowing with soft, calming hues. The walls shifted colours with the environment, transitioning from warm reds and yellows to cooler blues and purples as they moved further in. The floor rippled underfoot but felt solid and secure.

"This.... This is amazing," Ethan muttered, his voice hushed in awe. "It's like the shuttle is breathing."

"And the sound," Mira added, noticing the soft hum that surrounded them. "It's like a heartbeat."

"The shuttle is designed to harmonise with its crew," Gibil-Zababa explained. "The atmosphere, sound, and even the subtle scents are all meant to create a calming environment. The air smells like... nature on our planet of origin."
"Yeah," Ethan agreed, taking a deep breath. "It smells like

a forest after rain."

The shuttle door closed behind them, leaving no trace of its existence, seamlessly blending into the walls. It lifted off the hangar floor effortlessly, with no engines roaring, no energy blast, just a smooth, silent ascent.

"We've been cleared for departure," Ningal-Uruk announced, turning to face the others. "We'll be heading directly to the impact zone where the unexploded Quantum Starfire shell is lodged."

As the shuttle sped out of the hangar, passing through the shield, Ethan couldn't help but marvel at how fast it was moving. "This thing's got some serious speed," he said, leaning slightly to peer out of the transparent wall that seemed to appear out of nowhere.

Ningal-Uruk pressed a few buttons on a floating control panel. "Captain Enki-Marduk, we are approaching the impact zone. We will reach the entry point to the unexploded Quantum Starfire in two quantum rounds."

Ethan blinked. "Wait, two quantum rounds? You mean two minutes, right?"
Ningal-Uruk smiled apologetically. "Yes, my apologies.

Two minutes."

Mira couldn't help but chuckle at Ethan's confusion. "Get used to it, Ethan. We're not in Kansas anymore."

With a final smirk, Ethan settled into his seat as the shuttle silently made its approach, ready for the dangerous task that lay ahead.

Ningal-Uruk's voice came through the intercom, steady and calm. "Captain Enki-Marduk, we're in position and ready to manoeuvre the shuttle through the breach created by the thermonuclear shell."

Captain Enki-Marduk, standing at his command console aboard the Nergal, replied, "I can see that on the main viewer. Proceed carefully, Ningal-Uruk."

At that moment, Captain Zulu chimed in through a shared channel. "Odyssey to shuttle team: proceed with extreme caution. That shell is ancient and unstable. We don't want any surprises."

Mira glanced over at Ethan, who seemed more focused than usual, and responded, "Acknowledged. We'll be careful." Ningal-Uruk gently guided the alien shuttle forward.

"Entering the crack caused by the impact now. Moving slowly."

Mira peered out at the widening breach as they advanced. "Wow, that's a big opening.... I'm surprised it didn't detonate on impact."

The shuttle crept forward, moving cautiously into the dark, jagged wound in the outer hull of the Nergal. Within seconds, they were 150 meters deep into the outer layer. The tension inside the shuttle was visible, but the team remained focused.

"There it is," Gibil-Zababa and Ethan said simultaneously as they spotted the thermonuclear shell on the shuttle's organic-like display screen.

Gibil-Zababa glanced at Ethan with a slight smirk. "Shall we begin?"

Captain Enki-Marduk's voice cut in over the comms. "Are you seeing this on your NÍG-LAGAB GUB-BA reader?"

Ethan, momentarily confused, muttered, "Uh, what?"

AI Aria interjected, "Ethan, they're referring to a Geiger

counter, a radiation detector."

Ningal-Uruk nodded at the captain's holographic image. "Yes, Captain, we're seeing it. The shell is leaking radiation. The shuttle has already activated the LAGAB protocol."

"Aria," Mira called, "confirm we're in radiation protection mode?"

The AI responded instantly. "Yes, the shuttle has entered full radiation protection mode."

Mira exhaled. "Good. What kind of radiation levels are we talking about?"

Ningal-Uruk, checking her console, replied with concern, "We don't want to stay close to that thing for too long. It's leaking alpha radiation, but the real danger is the pulsating cosmic rays. Lethal to anything organic."

Ethan, slightly uneasy, asked, "Right. How quickly can we get this thing out?"

Gibil-Zababa, with a steady tone, answered, "Once we grab hold of it with the energy beam, we can't afford to release it. If we do, there's a high risk of triggering an explosion."

Captain Enki-Marduk's voice returned, firm but calm. "Proceed with the extraction. Begin."

"Energy beam activated," Gibil-Zababa announced. "It's your turn, Mira and Ethan. Hands on the controls."

Mira and Ethan placed their hands on the shuttle's organic interfaces. Ningal-Uruk, guiding them, said, "As we rehearsed earlier, think of cutting through the outer layer."

Suddenly, two beams of low-intensity energy emerged from the shuttle's exterior stripes, focusing on the shell.

"Good," Ningal-Uruk praised. "You're doing great. Now follow the outline marked by the computer."

The beams cut smoothly on either side of the unexploded shell, tracing a perfectly circular path around it. Slowly but surely, the thermonuclear shell dislodged from the ship's inner layer.

"Nice work," Gibil-Zababa said, her voice calm but impressed. "The shell's free. Let's get it out of here."
Ningal-Uruk carefully began manoeuvring the shuttle out

of the breach, the massive shell floating alongside them, nearly the size of the shuttle itself. "Backing out now," Ningal-Uruk reported.

Just as they cleared the breach, proximity alarms sounded inside the shuttle. The alert was sharp, making everyone in the cockpit tense up.

Captain Enki-Marduk's voice broke the tense silence. "Don't be alarmed, but we have company."
Aria, with her usual precise timing, added, "Seven spaceships have just entered close proximity to the Nergal."

Ethan's face turned grim. "Well, that's just great. I was hoping for a quiet mission."

Mira smirked. "You know we're never that lucky."

Ningal-Uruk, keeping her eyes on the controls, said, "No time to worry about them now. Let's focus on securing this bomb."

Captain Zulu's voice returned on the shared channel. "We'll hold them off, but you need to finish your task and get that shell out of here."

"Understood," Ningal-Uruk replied. She glanced at Gibil-Zababa. "The Shell is out and moving off?"

With the shell in tow and the shuttle team focused, the mission continued, but the looming threat of the unknown fleet cast a shadow over their success.

Chapter 7 – Tip of the spear

Aboard the Odyssey, Commander Reyes's voice crackled over the holographic intercom. "Captain Zulu, we've detected seven vessels entering our surveillance zone. They're slowly approaching the Caral's mothership."

Captain Zulu turned towards the comm holographic panel, his brow furrowing. "Acknowledged, Commander Reyes." "Lieutenant Vega," he called, "get the engagement tactics targeting coordination ready. I don't like the look of this."

Vega's voice came through crisp and clear, "On it, Captain."

"Arno," Zulu continued, "plot a course directly between the Nergal and those seven ships. Keep us 200,000 kilometres from the Caral mothership. Let's be ready in case they try something."

Arno nodded from his station, fingers flying over the console. "Plotting course now, Captain. Distance set, moving out."

Zulu leaned back in his chair, thinking aloud. "Good thing we positioned close to the Nergal. Get the dart fighters prepped, Commander Nin. If things go sideways, we might need them for evac, our people and the awakened Caraliens, especially Princess Odriin.”

As the Odyssey shifted into position, two of the alien vessels suddenly altered their course. Commander Reyes's voice was urgent over the intercom. “Captain, two of their ships have changed heading, directly toward us. They've accelerated and will intercept in minutes.”

Zulu's jaw tightened. “Reyes, coordinate with Jessica Thompson. I want the gamma burst cannons primed and ready. Get all weapons on full alert. We might need every bit of firepower we've got.”

Reyes hesitated for a second. “Captain, are you saying, all weapons? Plasma cannons, antimatter torpedoes, everything?”

Zulu responded without hesitation. “Yes, all of them. And make it quick. We don't have time to argue.”

“Affirmative, Captain. We'll be weapons-ready in minutes.”

As Reyes got to work, one of the Tot vessels accelerated further, positioning itself directly in front of the Odyssey, forcing it to halt. “Captain, we're being scanned,” Vega reported, her eyes on the sensor readouts.

"Stay sharp," Zulu muttered. "Let's see what they want."

A moment later, the Odyssey's comm system activated. The screen flickered, and the visual feed revealed a humanoid figure, clad in a sleek white robe with golden strips outlining the intricate design. The figure's face was obscured by a white helmet, and behind the humanoid, eight soldiers stood in menacing black tactical armour, their weapons at the ready.

"I am High Priest Uttu of the Tot Empire," the white-robed figure announced, his words seamlessly translated by the auto-translation system due to the striking similarities between his language and that of the Carals. His voice was cold and commanding. "Identify yourselves. We hold no hostility toward your species, but we have detected your presence aboard the Caral vessel. We've also detected technologies belonging to our enemies on your ship. Prepare to be boarded. Failure to comply will result in your destruction."

Zulu's eyes narrowed as he took in the sight of the towering Tot battleship, easily twice the size of the Odyssey. However, even these imposing vessels seemed dwarfed by the colossal Caral mothership. He didn't like being threatened, especially after being in a war with the

Fanatics 40 years ago.

Reyes cut into Zulu's thoughts. "Captain, the Tot ships are disrupting our comms with the Nergal. We've lost contact. I can't tell what's happening over there, but I'd bet Commander Shepard's already gearing up to defend the Carals."

Zulu nodded, his fingers tapping rhythmically on the armrest. "No doubt. But we can't just sit here and wait to be boarded like some passive freighter."

"Captain," Reyes added, her voice tense, "the Tot ships are closing in on the Nergal. Our sensors show they've powered up weapons. They're ready to fire."

Zulu's eyes flicked to the battle display, watching as the Tot ships inched closer to the Caral mothership. His mind raced there was no way he'd surrender to these aliens after spending half his life fighting the Fanatics for freedom.

He rose from his chair. "Reyes, keep the weapons hot. Prepare for evasive manoeuvres. And if that High Priest wants a fight, we'll make sure he regrets picking one with us."

Reyes grinned. "Let's show these Tots who they're dealing with."

Captain Zulu turned back to the comm panel, locking eyes with the white-robed figure on the screen. "This is Captain Zulu of the Odyssey. We don't intend to surrender, nor will we let you harm our friends on the Nergal."

The High Priest's face remained obscured, but the coldness in his voice was unmistakable. "So be it. Your defiance will be your undoing."

Zulu smirked, glancing at his second-in-command. Without a word, Nin swiftly muted the communication with the Tot's vessel, meeting Zulu's gaze. "We'll see about that," Zulu muttered. Then, turning to Lieutenant Stella Vega, he said with determination, "Let's show them what the Odyssey is capable of."

The Tot battleships are beautiful, this colossal *Tot's Empire* battleship, is an awe-inspiring fusion of elegance and power that dominates the cosmos with its striking design. The vessel is immense, easily the size of a small city, with a sleek, elongated shape that tapers at the ends, giving it a graceful yet imposing presence as it glides through space.

The ship's exterior is pristine, gleaming white, smooth as polished marble, reflecting distant starlight and lending it an almost divine aura. Intricate gold accents trace along the hull in regal patterns, their delicate filigree serving both as decoration and housing for energy conduits or shielding. These golden lines pulse softly, hinting at the immense power contained within.

At the front of the battleship, a large, spear-like prow juts forward, reinforced with layered armour and edged in gold, giving it a threatening, predatory look. This prow functions not only as a weapon of intimidation but also houses powerful projectile cannons capable of devastating entire fleets with its thermonuclear shells. Along the sides of the vessel, massive gun turrets are mounted, sleek and integrated into the ship's hull, ready to unleash devastating firepower.

The battleship's command tower rises gracefully from the central spine, crowned with a shimmering golden dome that houses the bridge. The tower's windows are tinted, reflecting a dark shimmer that hides the inner workings, adding an air of mystery. Surrounding the main hull are smaller auxiliary ships or drones that dart around like golden fireflies, loyal to the empire's cause.

Despite its beauty, the battleship radiates a sense of menace.

Its imposing size, combined with the flawless, cold design, projects a feeling of invincibility as if it's a weapon forged by the gods of war. While giving it a majestic look, the golden highlights also frame its destructive potential, making it clear that this is not just a vessel of beauty, but one capable of delivering unmatched devastation to its enemies.

As it cuts through the void of space, the battleship leaves behind a faint trail of glowing energy, as if marking its territory across the stars, a symbol of the Tot Empire's grandeur and their unyielding dominance over the cosmos.

Captain Zulu stood on the bridge of the Odyssey, a calm but intense expression on his face as he stared at the looming vessels of the Tot Empire on the viewscreen. The tension in the air was perceptible, every crew member awaiting his command. He looked at Nin and then turned to Lieutenant Vega, who was manning the tactical station.

"Lieutenant Vega," Zulu said, his voice firm but measured. "You are clear to fire the Gamma Burst Cannon."

Vega nodded and quickly tapped her console. "Gamma Burst Cannon, online," she reported. "Firing in three, two, one...."

Outside, the Odyssey's Gamma Burst Cannon, barely visible from a distance, unleashed a brilliant ray of high-energy particles. The beam sliced through the cold vacuum of space like an arrow loosed from a bow, homing in on its target, the massive Tot Empire battleship. The sheer speed of the beam made it seem as if the distance between the two vessels shrank in a heartbeat.

The Tot Empire's battleship had no time to react. The energy beam struck its shields, causing them to flare violently. A crackling overload rippled across the protective barrier, which buckled and failed within seconds under the overwhelming power. The beam then tore through the hull of the battleship, slicing into its core with devastating precision.

The bridge of the Odyssey was momentarily silent as the crew watched the impact unfold on their screens. A massive ball of fire erupted from the centre of the Tot battleship, followed by secondary explosions. The once-mighty vessel disintegrated in a spectacular display of destruction, fragments of its pristine white and gold hull scattering across the starry backdrop.

"Direct hit," Vega announced, unable to hide the

satisfaction in her voice.

Zulu nodded, his eyes still locked on the viewscreen. "One down."

Commander Reyes gave a low whistle on the holographic intercom. "That's one hell of a way to make an entrance, Captain."

But Zulu wasn't finished. His attention shifted to the remaining Tot battleships. One of them, witnessing the destruction of its companion, had halted its approach, beginning to turn away. Zulu wasn't about to let them regroup.

"Lieutenant Vega," Zulu said, his voice sharp. "Prepare two antimatter torpedoes. Plot an intercept course with the retreating vessels and get the plasma cannons ready. We'll be moving in closer."

"Antimatter torpedoes armed and ready," Vega confirmed, her fingers dancing across her console.

The first of the antimatter torpedoes launched, streaking toward the Tot battleship. The crew held their breath as it sped through space. The torpedo hit the battleship's shields, which flickered but held. Then, the second torpedo hit, timed perfectly. The enemy's shields collapsed, leaving the ship vulnerable.

"Plasma cannons, full spread," Zulu ordered.

The Odyssey's plasma cannons fired in unison, unleashing a barrage of concentrated energy bolts that slammed into the side of the Tot battleship. The once beautiful ship, with its elegant white hull and golden accents, now sported a gaping crater. Sparks and debris flew from the wound, and moments later, the lights on the Tot ship flickered and went dark.

"They've lost power!" Nin shouted, a note of triumph in her voice.

"Commander Arno," Zulu added, turning to his navigator, "bring us within two hundred thousand kilometres of the Nergal, but keep a distance. We don't want to be caught off guard."

"Aye, Captain," Arno said, steering the ship with careful precision. The Odyssey moved with grace, positioning itself between the Caral's mothership, Nergal, and the Tot ships.

Zulu's gaze swept the bridge, taking in his crew's readiness.

"Vega, status on the other Tot ships."

"Five remaining ships, Captain," she replied, her eyes narrowing at her console. "They're retreating, sir. They've stopped advancing and are turning around.... Wait, they just jumped out of our interstellar system."

Zulu allowed himself a small, satisfied smile. "Good. Let them run."

Commander Nin reported, "Captain, the smaller vessels surrounding the disabled Tot battleship appear to be inactive. I can't detect any energy signatures from them like before, and their once-golden hue has turned greyish. Requesting permission to bring one on board for closer examination."

The Captain nodded thoughtfully and replied, "Permission granted. This will give us valuable insight into their technology and help us better understand who we're dealing with."
Just then, the comms crackled back to life, and Commander Shepard's voice came through, clear and strong.

"Captain Zulu, we've regained communication on this end. What a show you put on. We were watching from here, and

I've got to say, it was impressive to see the Odyssey take down those Tot battleships."

Zulu gave a modest nod as he looked at Nin, though there was a hint of pride in his eyes. "Commander, there was too much at stake to let them get the upper hand. If we had surrendered or hesitated, that would have been the end of humanity as we know it. I wasn't about to let that happen."

Shepard's chuckle echoed through the comms. "You've always been one for grand gestures. But we appreciate it. The Caraliens do too."

Zulu's expression softened. "We stand ready to defend the just cause, Commander. That's what the Odyssey is here for."

Nin turned to Zulu. "Captain, we've got the all-clear from the Caral's mothership. No further hostiles in range. Looks like the Tots weren't expecting that kind of firepower."

Zulu crossed his arms, his gaze still on the viewport where the debris of the Tot battleship drifted like cosmic wreckage. "No one ever expects a Gamma Burst Cannon to the face."

Nin smirked. "I'm just glad they didn't stick around to find out what else we've got in our arsenal."

Zulu turned to his crew. "Let's not get too comfortable. Commander Reyes, I want those torpedo bays restocked, and the Gamma Burst Cannon is going to take another five hours to recharge. Make sure we're prepared for any surprises."

"Aye, Captain," Reyes said over the comm, already relaying the orders.

"Arno," Zulu added, "keep us at a safe distance from the Nergal, but maintain close proximity. I don't want anyone getting between us and the Carals."

"Understood, sir," Arno replied, adjusting their course.

Ethan stepped back as the shuttle controls retracted into the floor, leaving no sign they had ever been there. His voice crackled over the intercom, breaking the tense quiet on the Odyssey's bridge. "Captain Zulu, that was quite a show of force. The Odyssey really flexed its muscles out there. We've successfully extracted the thermonuclear shell, and it looks like the damage it caused to the Nergal's hull is healing itself. The ship's auto-repair system is kicking in much faster than expected."

Captain Zulu leaned forward, eyes focused as he absorbed the update. "Good job, Ethan. Keep monitoring the repairs and report any changes."

Mira, finishing her task, disengaged from the shuttle control as well and chimed in, "Captain, we're moving the shell a safe distance away from the Nergal. It'll be out of range in a few minutes."

Before Zulu could reply, a sudden flicker of light captured the crew's attention. A holographic figure began to materialise right on the Odyssey's bridge, slowly taking on a humanoid form. The crew stood frozen, startled by the unexpected arrival.

Captain Enki-Marduk had made his first visual connection with the Odyssey since the human crew had boarded the alien vessel. His holographic presence was tall, and regal, with an air of ancient wisdom.
"Captain Zulu," Enki-Marduk's voice resonated with calm authority, "I owe you and your crew a debt of gratitude. You have saved us all from the Tot's onslaught. Since the shell was removed, our systems are coming back online faster than expected. Life support, communications,

navigation, all are returning to full capacity."

Zulu gave a respectful nod. "We're just glad we could help. It was touch-and-go for a while, but the Odyssey will always be ready to stand with our allies."

Enki-Marduk smiled, a gesture that somehow carried warmth despite the cold distance of the hologram. "And for that, we would like to offer something in return. Once our systems are fully functional, I would be honoured to give the Odyssey a ride through the cosmos. We can reach Alpha Centauri in less than five Earth days. Consider it a gesture of our gratitude."

A ripple of excitement spread through the bridge. The crew exchanged glances, their eyes lighting up with the prospect of finally reaching Alpha Centauri so quickly.

Zulu noticed the energy in the room but remained composed. "That's a generous offer, Captain Enki-Marduk. We'll gladly accept once everything is stable on your end." As Enki-Marduk's holographic form flickered, he continued, "I've also reviewed the signal shared with my Princess. It originates from our sister clan, the Namzir, who serve as our Mystics and advisors. They are believed to possess foresight and guide the Caraliens through visions of the future. It's unusual for them to reach out in this manner. Unfortunately, without the codec; the missing key, we can't fully decode the Codex message or understand its intent. That said," he added thoughtfully, "what you've deciphered so far is accurate. Once the Nergal's AI is fully operational, she might be able to provide further assistance."

Captain Zulu nodded thoughtfully. "Understood. We'll wait until your systems are fully back online. The message is the main reason why we are out here between the stars, but we'll need to be patient."

Aria suddenly joined the conversation. "Captain Enki-Marduk," her voice was smooth and curious, "I would be thrilled to meet your ship's AI once she's fully restored. I'd love to study her matrix, compare notes, so to speak."

Enki-Marduk chuckled. "Naturally, Aria. I imagine she'll be just as curious to meet an AI of human design. Once the Nergal's AI is operational, I'll arrange the introductions." With that, Captain Enki-Marduk gave a respectful nod to Captain Zulu, and his holographic form flickered out.

Zulu turned back to Ethan over the intercom. "Ethan, what's the status on that unexploded thermonuclear shell?"

Ethan's voice came back, steady and confident. "All secured, Captain. We've made a full scan of the internal workings for our records. We're ready to release it and detonate remotely once we're a safe distance away."

"Good," Zulu replied. "Make sure your shuttle is clear before we detonate."

Just then, Nova Rodriguez stepped forward from her station. "Captain, the Nergal is healing itself faster than anticipated. Systems are coming back online, one by one. It won't be long before their entire population comes out of stasis."

Zulu allowed himself a moment of relief. "That's excellent news, Rodriguez. Keep monitoring the process."

As the crew settled into their tasks, preparing for the next phase, Commander Shepard's voice crackled through the comms. "Captain, we've finished the systems check on the Nergal. The Carals are extremely impressed with the Odyssey's offensive capabilities. And, " Shepard's message was suddenly interrupted by a softer yet commanding voice.

Princess Odriin's voice cut through the comm. "Captain Zulu, the protection your crew provided to my people will not be forgotten. You have our eternal gratitude. With allies like you, we stand a fighting chance against the Tot Empire."

Zulu's expression softened as he listened to the alien princess. "We're honoured to stand with you, Princess. We'll do whatever it takes to ensure peace and our survival."

Odriin's voice carried a quiet strength as she responded. "With you on our side, Captain, we may finally have the strength we need to end this endless war."

Zulu glanced at the screen, where the drifting debris of the Tot battleship still floated and smiled. "Let's hope so, Princess."

With that, the bridge of the Odyssey returned to its usual hum of activity. The crew, though buzzing with excitement, worked with focused determination. Zulu observed them for a moment, appreciating their discipline. They had proven themselves today, not just to their allies, but to themselves.

The Odyssey had come through again, and as long as Captain Zulu and his team were at the helm, they would fight to protect their allies, their mission, and the future of humanity.

As the Caralien engineers continued their work alongside the humans, Utu-Dumuzi called out from her station. "We are nearly ready to restart the exotic matter engine, Captain. It will take a few moments, but once we activate it, the ship's repair systems will function at full capacity again."

Shepard, observing the interplay between the Caraliens and his team, was impressed by how quickly the two species had begun to work together. "You've got a talented crew, Captain Enki-Marduk," he commented.

Enki-Marduk nodded slowly. "Yes, Commander. And I see the same in your people. Perhaps we are not so different after all."

Just as the tension on the bridge began to ease, an alarm sounded from one of the consoles. Utu-Dumuzi frowned and quickly tapped on the display. "Captain, we have detected an anomaly in the outer hull. Something.... or someone.... is approaching the ship."

The atmosphere on the bridge shifted immediately, the earlier camaraderie giving way to alertness and readiness.

Captain Zulu's voice echoed over the comms from the Odyssey. "We've got debris from the destroyed Tot ship heading our way. I've already sent out the dart fighters to intercept the larger pieces," he informed, his tone calm but focused.

Captain Enki-Marduk appeared on the screen, his expression serious. "Understood, Captain Zulu. The Nergal's shields won't be fully functional until the exotic matter engine is fully stabilised, and that's going to take some time."

Zulu leaned forward slightly, sensing the urgency. "How much time are we talking about?"

"Exotic matter is.... temperamental," Enki-Marduk replied, choosing his words carefully. "It requires delicate handling. We'll need a bit more time to ensure it's fully operational. Until then, the ship is vulnerable."

"I hear you," Zulu said, nodding. "We'll cover you. But if you need more support, let me know."

Enki-Marduk's eyes glinted with a sense of determination. "I'll be deploying our automated shuttle fighters as well. They'll assist in intercepting the debris."

"Good call," Zulu acknowledged. "We'll keep the area clear until your shields are back up."

With a nod of understanding, Enki-Marduk added, "Thank you, Captain. The Carals owe you much already." His holographic image flickered before disappearing, leaving Zulu to focus on managing the incoming threat. "Nin," Zulu called to his second-in-command, "keep an eye on the fighters and make sure none of that debris gets close to the Nergal."

"Aye, Captain," Nin responded, turning back to her console, the bridge once again buzzing with activity as they prepared to defend their vulnerable allies.

Chapter 8 – The close shave

As the Nergal released its four alien shuttles into the vacuum of space, their sleek forms darted out from the massive hull of the Caral's mother ship. From a distance, they could have been mistaken for humanity's experimental stealth craft. But as the Odyssey's main viewer zoomed in, the shuttles revealed their bizarre and organic appearance.

Each craft seemed to pulsate as if it were alive, covered in deep, almost living, shades of crimson that shimmered in the distant starlight. Stripes of yellow and white crisscrossed their surfaces, not in rigid lines, but more like glowing veins of light, pulsing gently as they moved. It was clear these shuttles were completely controlled by the Caral's advanced onboard AI systems, tasked with a singular purpose: intercept the incoming debris before it reached the vulnerable Mother ship.

On the bridge of the Odyssey, Captain Zulu studied the view closely, intrigued by the strange craft. "What are we looking at, Nin?" he asked, leaning forward, eyes narrowing at the shuttles.

Commander Nin, standing beside him, replied thoughtfully. "It looks like the Carals have launched their automated shuttles, Captain. But.... their speed and manoeuvrability, are impressive. I didn't expect their tech to move like that."

Zulu nodded. "Swift, yes, but notice their firepower. Those shuttles aren't built for war. They're scientists, not warriors."

"Agreed," Nin said, her gaze fixed on the screen. "Their weapons seem rudimentary compared to ours, despite their advanced tech."

Zulu tapped his console, activating the intercom. "Captain Enki-Marduk," he called, opening a line to the Caral ship, "are you sure you can't move the Nergal? It might be better to reposition your vessel out of the trajectory of the debris."

The holographic image of Captain Enki-Marduk flickered to life before Zulu, his expression calm yet firm. "Thank you for the concern, Captain Zulu, but we must remain in our current position. The exotic matter is delicate and unstable during its initial phases. Any movement could disrupt the process."

Zulu exchanged a glance with Nin but nodded. "Understood."

As the automated shuttles of the Caral zipped around, intercepting the debris at incredible speed, the Odyssey's dart fighters joined the fray. Their sleek forms shot out from the hangar, their fusion Ion thrusters burning brightly as they soared into the blackness of space. Captain Zulu had dispatched his best pilots to assist with the cleanup operation.

"Lara, Jason, Ethan, Sarah, you're up. Let's clear out the big stuff before it gets too close," Zulu commanded over the intercom.
Pilot Lara Chen responded first. "Copy that, Captain. We're moving into position."

"Roger that," added Pilot Jason Moors, his voice steady with focus.

"Dart Squadron Leader Ethan Cooper, ready to engage," came the voice of the squad leader, followed by a quick, " Sarah Mitchell here. We're locked in."

The four dart fighters streaked past the viewports of the Odyssey, heading directly towards the mess of debris from the shattered remains of the Tot's battleship. The larger pieces of debris, looming in the darkness of space, began to glow faintly as the dart fighters' laser cannons locked onto their targets.

The Dart fighter pilots moved in perfect sync, coordinating as though they had trained for this mission their entire lives. Smaller fragments of wreckage harmlessly struck their shields, flashing briefly before disintegrating. However, larger debris loomed ahead, posing a serious threat to the Nergal if not intercepted in time.

"We're closing in on the biggest chunk now," Lara's voice cut through the intercom. "Captain, this part is littered with Tot corpses and inactive drones. One of the Caral shuttles is already here, collecting the remains."

Commander Nin glanced at Zulu, arching a brow. "Looks like they're gathering biological samples."

Zulu gave a slight nod. "They finally got what they were after."

Nin smirked and turned back to the screen. "Are we planning to investigate the other Tot wreckage, Captain? We could send in a squad of Tengus and Ashigarus. They could gather technological samples without risking any human lives."

Zulu considered for a moment, then nodded. "Good idea. Organise a small battalion, Nin. Deploy them at your discretion. I want those Ashigaru units to prioritise retrieving any tech samples from the wreckage. The Tots' technology could prove valuable."

"Understood, Captain," Nin replied, her expression lighting up with enthusiasm. "I'll handle it personally."

As she made her way towards the exit, she turned back to Zulu, a small smile on her face. "I'll make sure we get the best out of this, Captain."

Zulu returned the smile with a nod. "I trust you will, Nin."

As she left the bridge, Zulu's gaze shifted back to the main screen, where the dart fighters and Caral shuttles continued to work in unison, clearing the debris field. The contrast between the two forces was stark: the human fighters, sleek and aggressive, versus the Caral shuttles, elegant and almost fragile in comparison. Yet together, they were an effective team.

Lara's voice came back over the intercom. "Captain, the largest debris are neutralised. We've made contact with the Caral shuttle, and they're finishing up the collection of Tot corpses."

"Good work, people," Zulu replied. "Return to base once the Caraliens have finished their retrieval."

On the other side of the comms, Ethan, the squad leader, chimed in. "Captain, all major debris has been dealt with. The area's clear for now."

"Well done, everyone," Zulu responded, his voice calm but filled with pride. "Return to the Odyssey. We'll maintain our position until the Nergal's engine is fully operational."

As the dart fighters began their return to the Odyssey, the crew on the bridge resumed their quiet hum of activity. Commander Nin, preparing her team for deployment, was already working in the background, organising the Tengu and Ashigaru soldiers for their mission to investigate the Tot wreckage.

Captain Zulu leaned back in his chair, watching the tactical displays as his crew worked seamlessly around him. He knew the danger wasn't over, but for the moment, they had gained the upper hand. The debris was cleared, and with each passing moment, the Nergal was becoming more stable. Still, in the back of his mind, he couldn't shake the feeling that this was just the beginning of something far larger.

The elevator pod slid open smoothly on Deck 15 of the Odyssey, revealing the wide expanse of the security and combat deck. Commander Nin stepped out with purpose, her polished boots hitting the deck with a soft but firm thud. As she walked past the stationed soldiers, they straightened up, offering her a nod of respect. "Boot on deck," they murmured, a traditional sign of acknowledgement to the Second-in-Command.

This massive, hangar-like deck always stirred something in Nin. Memories of battles fought and comrades lost, especially the brutal war with the Fanatics, flooded her mind. Blood and explosions, the smell of smoke and burnt metal, faces of the fallen, it was a past she was determined to not revisit, yet it haunted her. Her time fighting side by side with Captain Zulu had been one long, harrowing journey, etched in her memory like deep scars. But now was not the time for reflection.

She made her way directly to the robotic division, where the Ashigaru combat units and Tengu war dog machines were housed. The scent of oil and metallic servos filled the air as she approached the commanding units of both divisions.

"Commander," the Ashigaru unit leader greeted, snapping

to attention.

"Tengu squad leader," Nin acknowledged both, her tone sharp and authoritative. "Select ten of your best, fully serviced units for an incursion. We're boarding the disabled Tot battleship."

Both leaders nodded immediately. "Understood, Commander," the Ashigaru leader said.

Nin tapped her holographic arm pad, quickly pulling up the necessary mission details and sending the authorisation codes to the robotic units. "You'll be transported on the shuttle Nebula Runner, piloted by Mathew Macedo and Cindy Ortiz," she continued, her voice steady as she worked. "Your mission: secure Tot technology and capture any Tot alien beings if possible. But, and I can't stress this enough, only use lethal force if necessary."

The Alpha Ashigaru unit, the leader of the robotic soldiers, paused for a moment as the instructions downloaded into its systems. Then, in its modulated voice, it asked, "Commander, if I'm understanding correctly, you wish for us to.... capture Tot species? I mean, not just annihilate them?" A hint of robotic amusement could be detected in the machine's tone, almost like it was teasing.

Nin raised an eyebrow, not missing the faint trace of humour in the Alpha Ashigaru's query. "Yes, Alpha. Capture, not annihilate. We're scientists too, remember? We want to study them, maybe even talk to them. So, shoot to kill only if you must."

The Alpha Ashigaru's mechanical eyes blinked for a moment, and then its servos whirred. "Capture aliens, secure technology, minimal annihilation. Got it. Sounds.... almost boring. But we'll manage."

Nin allowed herself a small smirk. "Good. It's a quick insertion. Get in, map the ship, secure the tech, and find us a few Tot aliens for study. You have 20 minutes to arm yourselves and get ready. Shuttle bay 2. Move out."

The Ashigaru raised a salute, followed by a curt "Aye, Commander." The Tengu war dog machines, their red sensor eyes glowing brightly, flashed in acknowledgement as well.

With the orders set, the shuttle Nebula Runner, a sleek, silver spacecraft built for precision boarding operations, was loaded with the robotic units. Mathew Macedo, the shuttle's experienced pilot, sat at the helm while Cindy Ortiz, his co-pilot, ran through the final systems check.

"All systems green," Cindy reported, her voice clear over the shuttle's comms.

"Understood," came Commander Nin's voice from the bridge. "Shuttle Nebula Runner, you are cleared for launch. Proceed toward the Tot battleship and initiate boarding as planned."

"Copy that, Commander," Cindy replied, and the shuttle's autopilot engaged, guiding the craft out of the Odyssey's bay doors and into the vast expanse of space.

Four dart fighters flanked the shuttle, ensuring its safe passage as it approached the wreckage of the Tot battleship. The once-glorious alien vessel now drifted aimlessly, its lights dark and hull scarred from the Odyssey's plasma cannons. Sparks flickered from the edges of the crater the Odyssey's weapons had created.

As they neared, one of the dart fighter pilots, Lara from Hyperion-1, chimed in over the intercom. "Nebula Runner, this section of the hull looks unstable, but there's an entry point just around the crater. You should be able to breach safely here."

"Thanks for the update, Hyperion-1," Mathew responded,

his hands steady on the controls. "We're locking in on that entry point now."

On the bridge of the Odyssey, Commander Nin stood beside Captain Zulu, watching the operation unfold on the tactical display. Zulu, his arms crossed, observed the shuttle's progress intently.

"They'll be inside in no time," Nin remarked, her voice calm but focused.

"Good," Zulu responded, his eyes still on the screen. "This is a good chance for us to see what's left of the Tots' technology. Could give us an edge if they ever return."

Nin nodded. "And hopefully, the Ashigaru will secure a few live specimens for us to interrogate. It's better than trying to decipher their language from scraps of data."

"That too," Zulu agreed, though his mind seemed elsewhere, still pondering the larger implications of what they might find aboard the wreck.

Meanwhile, inside the shuttle, the Ashigaru units prepared for their mission. The Alpha Ashigaru, with its slightly playful nature, couldn't resist a remark as they approached the disabled battleship.

"Ah, the glamorous life of a robotic soldier," it quipped. "Boarding wrecked ships, sifting through alien junk, and trying not to kill too many hostiles. Makes you appreciate the little things in life."

"Focus on the mission," Mathew called out.

"Relax," the Alpha Ashigaru replied with a hum of amusement in its synthetic voice. "Just keeping things light. You know, to break up the monotony of imminent danger."

The rest of the robotic units stayed silent, as they were programmed to do, but it was clear that even in the tense moments leading up to a mission, the Alpha Ashigaru had its way of diffusing stress.

As the shuttle neared the breached section of the Tot battleship, Mathew called out, "We're in position. Prepare for boarding."

"All units, deploy," Cindy added.

The bay doors of the Nebula Runner opened, and one by one, the Ashigaru and Tengu units filed out, their mechanical limbs moving with precision. They descended onto the hull of the Tot battleship, their weapons and scanners at the ready.

Back on the Odyssey, Nin's eyes were glued to the screen. She turned to Zulu with a nod of confidence. "They're inside, Captain. Now let's see what they find."

Zulu leaned back in his chair; his gaze distant. "Let's hope it's more than just debris and dead ends."

Nin stood beside Captain Zulu on the Odyssey's bridge, her eyes fixed on the large monitor displaying live feeds from the Ashigaru and Tengu units. The visuals were stark and unsettling, destruction was everywhere, twisted metal and debris filled the corridors of the Tot's vessel. The robotic teams moved with precision, their sensors and cameras feeding the bridge crew real-time updates.

Aria broke the silence, her holographic body appeared on the bridge. "Captain, I can assist in hacking into the Tot systems. It seems their technology is old and vulnerable to infiltration."

Zulu glanced at Nin, who gave a curt nod. "Do it, Aria," Zulu replied. "We need as much information as possible."

Meanwhile, the Tengu war dog machines swiftly moved through the wrecked hallways, paired off as they used their energy cannons and retractable blades to cut through debris. They sliced through blocked passages with mechanical efficiency, making their way toward deeper sections of the ship. The Ashigaru robots followed closely, their heavy footsteps reverberating in the hollow corridors.

"Still no sign of any Tot survivors," Nin observed, watching the video feeds. "Just endless destruction."

"They were not expecting our firepower," Zulu said grimly. "They weren't ready for an attack."

For five minutes, the robots advanced, navigating through the lifeless ship at a fast pace. Their path finally led them to a heavily shielded door, the only part of the ship still intact amidst the devastation. The door's strange markings and reinforced structure made it clear something important was hidden behind it.

"Commander," the Alpha Ashigaru spoke up over the comms, "We've reached a heavily fortified section of the ship. The door is locked."
Aria's voice came in once more, calm and calculated.
"Allow me to try something." There was a brief pause as

the AI connected to one of the Tengu units. "Reconfiguring systems.... accessing interface.... It's strange, Captain. Their binary code is almost identical to ours, as if they share some technological ancestry."

"That is strange," Zulu muttered, his brow furrowing. "Aria, have you established a link?"

"Yes, Captain. I can access their system now. Would you like me to download all available data onto an isolated mainframe?" Aria asked, her voice cool and methodical.

"Do it," Zulu ordered. "Once the download is complete, disconnect immediately. We don't know what kind of traps or viruses might be embedded in that data."

"Understood, Captain," Aria replied.

As the data transfer began, the Ashigaru soldiers waited in front of the sealed door. Suddenly, Aria's voice came back. "The door is unlocked. You may proceed."

The Ashigaru soldiers moved forward, pulling open the door. What they saw inside stopped them in their tracks. The room was filled with hundreds of bodies, scattered across the floor in eerie silence. The artificial gravity was still active, keeping the bodies grounded, but there was no life in them.

On the bridge, Nin's hand instinctively flew to her mouth. "What in the world…?"

"Captain," the Alpha Ashigaru reported, "We are detecting four life forms in the room. It appears to be a communal area. I cannot explain why the rest of the Tot beings are dead, but four survivors remain, two adults and two small children."

Zulu's jaw clenched. "Bring four of the bodies back to the Odyssey for analysis, and place them in quarantine bags. I don't want any unnecessary risks."

"Copy that, Captain," the Alpha Ashigaru responded. It immediately relayed the order to the other units, which began bagging the bodies. Alpha continued moving deeper into the room, where the life signals were coming from.

Behind a long, overturned table, the four Tots cowered. Two adults, clearly parents, were shielding two small children, all in spacesuits. The Ashigaru had already detected them. As Alpha approached, the Tot adults made one last desperate effort to hide, but it was futile.

"They're alive," Nin said softly, watching the feed. "But why aren't they fighting back?"

"Fear," Zulu replied. "They probably don't know what's happening, and they're scared of us."

As the Ashigaru closed in, the four Tots seemed to give up hope. They closed their eyes and went limp, slipping into some kind of forced coma. The Ashigaru scanned them carefully, ensuring they weren't dead.

"Commander," the Alpha Ashigaru reported, "The four life forms have entered what appears to be a self-induced comatose state. Should we proceed with extraction?"

Nin's voice cut in, calm but firm. "Yes, bring them aboard. We need to analyse their atmosphere and physiological data. Make sure to handle them carefully during transport and ensure they are not harmed in any way."

As the units prepared the survivors for transport, Nin added, "And check their environmental suits. If they're in the same atmosphere as the rest of the ship, they might be relying on something similar to what we breathe."

The Alpha Ashigaru ran a quick scan and confirmed her

suspicion. "Captain, Commander, these beings require an atmosphere identical to Earth's. Oxygen-based, just like ours."

Zulu exchanged a glance with Nin. "Fascinating. They're more like us than we thought."

"They're pale blue," Nin added, studying the feed. "No hair, flat noses, and small white dots along their necks and no ears. But otherwise, their physiology is eerily similar to humans."

"Copy that," the Alpha Ashigaru said, moving efficiently as it finished retrieving the bodies. "We have secured both the living and deceased Tots. Heading back to the shuttle now."

The robotic soldiers carried the comatose aliens and the bagged bodies carefully, making their way back through the ruined corridors toward the waiting shuttle.

"Shuttle Nebula Runner," the Alpha Ashigaru radioed, "We are en-route with the cargo. Prepare for extraction."

On the bridge, Nin took a deep breath, her fingers flexing in anticipation. "We need to study them thoroughly, Captain. There's so much we need to understand about the

Tots."

"We will," Zulu assured her, his voice steady. "But let's take it one step at a time. First, we get them onboard. Then, we figure out why they're still alive, and what killed the rest."

"Agreed," Nin said, though the unease lingered in her chest.

As the shuttle prepared to return, the bridge crew silently watched the live feed, knowing that whatever secrets the Tots held, they were now in humanity's hands.

Suddenly, the sharp sound of a proximity alert filled the Odyssey's bridge, breaking the tense silence. Alarms blared on both the Odyssey and the Caral vessel. Commander Reyes, at her station on Deck 3, quickly brought up the holographic display to see what had triggered the alert. At first, there was just one small dot in the distance, but as Reyes zoomed in, more dots started to appear, dozens, then hundreds. Tot battleships, each with a unique and menacing design, materialised on the horizon of space.

Reyes's voice cracked through the comms. "Captain, we've got company. A lot of company."

Zulu's gaze darkened as he turned to the main view screen, which now showed a massive fleet of Tot warships slowly advancing. "How many?" Zulu asked, already dreading the answer.

"Over a hundred, Captain. They just keep coming," Reyes replied, her voice tight with tension.

Zulu wasted no time. He opened a channel to the Nergal, where Captain Enki-Marduk was overseeing the final preparations for their jump.
"Enki-Marduk, we need to move, now," Zulu said, urgency threading his words. "The Odyssey can't hold off a hundred battleships. We need to jump immediately!"

The holographic image of Captain Enki-Marduk flickered to life on the Odyssey's bridge. His calm demeanour didn't reflect the growing danger around them. "Our system will be ready to jump in exactly one hour," Enki-Marduk replied, his tone level. "Not a minute more, not a minute less. We will need to distract the Tot armada in the meantime."

"An hour?" Zulu muttered in disbelief, running a hand through his hair. "We don't have that kind of time."

Just then, Commander Shepard, who had been quietly observing, spoke up. "Captain, what if we use the thermonuclear bomb?"

Zulu turned sharply. "The thermonuclear bomb?"

Shepard nodded, excitement creeping into his voice. "We still have that unexploded atomic bomb we recovered. If we wait until the Tots get close and detonate it, the blast could stall them, give them something to think about. It might buy us the time we need."

Zulu considered the idea for a moment. "It's risky, but it might just work."
Opening a comm channel to the away team aboard the Tot battleship, Zulu spoke urgently. "Away team, report your status. How close are you to the bridge?"

The Alpha Ashigaru's voice came back over the channel, calm but mechanical. "Captain, we have not yet reached the bridge. However, we are gathering data and samples along the way. Do you wish us to continue?"

Zulu didn't hesitate. "No, don't risk it. Grab whatever useful intel or tech you can find and return to the shuttle immediately. We're short on time."

"Understood, Captain," the Alpha Ashigaru responded, and the robotic soldiers obeyed without question, quickly reversing course to return to the shuttle.

As the away team made their way back to the shuttle, Zulu turned his attention back to the massive fleet of Tot ships inching closer with every passing second. "Reyes, get our dart fighters in position to cover the shuttle's return. We can't afford to lose any time."

"Roger that, Captain," Reyes confirmed.

The dart fighters launched from the Odyssey, streaking through space to escort the shuttle back. Meanwhile, the Tot armada, sensing something was amiss, advanced cautiously, weapons at the ready. They were preparing for a full-scale assault.

Minutes ticked by, each one feeling like an eternity. The away team successfully boarded the shuttle, and the dart fighters led them safely back to the Odyssey's hangar bay. All the while, the Tot ships crept closer, a wave of destruction waiting to crash down upon them.

One hour had almost passed when Zulu opened another channel to Enki-Marduk. "We're running out of time!

What's the status of the jump?"

Enki-Marduk's holographic form reappeared, looking slightly more tense now. "We need five more minutes, Captain."

"Five minutes?" Zulu spat in disbelief. "We don't have five minutes!"

The Tot ships were now within striking distance, their guns locking onto both the Odyssey and the Nergal. Zulu had no choice. "Prepare the thermonuclear bomb for detonation."

Commander Shepard and the bridge crew quickly readied the bomb. Zulu watched the Tot ships grow larger on the screen. Sweat beaded on his forehead as he gave the final command. "Detonate."

The moment the order was given, the thermonuclear bomb exploded in a blinding flash of light. The force of the explosion rippled through space, brighter and more powerful than anyone had anticipated. The entire bridge of the Odyssey was bathed in an intense white light as the explosion engulfed the advancing Tot fleet.
When the light finally faded, the Tot ships had come to a halt, seemingly stunned by the sheer power of the blast. But

it didn't take long for them to recover. The lead ships in the Tot armada began powering up their weapons. The Odyssey's sensors screamed as hundreds of nuclear shells were launched, all hurtling toward the Caral vessel and the Odyssey at incredible speed.

"Here they come," Nin said, her voice grim.

Just as the first few shells closed in, Enki-Marduk's voice crackled over the comms. "Brace yourselves. We're jumping in three.... two.... one."

In an instant, a bubble of energy enveloped both the Odyssey and the Nergal. The jump sequence initiated, and they were ripped from their location, hurtling through space at an unimaginable speed toward Alpha Centauri. The sensation was dizzying, but Zulu kept his eyes on the displays, watching the Tot armada fade into the distance until it was nothing more than a memory.

When the jump was complete, the crew exhaled in collective relief. The Tots were gone, and they were safe, for now.

"Well," Zulu said, leaning back in his chair with a tired grin, "that was close."

"Too close," Nin added, shaking her head. "But we made it."

Captain Enki-Marduk's hologram flickered to life once more. "Congratulations, Captain Zulu. Your quick thinking and bravery have saved us."

Zulu nodded but didn't feel much like celebrating. "We got lucky. Let's just hope we don't run into another fleet like that anytime soon."

As the crew of the Odyssey settled back into their stations, they all knew the truth, this was only the beginning. The Tots weren't finished with them, and Alpha Centauri was still a long way off. But for now, they had survived, and that was all that mattered.

Chapter 9 –
Captains and the Ki-ág
Ceremony

The Ashigaru and Tengu units had done their job well. They had retrieved eight Tot corpses and four living Tot humanoids from the wreckage of the disabled Tot battleship. Now, the Odyssey's morgue was filled with the remains, with Doctor James and his specialist team meticulously examining the bodies. In a separate, isolated area, the four surviving Tots were monitored closely under strict atmospheric regulation to ensure their survival.

Captain Zulu stood on the bridge, staring at the monitors showing live feeds from both the morgue and the isolated chamber. His brow furrowed in thought as he considered the strange turn of events.

"Captain," Commander Nin interrupted his thoughts, stepping up beside him. "We've received a request from some of the Caralien scientists. They want to come aboard to assist in studying the living, Tots. What should I tell them?"

Zulu nodded slowly. "Tell them they're welcome. It's better if we work together on this. I'll authorise their visit. Also, I got a private request from Commander Shepard who requested to stay aboard the Caral vessel to help ensure their systems and crew are fully back to speed."

Nin raised an eyebrow. "That makes sense. Shepard's team is skilled and quick to adapt to new technology, plus the Caraliens trust us now. I'll check in with their captain to confirm."

"Good," Zulu replied. "Oh, and my wife, she's asked if she and her team can assist Doctor James in examining the Tot bodies and the living specimens. What's your take on that?"

Nin gave a small smile. "Tashia's one of the best. Doctor James could use all the help he can get, especially when dealing with something this.... unfamiliar."

Zulu smiled. "She's determined; that's for sure. Alright, I'll approve her request." He paused, turning back to the screen showing the Tot survivors. "It's strange, isn't it? How similar they look to us and the Caraliens."

Nin nodded. "Yeah, I noticed that too. The only real

differences are their pale blue skin, flat noses, and those strange white dots along their necks. Also, Captain, they have no ears. Other than that, they're almost indistinguishable from humans. It's unsettling."

Zulu folded his arms, his expression contemplative. "It really makes you think, doesn't it? The Carals bio-engineered the Tot species, and over time they've clearly evolved in various ways. Yet, as Princess Odriin and Captain Enki-Marduk have pointed out, they've retained their primal and predatory instincts."
Nin nodded with a casual shrug. "Absolutely, Zulu. They've definitely held onto those predatory instincts."

Just then, the comms buzzed to life, and a soft chime indicated an incoming message from the Caral vessel. Captain Enki-Marduk's voice came through, calm and composed as always.

"Captain Zulu, as a diplomatic courtesy, we would like to extend an invitation for a formal visit aboard the Nergal. Given our current speed and the unique nature of this bubble between space and time, traditional shuttling between vessels is impractical. We offer our A.R.T system as a means of quick and seamless transport."

Zulu glanced over at Commander Nin, a look of confusion on his face. She raised an eyebrow, shrugging as if to say, I have no idea either.

Clearing his throat, Zulu leaned back toward the comms. "Captain, forgive my ignorance, but could you clarify what exactly A.R.T. stands for?"

There was a brief pause before Enki-Marduk responded. "Of course, Captain. My apologies. A.R.T. refers to our Atomic Rematerialisation Transportation system. It allows for instant travel between locations, rematerialising you on board our vessel without the need for traditional transportation methods."

Nin shot Zulu an intrigued glance, and Zulu couldn't help but smirk slightly. "Ah, well that clears things up," he replied. "Thank you for the clarification. I'll gladly accept your invitation. Diplomatic courtesy is always appreciated, especially under these circumstances."

Zulu paused for a moment before adding, "Where do I need to be for this.... A.R.T. transfer to take place?"

Enki-Marduk's voice remained calm and polite. "Simply remain aboard the Odyssey, Captain. When you're ready to come aboard, signal us, and we will initiate the transport from our side."

"Understood, Captain. I'll prepare for the transfer. Zulu out."

As Zulu closed the comms, he leaned back in his chair with a sigh, rubbing the back of his neck. "So ... I'm about to be the first human to try this A.R.T. system, huh? Guess that's what comes with the exploration, meeting alien races, trying out their tech as we go."

Nin chuckled, crossing her arms and shaking her head. "Well, it sure beats dealing with an angry alien armada on our doorstep."

Zulu grinned. "I'll take new tech over hostile fleets any day." He stood up and stretched, glancing at Nin with a hint of mischief in his eyes. "You're sure this thing won't turn me into space dust?" Nin raised her hands in mock surrender. "Hey, I have no idea how this thing works, but if it's anything like their other tech, I'd say you're in good hands." Her expression turned serious for a moment. "But I'll keep an eye on things here while you're gone." Zulu nodded, appreciating her confidence. "Good. I trust you to handle things while I'm gone. Just.... don't blow up the ship."

Nin chuckled. "No promises, but I'll do my best."

"Of course," Nin said with a smile. "And don't worry, Captain. I'll keep the ship intact while you're off playing diplomat."

Zulu gave her a mock glare. "Let's hope I don't get stuck over there too long."

A few minutes later, Zulu stood in the command centre, taking a deep breath. He activated the comms, signalling to the Nergal.

"This is Captain Zulu. I'm ready for transport."

A moment later, a soft hum filled the room, and the air around Zulu shimmered faintly. He felt an odd tingling sensation wash over his body, as though his molecules were being gently rearranged. In a blink, the bridge of the Odyssey disappeared, replaced by the sleek, organic metallic-looking interior of the Nergal.

Captain Enki-Marduk stood tall before him, his serene face framed by the gentle glow of Caral technology. He greeted

Zulu with a slight bow. "Welcome aboard, Captain Zulu. I trust the transportation process was.... comfortable?"

Zulu gave a short laugh, more out of relief than humour. "Comfortable? Sure. Let's just say it was a new experience. Fast, though, I'll give you that."

Enki-Marduk smiled. "Our technology is designed to be as efficient as possible. We have created the A.R.T. to eliminate unnecessary delays."

Zulu raised an eyebrow. "I bet. It sure beats waiting around for a shuttle." He glanced around at the sleek, alien architecture of the Nergal. "Impressive ship you've got here, Captain."

Enki-Marduk motioned for Zulu to follow him. "Thank you, Captain. Our focus has always been on exploration and understanding rather than conflict, though recent events have shown us that we must adapt to the more.... aggressive tendencies of the universe."

Zulu nodded, following Enki-Marduk through the corridors of the Caral ship. "Yeah, I've noticed that about your people. You're not warriors, but you've got brains. That's a valuable asset, especially when you're dealing with species that don't always care for diplomacy."

Enki-Marduk's expression remained calm, but there was a hint of amusement in his voice. "Indeed. We prefer to avoid conflict whenever possible, though your species has shown us the value of strategic defence."

Zulu grinned. "You can thank a few millennia of wars back on Earth between our species for that. We've gotten good at surviving."

As they walked, the two captains continued to exchange insights about their respective cultures, their technological achievements, and their visions for the future. Though their worlds were vastly different, there was a mutual respect growing between them, one that would likely shape the future of their alliance.

Enki-Marduk stopped in front of a large observation window, gazing out into the vast expanse of space. " Captain Zulu, I believe our strengths complement each other. You bring fire and determination, and we bring knowledge and discovery."

Zulu stood next to him, gazing at the stars streaking past. "Let's hope that's enough to get us through whatever comes next."

Enki-Marduk nodded solemnly. "Yes, Captain. Let us hope."

Captain Enki-Marduk looked at Captain Zulu, his eyes calm but filled with a weight of knowledge. "Captain Zulu, would you like to share in some of our ancient memories?" His voice carried a tone that suggested more than just casual curiosity.

Zulu furrowed his brow. "I'm not sure I understand what you mean," he replied cautiously, leaning slightly forward.

Enki-Marduk smiled gently and elaborated, "We Carals have the memories of our ancestors stored in what we call Memory Crystals, scattered throughout the universe. When a Caralien dies, our Corporeal memories are uploaded through a quantum transfer somewhat like what humans call quantum entanglement. Our Corporeal, and these Memory Crystals, are linked, no matter where we are. This technology was developed a long time ago with the help of the Celestial beings. Ninil and Ishtar's race, the multidimensional realm species who came to aid us during a crucial time in our history."

Zulu looked out at the stars again, absorbing the magnitude of what Enki-Marduk was saying. "So, you're saying.... you have access to the memories of every Caraliens who's ever lived?"

"Precisely," Enki-Marduk confirmed. "Our ancestors, especially the first generation of pure scientists, rejected violence in favour of knowledge and wisdom. We were on the brink of annihilation while trying to perfect our Zero Point Energy system, ZPE, as we call it. You might recognise it as the Casimir effect or entropy-harnessing energy from the vacuum of space."

Zulu nodded, intrigued. "I've heard of it, though our scientists are still grappling with those theories."
Enki-Marduk continued, "At our peak, we sought to create the ultimate unlimited energy source, Exotic Matter. But in our pursuit of perfection, we made catastrophic errors in our calculations. The result was a dangerous fracture in space-time. Out of nowhere, five beings appeared. We call them, Celestials, much like the ones currently aboard your vessel. They corrected our mistakes and stayed with us for many years, teaching us and guiding us. When they passed, they didn't leave behind their corporeal bodies as we do. Instead, they evaporated into pure energy, like they had transcended our physical realm."

Zulu sat silent for a moment, digesting the story. He had faced strange and unknown technologies before, but this was something else entirely. "So, you're saying.... I could connect with these memories?"

Enki-Marduk nodded. "Yes. Princess Odriin could act as a conduit, helping you receive the memories from one of our Memory Crystals. It is a great honour among our people, something we call the Ki-ág. You would receive a brief but rich history of our species, our struggles, and our triumphs. The process takes about one hour, but it's profound."

Later that day, Zulu met with his crew. They gathered around a long table in the ship's canteen, mingling with the Caralien engineers. The atmosphere was light-hearted, but the weight of the upcoming memory-sharing ceremony hung in the background.

Commander Shepard sat close to Mira, who was absorbed in conversation with a female Caralien engineer, Ningal-Uruk who had helped with the removal of the thermonuclear threat. Captain Zulu noticed Ethan laughing heartily with the same Caralien, seemingly engrossed in whatever tale he was telling her.

"You seem to be enjoying yourself, Ethan," Zulu teased, smiling as he approached.

Ethan looked up with a cheeky grin. "Just building some friendships, Captain!" He held the captain's gaze for a moment, his smile unwavering, before casually returning to his conversation, completely relaxed.

Across the room, Alexander and Ninil sat together, their closeness unmistakable. They spoke in hushed tones, but their affection for each other was clear. Zulu smiled as he watched them, briefly reminded of his early days with Tashia after his life-saving operation. Love, it seemed, transcended species and circumstances.

Princess Odriin sat at the table, sipping from a small cup of kaš, a Caralien drink with a flavour similar to coffee from their perspective. She turned to Zulu. "Captain, I hear you've been invited to experience the Ki-ág, sharing the memories of many important Caraliens. I'll be guiding you through the process, helping you manage the influx of information."

Ninil, who had been eavesdropping on their conversation, couldn't resist chiming in. "I'd like to participate as well, if that's possible. There's so much about the Caral history I don't know, and I'm particularly interested in how the war with the Tot Empire started."

Odriin smiled warmly. "Of course, Celestial. I will add you to the authorisation list. It is an honour to share our history with you, my beautiful Celestial. May peace be upon your universe."

Ninil smiled back and wrapped her arms around Alexander, clearly touched by the gesture. Zulu observed them, chuckling inwardly. Ninil seemed almost lovestruck, something he found "super cool," as he privately mused.

Princess Odriin set her cup down and turned serious. "For the Ki-ág ceremony, Captain, you and Ninil will be placed in separate pods connected to mine. We'll need to remove our clothes, allowing our bodies to fully relax within the pods. These will be linked to the AI An Ama, which regulates the flow of information from the Memory Crystals. I'll process the data first and relay it to you. Without me as the conduit, the raw data would overwhelm you, leaving you with an incomprehensible flood of memories."

Zulu nodded, understanding the significance of what was about to happen. "And you've been through this yourself?"

Odriin smiled wistfully. "Yes, Captain. When I was chosen
to receive the Ki-ág, it was the most glorious day of my life.
Through it, I learned the full history of our people,
including the tragic conflict with the Tot Empire. We've
lost countless motherships trying to reason with them, to
find peace, but it's like trying to convince a hungry wolf
not to eat a sheep."

Zulu gave a thoughtful nod. "And yet, here we are, still
trying to make sense of it all."

Odriin met his gaze. "Exactly. But once you experience the
Ki-ág, Captain, you will see for yourself. You'll understand
the depths of our struggle."

"How long will the preparation take?" Zulu asked.

"One full Earth day," Odriin responded. "It's a significant
process, Captain. But I promise you, it will be worth it."

Zulu leaned back in his chair, taking a deep breath. "Alright.
I'll need to spend some time with my wife before we
proceed, but I understand the importance of this ceremony.
I'll be ready."

Odriin smiled gently. "Take your time, Captain. The

memories of the Caraliens await you."

Back aboard the Odyssey, a soft hum filled the Captain's quarters as the air shimmered, gradually materialising Zulu's form. He glanced around, mildly disoriented at first, before realising he was back in the familiar surroundings of his own living room. After having used Caral's A.R.T. system on the Nergal, he couldn't help but smile. It had been a surreal experience, alien technology lightyears ahead of humanity's current capabilities.

He made his way to his private kitchen and ordered a cappuccino from the Molecular Gastronomy Module. As the machine whirred quietly, Zulu mused on how incredible it would be for Earth vessels to incorporate such advanced technologies. His children would be over the moon if they got their hands on alien tech thousands of years more advanced than humanity's. Holding the warm cup in his hand, he took a slow sip, enjoying the rich flavour as he sank into his chair.

As he sat, his holo arm pad beeped. The voice of his second-in-command came through. "Captain, are you onboard the Odyssey? We're registering your life signs in your quarters."

"Yes, Commander," Zulu responded quickly. "I've just used their teleportation system and beamed back. I'll be in my quarters for a little while."

"Understood, Captain," Nin replied. "Shall I prepare a meeting?"

"Yes, please. Get the Doctor, our engineers, and Aria. Let's meet in two hours on deck 2, the meeting room," Zulu said.

"Copy that, Captain," Nin confirmed.

As soon as the call ended, Aria's holographic avatar shimmered into existence in Zulu's quarters. "Captain, how are you feeling after using the A.R.T. system?" she asked, her voice curious but calm.

Zulu leaned back, considering for a moment. "Disoriented at first," he admitted, "but after a few seconds, you find your footing. It's smoother than I expected."

Aria nodded. "Do you think Captain Enki-Marduk would allow me to interface with their AI systems? It would be an interesting opportunity to learn from their technology."

Zulu smiled. "Their AI goes by the name An Ama. It's

translated to something like 'Mother Sky,' if I recall correctly. And yes, I don't see why not. I spoke to the Captain and Princess, and they didn't raise any objections to you interacting with her."

"Mother Sky," Aria mused. "A fitting name for a sophisticated AI. Thank you for confirming, Captain."

"I'll need you at the meeting later," Zulu added. "But for now, I have a diplomatic mission of my own. I'm about to undergo a procedure to absorb part of their history, through their memory crystals, using one of their alien pods. Princess Odriin will help facilitate the process, and Mother Sky will be overseeing it."

Aria's expression didn't change, but her tone became more serious. "That sounds… intense, Captain. Are you prepared for the amount of information you'll be absorbing?"

"That's why I'm calling Tashia to talk it through," Zulu said with a chuckle. "I'm sure she'll have a few words about it."

Aria smiled before disappearing with a flick of light, and moments later, Tashia stormed into the room, her eyes flashing with a mix of worry and frustration. "Zulu, are you serious about this memory transfer? You didn't even talk to me or the Doctor about it first!" she scolded, crossing her arms.

Before she could continue, Zulu stood and held out a steaming cup of cappuccino, offering it with a soft smile. Tashia paused, eyeing the cup with reluctant appreciation. "You always know how to calm me down," she muttered, taking the cup from him. "But this is still too dangerous! You just accepted this memory transfer without even considering the risks!"

Zulu raised his hands defensively, the smile never leaving his face. "Tashia, love, it's not dangerous. It's just an hour lying in a pod, receiving historical information. I'm not boarding an enemy ship or heading into a firefight." Tashia scoffed. "Oh, really? This isn't like the time you wanted to board The Spirit of Glory. That nearly got Commander Shepard killed!"

Zulu waved it off. "You're exaggerating! And besides, I wasn't actually going to do that. I was just joking."

"Joking," she repeated, her tone exasperated. "This is serious, Zulu. These are alien memories, potentially thousands of years of information, and you're treating it like it's nothing."

"I am treating it with respect," Zulu said, gently correcting her. "But this knowledge is crucial, Tashia. It might help us uncover why they sent the enigmatic signals in the first place. Princess Odriin mentioned that these signals date back to when they first arrived in this galaxy, and the fact that they originated from Alpha Centauri raises even more questions. We need to understand this before we reach that star system. Unlocking their memories could hold the key to understanding the true nature of the Carals."

Tashia sighed, her earlier fire dimming. She took a sip of the cappuccino, letting the warmth soothe her. "I know you're right. I just worry. But if you're going to do this, I want Doctor James and I there with you. We'll monitor everything."

"Of course," Zulu agreed quickly. "You and the Doctor can be there, and you can bring all the medical kits you need." Tashia finally smiled, albeit faintly. "Okay, fine. But you better not do anything reckless."

Zulu grinned. "Me? Reckless? Never." He gave her a playful wink.

Tashia shook her head, half-smiling. "I'll hold you to that. And I'll be at the meeting too. After all, someone has to keep an eye on your 'adventures.'"

She turned and walked toward the bedroom, pausing at the doorway to glance back over her shoulder with a mischievous look. "Are you coming, Captain?" she asked with a playful smile before disappearing into the room.

Zulu laughed quietly to himself, finishing his cappuccino. He could face dangerous aliens and explore uncharted territories, but keeping Tashia calm? That was a challenge on its own.

Two hours later, the meeting room aboard the Odyssey buzzed quietly with activity. Doctor James, Commander Nin, Commander Reyes, and Senior Engineer Jessica Thompson sat at the long table, their holographic displays floating in front of them as they worked on their daily tasks. Aria's holographic avatar was already in discussion with Doctor James, explaining the intricacies of the upcoming Memory Transfer Ceremony.

The door slid open, and Tashia entered the room, followed closely by Captain Zulu. The air shifted as the group straightened slightly, turning their attention toward their captain. Zulu greeted them with a nod, his eyes sweeping across his trusted crew. "Good to see you all," he began, saluting his friends and close colleagues. "I believe Aria has briefed you all on the exchange of memory I've been invited to participate in."

The room was quiet, save for the soft hum of the ship's systems as they listened. Zulu continued, "As you all know, I've been invited to participate in a memory-sharing ceremony called the Ki-ág by the Carals. Ninil has requested to join me as well. During this process, we'll both be placed in separate pods that will be connected to Princess Odriin's. Now, I know this sounds unusual, but we'll need to be completely…well, naked inside the pods to ensure our bodies are fully relaxed." He paused, allowing the group to absorb that detail. "These pods will be linked to their AI, An Ama, translated as 'Mother Sky.' This AI will regulate the flow of information from their storage systems, Memory Crystals, which have stored their entire history for over a millennium. Princess Odriin will act as the conduit, processing the data before it reaches me. Without her involvement, the raw data would overwhelm me, leaving me lost in an incomprehensible flood of memories."

There was a brief silence after Zulu's explanation, until

Doctor James raised his hand, his brow furrowed. "Captain, what if the process isn't compatible with the human brain? What happens then?"

Zulu nodded at the valid concern. "Good question, Doctor. They're modifying the pods as we speak to ensure that they're safe for humans. And remember, Princess Odriin is part human herself, her transformation was brought about by her stasis pod to adapt her body for survival aboard the Odyssey. Ninil, of course, is a different case entirely, but we all know she's more than human in ways we still don't fully understand."

Commander Reyes leaned forward, curiosity etched on her face. "Captain, I'd like to speak with their engineers, particularly about the data flow. For example, what's the bit rate? And what's the bit error rate? I'm also wondering if we could get a blueprint or schematic of these Memory Crystals. This tech is something we should definitely study and perhaps adopt ourselves."

Zulu smiled at Reyes' enthusiasm. "I'll make sure you're able to talk to them about those specifics. And yes, if they're willing, we'll get a blueprint of the crystals. It's the kind of technology we could learn a great deal from."
Jessica chimed in next. "Captain, while you're at it, I'd love

to get a close look at their ZPE systems. I know the exotic matter they use might be beyond our reach for now, but even having a solid understanding of their Zero Point Energy tech would be revolutionary for us. One of their batteries could power the Odyssey for years without needing to recharge, and without relying on fusion reactors or magnetic containment fields that demand massive amounts of energy."

Zulu leaned against the table, nodding. "You're right, Jessica. I know my daughter would love to study this too, and Tashia's been talking about it nonstop. A ZPE system could completely change the way we manage power on board our vessels. I'll speak to the Caraliens and get you the clearance to come onboard the Nergal to examine their systems."

As the crew absorbed the captain's words, it was clear they were not only intrigued but excited about the possibilities. "All right," Zulu continued, clapping his hands together. "We'll have the Caral transport us onboard in five hours. Use that time to get your gear ready, and we'll make sure everything is set on our end."

The room was filled with a palpable sense of anticipation as Zulu's senior staff began to gather their things and prepare for the task ahead. There was an energy in the air that hadn't been there before, each of them eager to explore the advanced Caral technology and unlock the secrets it held.

As they stood to disperse, Tashia lingered by Zulu's side. She gave him a concerned look, but there was also a hint of pride in her eyes. "You've always been good at getting everyone motivated," she said softly.

Zulu smiled, watching as the last of the crew filed out. "It's easy when we're standing on the edge of something this big. This could be our chance to really understand the Carals, maybe even understand the universe a little better."

Tashia sighed, her concern still evident, but she didn't argue. "Just promise me you'll be careful during that ceremony."
Zulu leaned in and kissed her on the forehead. "I always am," he whispered. "Besides, I have you and Doctor looking out for me."

She rolled her eyes but smiled. "That's what worries me," she teased.

They both shared a quiet laugh as they stood in the now-empty room, knowing that soon enough, they'd be embarking on a journey into the unknown once again.

The following morning on the Nergal, Captain Zulu, Ninil, and Princess Odriin stood quietly, wrapped in a sheer, ethereal white fabric that draped over their forms, nearly weightless as they prepared for the Ki-ág Ceremony. The chamber they stood in was vast, the size of a small stadium, its vaulted ceiling shimmering as though it was alive. Around them, newly awakened Caraliens gathered, observing with quiet reverence. Some, like Captain Enki-Marduk and his second-in-command, Geshtu-Ea, had distinctive angular features, translucence skin, and a subtle grey-blue hue. Others, like Princess Odriin, appeared entirely human, with deep brown or white skin, blonde hair, and eyes that gleamed a bluish-green, melding them visually with Zulu and Ninil.

The chamber itself was breathtaking, a grand elliptical amphitheatre with multiple tiers, each tier styled with architecture reminiscent of Earth's classical ages. The lower levels evoked the simplicity of Doric columns, progressing upward to Ionic elegance and finally, Corinthian-style columns intertwined with intricate golden designs resembling lotus flowers and vines.

The central arena was dominated by a massive obelisk, the Memory Crystal. Intricate circuits spiralled outward from its base, connecting the dozen pods encircling it. The crystal pulsed, glowing and shifting in colour, like a living organism breathing in and out. The entire setup was a mesmerising fusion of organic and technological design, giving the impression that this place was as much alive as it was engineered.

As they walked toward the Memory Crystal, Zulu whispered to Ninil, "Feels like we're standing inside a living entity."

Ninil nodded, eyes wide, "It is Captain, it's almost like… it's aware of us."

Princess Odriin smiled faintly, leading the way, "It is. My people believe in living architecture, so this chamber responds to those within it."

They reached the pods situated around the base of the crystal, and the chamber hushed as twenty Caralien priestesses, clad in diaphanous white robes, approached. Their forms were visible beneath the fabric, their features both regal and haunting. The priestesses moved with a delicate, practised grace, flanking Zulu, Ninil, and Odriin to guide them to the pods.

In the front rows of spectators sat Tashia, and Doctor James with his Nano-Medic kit, handheld vital scanner, and resuscitation device, along with the senior crew from the Odyssey. Tashia's eyes stayed locked on Zulu, her expression a blend of pride and concern. She murmured softly under her breath, "Stay strong, my love."

Once Zulu, Ninil, and Odriin were settled into their pods, Zulu looked up, mesmerised by the ceiling. It arched above like a single interconnected entity, glowing with deep hues of blue, green, purple, and gold. The structure breathed, colours pulsing in sync with some invisible rhythm that felt like a heartbeat. It was almost as though the ceiling were aware of its inhabitants, the light shifting subtly in response to the presence of the priestesses moving beneath it.

Doctor James leaned forward, studying the ceiling's intricacies. "It's almost like a vascular system," he muttered, noting the vein-like patterns. "Never thought I'd see something like this."

"It's more than a ship," Reyes replied, equally captivated. "It's an organism, something between the material and the living."

The priestesses began chanting, their voices clear, harmonious, and hauntingly beautiful, resonating within the chamber. The crew members were spellbound, the words both alien and comforting.

"(Enlil, bringer of wind and life)"
"(Anu, keeper of the high sky)"
"(Ninhursag, mother of all, great upon the earth)"
Each name was enunciated with deep reverence. Tashia's grip on her hands tightened, her gaze locked on Zulu's pod, and she whispered in her mind, "Zulu…be safe."

"(Guide our hands, where the river flows)"
"(Carathys, hear our plea)"
"(Bless the fields and calm the stormy sea)"

The chants grew louder, though never harsh. The chamber itself seemed to amplify their voices, a warm echo wrapping around everyone. The Odyssey crew watched in awe, the words resonating with a strange familiarity that tugged at the edges of understanding. Doctor James murmured to Aria, "It's almost as if the words are… reaching us in some primal way."

"(By the stars we light our path)"
"(Guard us through night, lead us through day)"

As the chant intensified, each word resonated with deeper meaning. The amphitheatre pulsed with energy, the lights shifting and dancing with the rhythm of the voices, and the memory pods began to close around Zulu, Ninil, and Odriin. The organic material of the pods moved smoothly, enveloping them as if it were an extension of the living chamber itself.

Doctor James leaned close to Tashia. "They'll be fine," he assured her, reading her tension. "This is an incredibly advanced process. We're witnessing something humanity has only imagined."

She nodded, trying to take comfort in his words, but her gaze didn't waver from Zulu's pod as it finally sealed, the shifting colours now mirroring the rhythm of the chanting.

The priestesses continued:

"(From the ancient clay, we rise again)"
"(In your hands, our fate unfolds)"
"(Through your will, we grow bold)"

At that moment, the entire chamber seemed to pulse with life. The Odyssey crew could feel it, almost like a gentle heartbeat beneath their feet. Tashia held her breath as the pods around the Memory Crystal began to glow in unison, colours shifting and merging, creating an ethereal display of light and shadow that filled the entire space. Each pod pulsed with a breath-like motion, as if alive, a symphony of colours and lights reflecting the wisdom and memories of millennia.

Zulu lay still within his pod, feeling a warmth seeping through him, calming and grounding him. He let his mind drift, surrendering to the experience. Thoughts of Tashia, of their life together, and the Odyssey floated at the edge of his consciousness as he prepared himself for the surge of ancient memories.

Princess Odriin's voice echoed softly in his mind, though she wasn't beside him, "Stay open, Captain Zulu. Let the memories flow through you without resistance. I am here with you, as is An Ama. We will guide you."

He exhaled, releasing any lingering doubts. Let the memories come, he thought.

Outside, the chamber's lights pulsed in sync with the chanting. The Odyssey crew could feel something profound in the air, an ancient energy older than they could fathom, yet strangely comforting. It was as though the chamber itself was sharing a story, one as old as the stars.

Aria's voice came softly through the earpiece of Doctor James and Professor Tashia, her usual calm laced with awe as she observed the entire scene through Tashia's handheld holo-camera. "This goes beyond anything we've ever recorded," she murmured. "It's a history that transcends understanding, a memory alive and breathing."

As the chants reached a final crescendo, the colours intensified, casting the entire amphitheatre in a kaleidoscope of light that seemed to come from the depths of the universe itself. The final words hung in the air like a benediction, soft and resonant:

"(In your hands, our fate unfolds)"
"(Through your will, we grow bold)"

With that, the chanting stopped, and a profound silence fell over the chamber. The light from the ceiling softened, bathing the room in a gentle, golden glow. The priestesses stood back, their heads bowed, and the Odyssey crew watched, transfixed, as the pods continued to glow faintly, holding Zulu, Ninil, and Odriin in a deep, meditative trance.

Tashia's eyes glistened as she kept her gaze on Zulu's pod,

silently willing him to return safely. Doctor James placed a comforting hand on her shoulder. "He's strong, Tashia. He'll make it through."

She nodded, her voice barely a whisper, "I know… but I can't help worrying."

In the silence, they could only wait, watching as the living chamber pulsed gently, holding its ancient memories and sharing them with his brave soul who had dared to enter its depths.

Chapter 10 – Memory Crystal

Captain Zulu found himself in a vast, white expanse, a world that seemed to stretch endlessly in every direction. No walls, no horizon, just an infinite void. Disoriented, he took a few tentative steps, looking around.

"Where… where am I?" he murmured, his voice echoing slightly, as though the silence itself absorbed sound.

"Hello?" he called out, and the emptiness answered with stillness. Is this some kind of dream? he wondered, trying to recall the events that brought him here.

Suddenly, two shadowy figures appeared in the distance, approaching steadily. His body tensed instinctively, preparing to defend himself. "Who's there?" he demanded. "What do you want?"

The figures came closer, their forms becoming more distinct. One was tall, and graceful, with unmistakable golden hair and piercing blue-green eyes. The other was familiar, her presence both commanding and calm.

"Captain, it's me, Odriin," said the first figure, her voice warm and reassuring. "And me, Ninil," added the second with a gentle smile. "Do you remember us, Captain?"

Zulu relaxed, the tension easing from his shoulders. "Odriin, Ninil. Right… It's coming back to me now. We're… we're in the memory pod, aren't we?"

Odriin nodded. "Yes, Captain. We've only just entered. How are you feeling?"

He glanced around the endless white again. "Like I've been in here forever. How long has it actually been?"

"Barely a few seconds," Odriin reassured him.

"Twenty seconds, to be exact," Ninil added with a light smile.

Zulu exhaled slowly, nodding as he gathered his thoughts. "All right. So we're here for the Ki-ág ceremony. Correct?"

"Exactly, Captain," Odriin confirmed. "The pod is adapting to the.... unique technology within you."

Zulu raised an eyebrow. "My nano-bots, you mean? I forgot to mention those might complicate things."

"They are quite unique," Ninil agreed, amusement in her voice. "We detected them during our first encounter with your people, Captain. For such a young species, humans show remarkable ingenuity in crafting technology. Quite impressive."

Odriin nodded. "Humans are advancing at a rate even we find astonishing. Someday, Captain, I believe your people could become a leading force in this galaxy and perhaps beyond."

Zulu smiled at their words, a sense of pride swelling in his chest. Suddenly, a warm glow began to descend from above, illuminating the empty space. The light grew brighter until it revealed a figure, a stunning woman made of radiant light, her skin glowing like molten gold. She drifted toward them, her presence both awe-inspiring and serene.

"An Ama," Odriin breathed, her face lighting up with joy. "It's been so long… I've missed you."

An Ama's voice resonated gently through the space, soothing and warm. "My dear Princess, I am always with you, as you well know."

Odriin stepped forward, her voice tender. "Of course, An Ama. You've always been a part of me." She opened her arms, and An Ama enveloped her in an embrace of light.

"Mind if I join?" Ninil asked, glancing at the two of them with a playful smile.

An Ama extended an arm, and Ninil joined in the embrace, while Zulu looked on, amused. He chuckled softly. "This is… definitely a 'girl thing,'" he murmured.

An Ama, sensing his gaze, turned her attention to him. Her expression softened as she met his eyes. Before Zulu could react, the space around him shifted, the white void replaced by a vibrant scene. He found himself standing in a large, bustling laboratory filled with figures, Caralien ancestors, their skin a deep indigo hue with faint, luminescent patterns trailing along their necks. They had flat noses and pointed ears, features both alien and beautiful.

Odriin appeared beside him, her voice warm. "Captain, welcome to a vision of our past. This is Kalā Sur, my home world. In your language, it translates roughly to 'Great High One.' It lies far from here in another galaxy, the Triangulum Galaxy, or M33, as humans call it. Our galaxy, known to us as Má Mul, meaning 'Boat of Stars,' is situated close to Andromeda. Here, you're seeing our ancestors at a pivotal moment. They are preparing to create the very first Memory Crystal."

Zulu looked around in awe, absorbing every detail. The room was filled with advanced equipment and the hum of scientific activity. Caraliens in long, flowing robes moved with precision, their hands delicately handling crystalline structures and energy fields that glowed with an otherworldly light.

Odriin pointed to a large, transparent crystal at the centre of the room, connected to various instruments. "This is the original Memory Crystal, powered by Zero Point Energy, or ZPE. Inside each of our Memory Crystals lies a ZPE core. It's a power source so efficient, some of our scientists speculate it could last until the end of the universe."

Zulu leaned closer to the crystal, fascinated. "You mean every memory, every thought, and experience your people have had since this moment… it's all stored in crystals like this?"

"Precisely," Ninil chimed in, appearing on his other side. "These crystals are made from highly resistant quartz glass, capable of withstanding cosmic radiation and extreme conditions. The information is etched at the femtosecond scale, each 'memory' is marked in tiny voids only 20 nanometres in size. This encoding spans five dimensions: height, length, width, orientation, and position. Each Caralien, from birth to death, has their life seamlessly transferred to these crystals."

The voice of the alien AI, An Ama, resonated softly. "These memories, Captain, span across ages, aeons filled with history, discoveries, and vast journeys. It was here, in this very lab, that our people first unlocked the technology to capture our daily lives and project it through time. My own AI sub-routines were built on these foundation principles a few centuries before the memory crystals' era."

Zulu's vision shifted once more, memories flooding his mind. Days passed, then years, then centuries, in a rapid cascade. He saw Caralien families growing, generations rising and falling, each memory adding layers to the collective consciousness. Love, loss, triumph, and sorrow, the kaleidoscope of life unfolded before him. He felt the weight of their journey, the discoveries, and the burdens they carried across the ages.

As memories, images, and data streamed through Zulu's mind, Odriin's voice resonated softly in the background, carrying a tone of reverence. "Captain, for us, the cosmos has always been our home. But our earliest journeys into the stars almost ended in disaster due to a mis-calibrated

Exotic Matter engine. It was the celestial beings who intervened, guiding us back before we drifted into oblivion."

Ninil nodded. "Captain, as you know already, our existence unfolds in realms where time and space lose all meaning. Occasionally, civilisations like the Carals, and now humans, pierce through dimensional barriers. When the Odyssey's Tachyon subspace field was mis-calibrated, it caused a dimensional fracture. The Carals experienced a similar effect with their use of Exotic Matter."

Zulu's eyes widened as he recalled what the trans-dimensional being had already revealed to him and his crew aboard the Odyssey. Reflecting on the overwhelming data flooding his mind, he tried to piece everything together. "Right, you mentioned this before. Tashia lost sleep over it for days. This is why you are here?"

Ninil nodded. "Exactly. We project fragments of ourselves into simpler forms across dimensions, not just to repair the disruptions but to experience existence as you do. Your reality, your way of living and dying, is unlike ours. Each encounter deepens our understanding. By living as you do, we grow, and when our time in this form ends, we return to our multidimensional state, forever transformed by what we've learned and felt."

The visions intensified, drawing Captain Zulu deeper into the Caraliens' memories. He found himself in a vast cosmic landscape, where they were discovering new star systems and making first contact with alien civilisations. He witnessed their first encounter with the Tots, a species resilient and adaptable, living within a neutron star system.

Odriin's voice floated beside him, soft and reverent. "We discovered the Tot's system orbiting a pulsar. Their world was ancient and hostile, yet they thrived, adapting to radiation and scarcity with extraordinary resilience." Her tone held both admiration and a hint of sorrow. "Their existence.... it humbled us."

Zulu watched as scenes unfolded, showing Caralien explorers and the Tot exchanging knowledge. Their alliance was cautious yet profound, grounded in mutual respect and curiosity. "These planets," Zulu asked, his voice filled with wonder, "are they all orbiting this neutron star?"

Odriin nodded, her expression thoughtful as if the memories were as vivid for her as they were now becoming for Zulu. "Yes, Captain. The Tot system has fifteen planets, five of them within the habitable zone, seven are gas giants, and two are frozen worlds. One planet, the closest to the pulsar, is revered by the Tot as their 'Pulsar God.' Our ancestors first discovered this system nearly a million years ago."

As she spoke, vivid memories of countless Caralien scientists and explorers began flooding Zulu's mind, allowing him to see what they saw, to feel the awe and wonder they felt as they first experienced the Tot's world.

Zulu raised an eyebrow. "And what was the alliance like?"

Odriin paused before continuing, "The Tot were bipedal predators, their faces resembling wolves from your world, complete with sharp fangs. Primitive, yet undeniably intelligent. At a certain point in our alliance, we began sharing technology, and they permitted us to mine Quantum Crystals from beneath their planet's surface. But things… grew complicated." Her expression turned distant. "In our hubris, we believed we could 'enhance' them, genetically altering the Tot to be more compliant and controllable. We thought we were creating ideal intellectual companions… even forging a deeper bond of friendship."

Zulu studied her, picking up the regret in her tone. "So, your people interfered with their evolution to make them more submissive?"

Odriin nodded solemnly. "It was… a mistake. We educated them and taught them things we shouldn't have. When the Tot realised why we were mining their quantum crystals, they wanted to harness Exotic Matter, an immensely complex and dangerous technology. But we refused to share it. From there, relations grew strained."

Zulu's expression darkened. "And that led to conflict?"

Odriin sighed. "They turned on us. The Tot began to reverse-engineer Carals technology, constructing their own spaceships inspired by our early designs. With their sheer numbers, they built a formidable fleet and turned the rudimentary weaponry we had shared into powerful arms. They pushed us out of their system and denied us access to Quantum Crystals on nearby non-habitable planets."

Zulu let out a low whistle. "From allies to rivals, just like that?"

Odriin's tone grew firm as she recounted the events. "That's correct. They drove us out completely, forcing us to retreat." She gestured toward Zulu, who turned to the side, his mind immediately flooded with a fresh stream of memories. Odriin continued, "What this great ancestor witnessed through his neural receptors, connected to spy satellite stations across their territory, was chilling. The Tot began conducting their own genetic experiments on other species in their star system, manipulating their evolution to suit their needs. Eventually, all contact with them was lost."

A pause hung between them before Odriin continued, "But they didn't stay gone. Hundreds of years later, the Tot returned, with a vengeance."

Zulu frowned. "So, they just… showed up at your doorstep?"

"Yes," Odriin said, voice weighted with memory. "They arrived as a coalition, few alien races led by the Tot, obsessed over control and demanding our technology to produce Exotic Matter. They wanted our secrets, but we knew the danger of unleashing such knowledge. They brought a vast fleet of battlecruisers, each ship more formidable than the last. Their strength lay in sheer numbers."

Zulu shook his head, processing the vivid imagery and details flooding his mind. "So, they began launching attacks on your colonies?"

Ninil nodded gravely. "One by one, our colonies in Andromeda star cluster fell to their advance. We tried to defend them, but the Tot were relentless. Our people were forced to evacuate every outpost across the galaxy."

Odriin's voice grew sombre. "In the end, we had no choice but to retreat. Our people gathered at the Jump Space Station, one of the few still functioning. It was an immense and complex structure powered by Exotic Matter, serving as both our final line of defence and our only path to escape."

Zulu leaned forward, captivated. "What happened then?"

Odriin's voice softened, steeped in the weight of memories. "We barely made it out. Of the few remaining ships, three successfully jumped to this star cluster, while the others reached the Magellanic Cloud, a small dwarf star cluster now merging with the Milky Way. Those three vessels jumped here, and one should have settled near Alpha Centauri and the other one on a distant planet we named Ninshubur, far across this star cluster."

Zulu looked at the Quantum crystals, awed by their enduring power. "These Crystals, the Quantum Crystals…

they're powerful enough to fuel entire galactic stations, aren't they?"

Ninil nodded. "These crystals were formed under extreme conditions, within neutron stars or near black holes. They're capable of superluminal conductivity, manipulating gravity, negative energy and much more. For millennia, the Tots and Caraliens mined them, but with the outbreak of hostilities, access to these precious resources became a matter of life and death."

Zulu took a deep breath, a new understanding dawning on him. "So, these crystals are not just fuel; they're keys to the cosmos."

Odriin gave a solemn nod. "Yes, Captain. The Quantum Crystals contain energies that reach beyond our dimensions. Used wisely, they can advance life beyond imagination. But in the wrong hands… they bring devastation."

Ninil spoke gently, "Now, Odriin, I fully grasp the entirety of your people's history so far."

As Zulu listened, he felt the weight of both Odriin's words and her ancestors' histories. The Tot were once allies, but that relationship was twisted by ambition and the quest for power. And now, as he stood amidst these memories, he saw just how thin the line was between ally and adversary, between creation and destruction.

"Respect," An Ama, intoned softly, "is the core of every true alliance. Without it, our progress means nothing."

The space began to fade, drawing Zulu back to the present. He blinked as the visions melted away, replaced once again by the vast white void. Odriin and Ninil stood beside him, their expressions calm, yet filled with unspoken emotion.

Odriin placed a gentle hand on his shoulder. "Captain, you have now seen the origins of the Carals, the beauty, and the burdens of our past. This memory, this knowledge, will be part of you now."

Ninil added, her voice barely above a whisper, "Your species is young, Captain, yet your spirit resonates with the wisdom of ages. Perhaps one day, humanity will walk this same path, leaving memories of its own for others to cherish."

Captain Zulu, still absorbing the vast knowledge and emotions he had experienced, looked at his two companions, nodding slowly. "Thank you... for sharing this part of your lives with me. I'll carry it with respect, and honour its weight."

As the scene faded, he took a deep breath, grounding himself. The white expanse around them grew brighter, and then, with a rush of warmth, he felt himself returning to the present, back to his pod, carrying the ancient memories of the Caraliens deep within his heart.

Captain Zulu slowly opened his eyes, finding himself in a beautifully decorated room aboard the Nergal vessel. The bed beneath him was soft and comfortable, surrounded by elegantly woven fabrics, polished metals, and soft, warm lights that cast a calming glow. As he took in his surroundings, he realised he wasn't alone. By his side were Tashia, looking at him with a gentle smile, Doctor James monitoring his vitals and the activity of his multifunctional nanobots, Commander Shepard, Captain Enki-Marduk, and both Ninil and Odriin, already dressed and ready.

With his voice slightly groggy, Zulu asked, "How long was I out?"

Doctor James glanced up, giving a reassuring nod. "Only an hour since the ceremony ended. You've been transported here to this specially designed room for recovery."

Zulu looked around the room, his gaze finally resting on a group of four Caralien diplomats standing behind Captain Enki-Marduk. Tall and striking, they held a calm yet intense presence and were in deep conversation with the human team of diplomatic scientists nearby.

"New visitors?" Zulu asked, a bit surprised.

Odriin stepped forward, her expression warm yet serious. "Yes, Captain. These are Caralien diplomatic officials, here to witness your awakening after the Memory Exchange."

Zulu nodded slowly, still processing the events of the day. The intensity of the ceremony began to catch up with him, and he felt a mixture of awe and fatigue weigh on him as he lay back.

Odriin continued, her voice filled with reverence. "We've seen a glimpse of your history, Captain. It's an unintended effect of the Memory Crystal. What we witnessed…" she hesitated, finding the right words, "…. showed us that humanity may be the greatest ally we Carals have ever encountered. Despite all the alien civilisations we have met, humanity is unique. You were willing to help us when we needed it most."

She paused, emotion evident in her eyes. "You saved our mother ship during the last encounter, Captain. Our people honour you not just as warriors, but as a species we can trust."

Zulu managed a tired smile, looking over to Tashia and nodding at her reassuring presence. Exhausted, he let his eyes close, drifting back into sleep. Doctor James adjusted Zulu's monitor and gave a gentle nod to Tashia.

"I'll stay with the Captain to ensure he fully recuperates," James said, looking up.

Tashia smiled, determination in her eyes. "I'll stay too. He'll want a familiar smile close by when he wakes up."

Odriin, Captain Enki-Marduk, Ninil, and the others exited the room quietly, allowing Zulu to rest. They walked down the corridor and soon entered a large, open recreational area. Towering above them were what appeared to be tree-like organisms, unfamiliar in form and texture, enclosed in force fields shimmering with energy.

Mira, walking beside Shepard, couldn't hide her fascination. "These trees.... they look alive but.... metallic… almost."

Ningal-Uruk nodded. "They are in a stage of acclimatisation. It will take them months to adapt to your atmospheric pressure and oxygen levels, but in time, they will adapt and thrive."

Engineer Jessica, Clovis, Ethan, Lieutenant Arvey, Masego, and Imka meticulously scanned the surroundings, their holographic arm pads capturing and analysing every detail. At the centre of the large Gardens Plaza Mall, a massive cubic boulder covered in Caral symbols and inscriptions hovered, held securely in place by a gravitational beam.

Mira pointed to it, eyes wide. "What if the power fails? Wouldn't it just drop and cause massive damage?"

Ningal-Uruk shook her head and gestured to the ground beneath the boulder, a soft and organic surface with a deep resilience. "The ground is designed to absorb the impact. If it falls, it will simply be cradled by the surface below, no harm done."

Satisfied with the answer, they continued their tour of the Nergal vessel, admiring the complexity and advanced technology around them. The walls had that organic metallic sheen, typical of the Caraliens' engineering prowess. Everything was intricately woven, showing an artistry and craftsmanship that both fascinated and inspired the crew of the Odyssey.

After a while, Gibil-Zababa turned to them. "Are you hungry? We have prepared food based on the information provided by the Odyssey. Our replicators have done their best to create your dishes."

They all agreed, eager to try a meal crafted by alien hands. As they made their way to the dining area, the anticipation grew. The humans were amazed by Caral's technology, which seemed like a glimpse into a future that could one day redefine their civilisation. They exchanged glances, each quietly realising that this alliance could change humanity's fate forever.

Meanwhile, Zulu awoke once more, fully refreshed to the delight of Tashia. He dressed and made his way with Tashia and the Docter to join the others, his mind still buzzing from the memories and visions imparted by the Memory Crystal. As he entered the dining area, the team turned to greet him, their faces lighting up with warmth and admiration. Zulu looked over the spread of dishes laid out before them, recognisable and yet strangely foreign interpretations of human cuisine.

Smiling, Zulu said, "Mind if we join in? After all that, I think I'm starving."

Zulu focused on the challenge ahead, determination gleaming in his eyes. "I'll get a message ready for Earth," he said confidently. "Once we reach Proxima B, we'll send it and await their reply. If they're willing to back us, I'll team up with the Carals to show them how to outmanoeuvre the Tots."

Captain Enki-Marduk looked at him thoughtfully. "Captain, we can transmit your message immediately, if you'd prefer," he said. "Our systems allow instantaneous communication within a 10-light-year radius powered by Exotic Matter. We could establish a full duplex communication link, meaning real-time communication with Earth if they respond, despite the distance."

Zulu raised his brow in surprise. "Real-time communication over ten light-years… that's incredible." He paused, considering. "But there's one issue. Based on the last memory exchange, I'm not certain if Alpha Centauri is still under Carals control or if it's been compromised by the Tots."

Odriin stepped forward, her expression earnest. "It may take a few days for the memories to fully integrate," she said. "Ninil and I feel the same. Our recent memory exchange has left things somewhat unclear. There's no way to be sure of the colony's status just yet."

Captain Enki-Marduk remarked, "I have the same impression. The instant communication link with the Alpha Centauri colony is being obstructed. Whether it's interference from the gravitational field of the trinary star system or someone deliberately blocking the transmission remains unclear."

Zulu nodded slowly, thinking it through. "Then perhaps we should approach with caution. What if we exited the sub-space bubble a safe distance from the colony to assess the situation first?"

Captain Enki-Marduk gave a nod of agreement, a subtle smile playing on his lips. "A prudent choice, Captain. We could jump just behind Proxima Centauri to mask our presence. From there, we'll deploy stealth shuttles to scout the area before revealing ourselves. Once we're sure the area is secure, we can proceed with communications or make our presence known."

Zulu's face lit up, impressed by the plan. "Yes, that's exactly the approach we need. Stealth first, then outreach."

Captain Enki-Marduk turned to his crew, issuing orders in the Caral's flowing language. Odriin, standing nearby, exchanged a knowing glance with the captain. They could sense Zulu's resolve, and his drive to protect both his people and theirs.

Ninil leaned closer to Zulu. "Captain, you embody the very spirit of what it means to be an ally. It's no wonder the Caralien people have put so much trust in you."

Zulu acknowledged her words with a nod. "Thank you, Ninil. But this trust goes both ways," he said. "We're in this together. The Carals, Earth, and whoever else stands against the Tots. The Carals paid too high a price to allow them to continue unchecked."

Odriin's gaze softened with appreciation. "Captain, the Carals haven't had an ally like you in countless ages," she said. "And your approach reminds me of how we once navigated diplomacy before... well, before we encountered the Tots."

The room grew quiet. Captain Enki-Marduk finally broke the silence, his deep voice steady and deliberate.

"Then it's decided. We'll approach Proxima Centauri under

stealth, staying close to the star. Our first priority will be to assess the situation and ensure the region is secure."

Captain Zulu nodded in agreement. "Once we've confirmed the area is clear, we'll establish a secure channel with Earth. I'll request the United Earth of Planets Council's formal approval to aid your species."

Enki-Marduk inclined his head. "And from there, we'll deploy scouting parties to gather additional intelligence."

Zulu continued, "We'll also initiate contact with the Alpha Centauri colony to request docking access and coordinate efforts."

Captain Enki-Marduk looked steadily at Zulu. "Captain, I believe the time has come for us to share some of our technology. We'd like to provide you with a Zero Point Energy module, which can be integrated into Odyssey's power systems. This will significantly enhance your energy capacity, allowing your weapons to charge faster."

Zulu considered the offer, nodding slowly. "We'd usually need Earth's authorisation to integrate alien tech into the Odyssey, but under the circumstances, especially after taking down two of the Tot's battleships, I'll gladly accept the ZPE. The Gamma Burst Cannon alone needs more power than our fusion reactors can provide in short succession. We'll need every edge we can get."

Enki-Marduk's team, headed by the Caralien engineers Ningal-Uruk, Gibil-Zababa, and Nanshe-Idnin, quickly arranged for transport to the Odyssey. Joining them were Captain Zulu's engineering team, Ninil, the onboard AI Aria, and the alien AI Cosma Matria, who would assist remotely from the Nergal. Together, they were fully prepared to carry out the intricate integration process.

"Let's get started," Zulu said, his voice steady but charged with anticipation.

After the crews teleported to the Odyssey, they assembled around the reactor chamber, where its fusion core pulsated with controlled energy. Ningal-Uruk projected a detailed hologram of the Odyssey's energy grid, and Cosma Matria provided a continuous feed of ZPE data. The energy module was unlike any human device, a sleek, crystalline structure that seemed to draw energy from an unseen dimension.

"This module operates in a state of quantum flux," Ningal-

Uruk explained, her voice rich with a Caral accent. "It's designed to pull Zero Point Energy from quantum vacuums, creating near-limitless power. However, it must be synchronised with the Odyssey's fusion matrix."

"Let's map it to the Odyssey's harmonics first," suggested Nova Rodriguez, activating her holo pad. "Aria, calculate potential interference patterns and determine the optimal alignment configuration."

"Working on it, Chief," Aria's voice echoed crisply. "Alignment will require sub-nanosecond precision. Syncing ZPE with Odyssey's systems will demand modifications at the subatomic level."

Gibil-Zababa nodded approvingly. "You have an excellent AI, Chief. With Cosma Matria's input, we can calculate the ZPE integration down to the quantum variables."

They worked with precise coordination, merging their skills and technologies in a remarkably seamless process. Chief Engineer Nova and her team managed the physical integration, carefully monitoring core temperatures and energy flow dynamics. Meanwhile, Ninil, using her holo-helmet system, interfaced directly with both the Carals and human AIs, offering insights that seemed to defy conventional physics.

"This process is remarkably smooth," Ninil mused, her voice reflective as she considered her multidimensional heritage. "When beings from different worlds come together and share their knowledge, it feels as though the very fabric of the universe aligns with us, resonating in harmony with our intentions."

After hours of intricate adjustments, Nanshe-Idnin confirmed the module's initial integration. "We're ready for a power-up sequence," she said, her eyes gleaming with anticipation.

Zulu looked to Aria. "Status?"

"Systems check complete," Aria responded. "We're ready for activation."

The team stood back as Chief Nova initiated the ZPE module. The Odyssey's reactor hum changed subtly, growing deeper and more resonant as the new energy source flowed through its channels. A faint, bluish glow spread throughout the reactor, signalling a successful connection.

"It's working," Nova said, almost in disbelief.

Cosma Matria confirmed, "ZPE is holding steady. All

systems are within operational parameters."

The Caralien engineers exchanged satisfied looks, and Ningal-Uruk spoke with quiet pride. "Captain Zulu, your Gamma Burst Cannon is now primed for immediate recharge cycles."

Zulu grinned, feeling a surge of hope. "With this power, we'll have the strength to stand against the Tot fleet, and defend our worlds."

As the final steps of the Zero Point Energy integration concluded, the engineers stepped back, admiring the steady glow of the Odyssey's newly enhanced power system. The hum of the ZPE resonated through the ship, thanks to the collaboration of humans, Carals, and Ninil's trans-dimensional expertise. The efficiency was undeniable; the Odyssey's systems, now revitalised, held a latent power far beyond its original design, and the team could feel it. Just then, a holographic figure of Enki-Marduk materialised in the Engineering bay, casting a steady gaze over the assembled crew and systems. "Captain Zulu," he began with a subtle nod of approval. "I've received confirmation from Cosma Matria that the ZPE has been successfully integrated into your ship's power core. Congratulations. This is a feat few in the known universe have ever accomplished."

Zulu looked around at his team, pride evident in his eyes. "Thank you, Enki-Marduk, and thank you all. This couldn't have happened without everyone's effort and trust," he replied, nodding to Chief Nova, the Caralien engineers, and Ninil, whose calm guidance had contributed a profound edge to the work. He glanced back at the ZPE core, its new energy streams seamlessly powering the weaponry systems and core functions alike. "This is a milestone for both our worlds."

Enki-Marduk continued, his tone more solemn. "As we prepare to exit the quantum bubble, there is an uncertain moment ahead. In a few minutes, we'll drop back into real space at Proxima Centauri.

Let's hope our colony remains untouched, that the Tot Empire hasn't reached it. But if we are met with hostility, rest assured we're ready."

Zulu's gaze hardened. "We'll be prepared. But let's hope diplomacy, not battle, awaits us."

As Enki-Marduk's hologram faded, Zulu turned to his team with a steady command. "Alright, everyone, stay sharp, we're on high alert. Chief Nova, keep a close eye on the ZPE's output and all critical systems." He opened a comm line to the bridge. "Commander Nin, prepare the bridge for immediate readiness." Then, glancing at Ninil, he added, "Ninil, stay on standby, we will be happy for any assistance you may provide."

Ninil gave a soft, knowing nod. "This collaboration has resonated deeply," she said quietly. "I trust it will carry us through whatever we face."

As the quantum bubble began to dissolve, the starfield shifted around them, revealing the vast expanse of the Proxima Centauri system. The Odyssey held steady, its new power systems ready to respond, the crew poised for anything that might await.

Chapter 11 – The Pale Red Dot

"Proxima Centauri," Tashia McColl murmured from the observation Deck 4, her eyes remained locked on the faint red dwarf star, visible through the ship's reinforced, transparent tungsten viewports. "A small, dim red dwarf, barely visible to the naked eye from Earth." She was accompanied by Ninil and Ishtar, who pulsed with a faint, calming blue light. The glow from their clothing softly illuminated the low-lit observation deck, casting an otherworldly sheen around them. Ishtar smiled warmly, her curiosity piqued.

"That was your destination from the start, wasn't it?" Ishtar asked, studying Tashia with deep, knowing eyes. "From Earth to here, Alpha Centauri."

Tashia nodded. "It's taken us a long time to get here, but seeing it up close… it's surreal."

Ninil, ever the more playful of the two beings, smiled. "Humanity is indeed remarkable," she remarked softly.

Tashia shot her a teasing look. "I think when you say 'humanity,' what you really mean is Alexander, don't you?" she said.

Ninil laughed, a sound as light as a breeze. "Well," she whispered with a mischievous smile, "perhaps it is Alexander. Humanity, Alexander, it all becomes the same to me. Though I will admit, he's rather exceptional."

Ishtar observed Ninil with mild amusement, a curious look crossing her face. "We've learned a great deal about humanity from you all, Tashia. Your passion, courage… and yes, even your tendency toward violence."

Tashia's expression grew defensive but still light-hearted. "Hey, we were only defending ourselves when we destroyed that Tot battleship. We didn't start this conflict."

Ishtar raised an eyebrow, clearly entertained. "Ah, now you're defending your husband's actions?" she asked with a knowing smile.

Tashia shrugged. "I'm just saying, that Captain Zulu's priority was to protect not only his crew but also to keep humanity from falling into the Tot empire's control. He was doing his duty, and he's damn good at it."
At that moment, the elevator pod doors hissed open, and the sound of friendly chatter and laughter filled the observation deck. Nova Rodriguez, Commander Nin, Commander Reyes Thalassa, and Mira Sanders walked in, each carrying steaming cups of coffee. They approached with broad smiles.

"Hey, ladies!" Tashia greeted them warmly.

"Did we hear right? You're all here just to stare at a red dwarf star?" Mira teased, grinning.

The group chuckled. Professor Tashia explained, "Well, it sounds silly, but yes. Captain Zulu's given us senior staff a short reprieve before the real work begins exploring Alpha Centauri, so we thought we'd soak in the view."

Reyes added, her tone thoughtful, "The Nergal and Odyssey are both positioned safely behind Proxima Centauri. With luck, we'll stay undetected if any Tot battleships are lurking."

Nin nodded, glancing at the rest of the group. "And speaking of the Carals, Princess Odriin has asked to come aboard this afternoon."

Tashia smirked. "Oh yeah, so, uh… speaking of the Caral, uh…, I think Princess Odriin might have a bit of a crush on Sergeant Major Masego Biko."

Ninil nodded, a glint in her eyes. "When we were in the memory pods connecting to the Memory crystal, I could sense that she was trying to mask certain emotions. Carals or humans, it seems some things are universal," she laughed. "She has a strong bond with Masego, maybe because he was the one who accidentally triggered her pod."

Commander Nin laughed. "Accident or fate, who knows? But I doubt Princess Odriin understands 'by accident' the way we do."

The women shared a laugh, and their light-hearted banter made for a well-deserved distraction from their current mission. In that moment, they weren't defined by their roles as scientists, commanders, and soldiers but were simply friends, finding connections beyond ranks and responsibilities. Captain Zulu recognised the power of this unity among his team, believing it to be one of the Odyssey's greatest strengths. He had carefully selected his crew, valuing not only their intellect but also their empathy, resilience, and the intuition that had seen him through countless challenges.

Nova kept her gaze on the distant star and said quietly, "Finally, Proxima Centauri.... so similar to our Sun and yet so different."

"Right?" Commander Nin responded, leaning forward. "It's technically a star, but the Sun would look like a blazing lighthouse next to this. Proxima is only about 12% of the Sun's mass and emits just a tiny fraction of its light."

Commander Reyes Thalassa peered out thoughtfully. "It may be faint, but Proxima has its own personality. It's notorious for violent flare-ups, blasting nearby space with intense radiation. Anything near it would be scorched."

"I can't wait to see Proxima Centauri B and C," Mira added, excitement in her voice. "Proxima B is right in the habitable zone. Imagine the potential here, especially with the Caral colonies orbiting these planets."

Tashia agreed. "It's unfortunate, though, that Proxima B has no magnetic field. Even if it had an atmosphere, it would've been stripped away by stellar wind long ago."

Commander Nin nodded. "Thankfully, the Nergal's shields are protecting us from any radiation spikes. Odyssey's shields could handle it, but they'd need a boost."
Nova grinned. "We're covered there. The ZPE integration is complete, so Odyssey has plenty of power now."

"Wait," Mira chimed in, "I thought the ZPE node was only allocated to the weapons system?"

Nova shook her head with a sly smile. "The Odyssey's been designed with versatility in mind. We can tap into the

ZPE if needed, thanks to the Caral's generosity."

The group exchanged knowing looks, each of them understanding just how significant that gift was.

"In a few hours," Nin added, "we'll deploy our prototype stealth dart fighter along with a shuttle to start mapping the system. Two Caral stealth vessels will accompany us, though they're more scouts than fighters."

Tashia raised an eyebrow. "We owe General Imhotep for our state-of-the-art weapons system. His relentless push to integrate the space station's Gamma Burst Cannon and other defensive systems onto the Odyssey almost didn't get Congress's approval. "Do you all remember when they said, 'The Odyssey is a space vessel for peaceful exploration and doesn't need weapons in the void of space'? Well, thanks to him, we now have the tools to protect ourselves."
Nin nodded but remained cautious. "That's true, but we're up against the Tot, and we don't know what to expect. Captain Zulu's experience in years fighting the Fanatics will certainly guide us, though."

Tashia gave a small nod, a silent affirmation of the trust they all shared in their captain. The group continued their lively discussion, seamlessly shifting from strategic planning to scientific wonder and, of course, a little light-hearted banter.

Captain Zulu leaned back in his seat, studying the holographic display hovering in front of him in the mess hall. Beside him, Commander Shepard was nursing a steaming cup of coffee, eyes fixed on the replay of their last skirmish with the Tot battleship. Aria had joined them, providing tactical support and retrieving essential snippets of the combat data for review. The scent of scrambled eggs and freshly brewed coffee filled the room, an unexpected but welcome reminder of Earth.

Shepard took a bite of his scrambled eggs, smiling with satisfaction. "These scrambled eggs are incredible, Captain. I think the chef really outdid himself."

Zulu chuckled, glancing at the display. "Aria, you're missing out on a fantastic meal here. You may be our AI, but you need to know just how good Chief Oliver Grant's cooking is."

Aria's avatar flickered, her face forming a playful smile. "I've heard tales of his culinary skills. I think Chief Grant might be one of Odyssey's finest assets," she teased. "I'll take your word on it, Captain. But maybe I'll persuade him to invent some recipes specifically designed for AIs."

Zulu smirked. "Good luck with that. I'll let him know you're eagerly awaiting your first digital meal," he joked before his tone shifted to business. "Aria, can you check on everyone's private messages and make sure they're queued up for transmission to Earth?"

Aria nodded. "Absolutely, Captain. It will take a few moments to ensure everyone's transmissions are ready." She paused, then added thoughtfully, "It's still fascinating to me that they can communicate almost instantaneously across these vast distances. I was just in conversation with Cosma Matria, and she still won't reveal the exact workings of this technology."

Zulu sighed, leaning back. "Trust me, I've asked Captain Enki-Marduk and even Princess Odriin about it. They're firm on not sharing. 'It's the law,' they said, something about humans not being ready for that kind of knowledge just yet."

Aria nodded in understanding. "I suppose humans have their own set of rules too. Some rules can be bent, but others… not so much. And this, Captain, is one of those times when breaking the rule is simply not an option. Perhaps when humanity reaches a new level of development, then… and only then… will the Carals be willing to share these secrets."

Shepard leaned in, cutting into the exchange. "So, are you all set to communicate with Earth today?"

Zulu nodded. "Yes. I'll transport to the Caral ship in four hours. But we're going to need Commander Reyes to connect to their transmission arrays an hour beforehand. She'll sync up the encryption protocols and establish a secure channel."

Shepard grinned. "The President, the Admiral, and the Generals are all going to want a word with you once we patch through."

Zulu smirked. "Right. I'll be standing in… what did they call it again, Aria?"
Aria's eyes gleamed as she completed his thought. "In a communication pod that resembles a classic telephone booth from the 20th and 21st centuries, Captain."

"Exactly." Zulu chuckled. "They've got an odd sense of style; I'll give them that."

The two of them shared a brief laugh before turning back to their work. Aria reactivated the simulation on the display, showing the moment their Gamma Burst Cannon obliterated the Tot battleship. The immense energy discharge was beautiful, even in the replay, a burst of gamma energy so intense it had penetrated their shield and incinerated the enemy craft in a matter of seconds.

"Aria," Zulu prompted, "what's the current replenishment rate after we fire a blast like that with our new ZPE in place?"

Aria's gaze focused as she ran calculations, her voice smooth and precise. "Right now, it's sitting at around one minute between charges, Captain. That's the minimum recharge time based on our energy reserves and the cannon's power requirements."

Zulu frowned, clearly not satisfied. "One minute? In a battle, with multiple Tot ships, we could be torn apart in that time."

Aria hesitated, her voice carrying a rare note of caution. "Captain, I must advise against trying to reduce the recharge time. The Gamma Burst Cannon wasn't designed for rapid-fire; it's a precision weapon, one of immense power but requiring careful handling. Altering its rate could lead to dangerous overheating or even irreversible damage to the system."

Shepard glanced at Zulu. "She's got a point. The Tot ships may be vicious, but we need that cannon operational, not fried by overuse."

Zulu nodded reluctantly. "You're both right. Still, we need to plan for contingencies. If there's an all-out battle, we'll need to be prepared."

Aria recalibrated the holographic display, pulling up scans and metrics from their last encounter. "Captain, I've tallied the Tot ships detected within our current zone," she reported. "Their fleet consists of eight classes, from destroyers down to a range of smaller fighter craft. Captain, I must warn you, that these numbers reflect only our latest scans by Commander Reyes' team using Odyssey and Nergal's sensors. We'll need to deploy reconnaissance dart fighters and shuttles to get a clearer count on the Tot fleet's actual numbers in this system. I presume that's still the plan after your communication with Earth?"

Zulu nodded, confirming, "That's right, Aria. As discussed in our team briefing, we'll move forward as planned."

Zulu studied the data with a furrowed brow, the weight of the numbers settling heavily on his mind. "If we're up against the full force of the Tot empire's fleet, one cannon won't be enough. We'll need multiple layers of contingency plans, exit strategies, fallback positions, and maybe even defences around the Caral colonies, assuming they're still intact." Shepard nodded solemnly, recognising the magnitude of what lay ahead.

Zulu looked at him, his eyes hard. "The Carals have shared knowledge, technology, and insights with us. We owe it to them to try to keep their people safe if we can. The Tots are relentless; they won't stop for no one. If the Caral colonies are still intact, they'll be the first line of defence in this system."

Aria interjected, "Captain, if we're looking at full-scale Tot engagement, then perhaps I could run simulations with Nova Rodriguez, Jessica Thompson and Commander Reyes on alternative weapon configurations and explore shielding options with the ZPE integration?"

Zulu's eyes lit up. "That's the kind of thinking we need. Start running those simulations and share your data with the Engineering team. We may need them to push the shields to their maximum output. As for the ZPE, let's consider drawing from it not just for the Gamma Burst Cannon, but for any other systems that could help in battle but first, I'll need approval from Earth Headquarters."

Shepard nodded. "Understood, Captain. I'll have Chief Rodriguez, Commander Reyes and their teams, run diagnostics on every weapon system and shield matrix. We're going to need all the power we can get."

Aria nodded, her holographic form shimmering slightly. "And, Captain, I'll coordinate with Cosma Matria, for any insight she can provide on Tot tactics. The Caral intelligence reports may contain strategies that we haven't yet considered."

Zulu took a long sip of his coffee, feeling the weight of their next steps. "If there's one thing I've learned in all my years, it's that preparation can mean the difference between survival and destruction. We have the tools, the intel… and we have allies willing to fight alongside us."

Aria's expression softened as if contemplating his words. "Captain, just a reminder, this conflict belongs to the Carals. While we're fighting alongside them, humanity isn't directly involved. Your commitment here is both admirable and… chivalrous."

Zulu's stern expression relaxed into a faint smile. "I know, Aria, but we're already in too deep. After taking down one of their ships and crippling another, there's no turning back now." He paused, glancing at her holographic form with a look of appreciation. "And thank you for the compliment. Just remember, if things go south, I'll count on you to pull us through."

Aria resumed the playback, and the holographic replay continued, with Captain Zulu, Commander Shepard, and Aria poring over every second of footage. As they dissected the Tot fleet's weaknesses and the Odyssey's strengths, the camaraderie in the room solidified into a quiet resolve. They were prepared to defend the Caral colonies and stand their ground, side by side, no matter what the Tot empire threw at them.

After a relaxed but productive meeting with Commander Shepard and Aria in the mess hall, Captain Zulu made his way back to the bridge. Commander Nin had already assumed her position, greeting him with a nod.

"Enjoyed the break, Captain?" Nin asked with a smile.

Zulu chuckled. "It was good to step back for a moment, but

no rest for the weary." He settled into his seat, the hum of the bridge systems around him both calming and energising.

"You should visit the observation deck before we move off behind Proxima," Nin urged. "Seeing the dwarf star with your own eyes is something else. It's a tiny red spark, but so vivid against the darkness, especially through the larger viewports. It's breathtaking."

Zulu raised an eyebrow, a hint of amusement in his expression. "Come on, Commander. The view from the bridge isn't bad either. Besides, there will be plenty of time to take it all in once we're finished dealing with our Tot friends." He glanced at the screens around him. "And after we make it out of this alive, we'll have a well-deserved celebration with the whole crew."

Nin's smile faltered slightly. "Captain, do you think it will come to that? That this situation with the Tot Empire will actually be resolved?"

Zulu looked thoughtful. "I believe so. But we're going to need to show them we're not pushovers. Predators like the Tots respect strength. If we can play this right, perhaps even beat them in this game of theirs, they might think twice about continuing hostilities."

Nin nodded, her expression serious. "So, you think they'll listen if we prove ourselves?"

"That's the idea," Zulu replied. "From what Captain Enki-Marduk and Princess Odriin have told us, the Tots are a lot like lions or wolves. They see weakness, they pounce. The Carals made the mistake of allowing themselves to be prey, hoping for peace. But with predators, you can't back down. You need to show resilience, maybe even a little aggression." He paused. "I didn't hesitate to fire on the Tot vessel because I wanted them to know we're capable of defending ourselves. They need to feel that resistance."

As he spoke, the intercom crackled, and Commander Reyes's voice came through, gently interrupting their conversation.

"Captain, we've just received all private messages from the crew and encrypted them for transmission back to Earth. The link between the Odyssey and the Nergal is established. Once you give the word, we're ready to transmit to Earth's current coordinates. And Captain," she added, "the Carals are also prepped for your instant holographic communication with Earth."

Zulu acknowledged her update. "Good work, Reyes. I'll contact Captain Enki-Marduk now."

"One more thing, sir," Reyes continued. "Princess Odriin will be visiting us soon."

Zulu smiled. "Understood. Aria, reach out to Tashia and the diplomatic team, I think they're planning to formally welcome the Princess on board."

Aria's holographic form nodded. "Understood, Captain. I'm on it."

As the intercom went silent, Zulu leaned back, taking in the readiness of his bridge crew. Turning back to Nin, he flashed a quick grin. "Looks like we've got a busy few hours ahead."

She smiled back. "Just another day at the office, right, Captain?"

Zulu chuckled. "Something like that." With that, he initiated the connection with the Nergal, preparing for the upcoming transmission to Earth.

The star was temperamental, spewing solar flares at

random. Through the filtered viewport of the Nergal, Princess Odriin and her companion gazed at Proxima Centauri, a dim red glimmer against the vast blackness of space. Smaller and cooler than their home star, this red dwarf emitted only a faint, subdued light. Yet Proxima was anything but calm, it frequently erupted in sudden bursts of radiation, flooding nearby space unpredictably.

Princess Odriin stood poised, ready to transport to the Odyssey, awaiting the go-ahead to activate the Atomic Re-materialisation Transportation system. Behind her, her loyal bodyguards, Momos and Moros, stood at attention. They had each changed into new attire, as had the princess herself.

Princess Odriin's clothes reflect Caral's mastery in design and technology. Her outfit is composed of a sleek, close-fitting suit with a primary colour of brilliant white, accented with shimmering shades of blue. The fabric, a soft material, clings to her form while allowing complete flexibility and movement.

At her shoulders, there are subtle yet elegant silver patterns, giving a regal, sophisticated look, while thin, blue iridescent lines extend down her arms and sides, glowing softly as she moves. Her suit, as all Carals attire, regulates her body temperature seamlessly, adjusting instantly to her environment whether it's an icy tundra or a blazing desert.

Around her waist, a blue sash drapes, appearing almost as if it's made of liquid light, symbolising her royal status. Her sleeves are fitted, and she wears an intricate, layered high collar that extends subtly up to her jawline, adding an air of mystique and elegance.

Her bodyguards, Momos and Moros, are clad in a more utilitarian yet equally sophisticated version of Caral attire. Their suits are darker, primarily in a deep blue with black undertones, to blend seamlessly with various surroundings, allowing them to move stealthily. The suits are reinforced with protective plates, almost invisible yet adding a faint sheen in key areas like the chest, shoulders, and forearms. Their attire, too, is temperature-regulating and resistant to extreme physical damage.

Unlike Princess Odriin's more ornate design, the bodyguards' suits are marked with subtle, angular lines in metallic silver that signify their roles. A high-tech belt around their waists carries various tools and small devices for protection and assistance. Each has a narrow, reinforced hood that can be raised to shield their heads. It is also equipped with a visor that adjusts based on light conditions.

Momos and Moros' attire is an elegant yet intimidating display of the Caral's protective technology, matching their silent and resolute loyalty to their princess.

"Princess, we've received the go-ahead from the Odyssey," one of Odriin's attendants said, gesturing toward the teletransportation pod. "You'll be arriving at the designated coordinates on Deck 4, also known as the Observation Deck. Professor Tashia and three other diplomats will be there to welcome you."

Odriin nodded, preparing herself for the jump, when the organic door hissed open, revealing Captain Enki-Marduk. He entered the room with a dignified nod, bowing his head to the princess in respect. "How long do you anticipate being gone, Princess?" he asked, concern subtly shadowing his features.

"Until we establish communication with our colonies," Odriin replied confidently.

The Captain nodded. "As you wish, Princess." He then turned to the two Caralien bodyguards accompanying her, meeting their eyes with a firm gaze. "See that she is well protected."

The bodyguards responded with a synchronised, silent bow. Enki-Marduk turned to the teletransportation operator, signalling the go-ahead. The operator initiated the process, and a soft, low hum filled the room, creating an iridescent shimmer around the princess and her guards.

On the Odyssey, the Observation Deck was bathed in the same shimmering light as Odriin and her guards began to materialise in front of the wide viewports, against the backdrop of the red dwarf. Professor Tashia stood ready with her diplomatic team, each wearing respectful smiles as Odriin fully materialised.

Tashia waved warmly, approaching the princess with an air of calm. "Welcome back aboard the Odyssey, Princess Odriin," she said. "We've taken the liberty of organising some of your preferred delicacies. Would you care to join us in the mess hall? Chef Oliver has truly outdone himself." Odriin's face lit up with genuine delight. "Thank you, Tashia. I appreciate the effort." She glanced around thoughtfully before asking, "Will Masego Biko be joining us? And, if possible, might I have the opportunity to observe the Tot captives, the ones who survived? I hope they're being treated well."

"Of course," Tashia replied smoothly, nodding to her team.

"Doctor James has been attentive to their care, and no harm has come to them. He's taken extensive precautions to maintain safe interactions, sealed behind transparent walls for now until he's certain there's no infection risk. But so far, they've adjusted well to the Odyssey's environment."

Jabari, one of the diplomatic scientists, added, "We've managed to establish basic communication with them. We're even translating parts of their language, it's been fascinating. They've shown a civil nature outside of their battle gear."

Odriin's eyes lit up with curiosity. "What about their dietary needs? I hear they eat vegetables too, which is quite a shift from their carnivorous nature. Have you been able to provide them with suitable food?"

Azibo stepped forward with a nod. "Indeed. We've examined their dietary patterns, learning from the Tot corpses' digestive tracts, and we've managed to replicate some of their typical food items. They seem to find our versions acceptable, which is a promising sign for further dialogue."

The Princess's expression softened. "Thank you, Azibo."

Mosi added, "Don't worry, Princess. The doctor is still being cautious, but he mentioned that the risk of contagious diseases is minimal. It's always better to be safe, and Doctor James insists we stay vigilant for now."

Tashia smiled at Odriin, gesturing toward the exit. "Shall we, then? We'll bring you to observe your… unexpected guests, and after, we'll join the others in the mess hall. I'll send word to Masego so he can join us."

Odriin gave a pleased smile, her excitement barely contained. "That sounds perfect. And, Tashia," she hesitated for a moment before continuing, "I'd like to request permission to stay aboard the Odyssey until we're able to establish communication with my people."

Tashia looked at her, considering the request with a slight smile. "I don't see why not. I'll inform Captain Zulu; it shouldn't be a problem. Your quarters are still available and awaiting you."

"Excellent," Odriin replied with a relieved sigh. "I'll have my belongings sent over once we're done here. I assume they'll need to be checked upon arrival?"

"Routine security, of course," Tashia replied, smiling

knowingly. "Nothing personal, I'm sure. But we'll handle it as discreetly as possible."

Odriin laughed lightly, waving off the concern. "It's only a change of clothes. I'll be cooperative, don't worry."

With that, the group began making their way down the corridor toward the medical bay, where the Tot survivors were kept under close observation. As they walked, Odriin cast sidelong glances, taking in the bustling activity of the Odyssey's corridors, a blend of human efficiency and Caral influence.

Upon reaching the medical bay, they found Doctor James engrossed in monitoring vitals on the main screen. He looked up, smiling as he saw the group.

"Princess Odriin," he greeted, inclining his head respectfully. "An honour, as always. I assume Tashia has briefed you on the Tot captives' condition?"

Odriin nodded. "Yes, Doctor and I'm pleased with how they're being treated. I understand you've managed to create a viable food source for them?"

James's face lit up. "Yes, indeed. We're careful, of course, with their unique physiology. They've been relatively compliant, although the language barrier remains challenging, we're learning."

Tashia smiled as she said, "The translation project has been really fascinating. The Tots' language is complex and surprisingly similar to yours."

Jabari added, "That's right. The cultural nuances are remarkable. Even in captivity, they show impressive discipline, which speaks volumes about their structure and values."

Odriin's eyes lingered on the large containment transparent metal walls where the four Tot captives were visible, quietly observing their visitors. She turned to Doctor James. "They seem… calmer than I expected."

"Agreed," Doctor James said, a hint of curiosity in his tone. "They're surprisingly introspective. I think they're assessing us as much as we're assessing them."

The Princess took in the sight, then turned back to the group. "This opportunity is unprecedented. It's rare that enemies have the chance to learn from each other."

"True," Tashia replied thoughtfully. "It's what makes this alliance with the Caral so crucial. And with the Tot, if there's even a chance of peace…"

Odriin nodded, deep in thought. After a moment, she looked back at Tashia. "Let's head to the mess hall. I could use a little sustenance before we delve deeper into diplomacy."

Tashia led the group to the mess hall, where the chef's meticulously prepared dishes were laid out in a welcoming display. The scent of freshly prepared delicacies filled the air, an array of vibrant colours and textures carefully crafted to appeal to Odriin's tastes.

Odriin glanced around appreciatively. "Chef Oliver has certainly outdone himself. He even made something that smelled similar to the Caral spiced fruits, remarkable."

"Nothing but the best for our esteemed guest," Tashia said with a smile, pulling out a chair. "And Masego should be joining us shortly."

True to her word, Masego arrived moments later, greeting the group with a warm nod. Odriin's face lit up as he approached, and she extended her hand. "Sergeant Major, it's been too long."

Masego took her hand briefly, a warm smile on his face. "Always an honour, Princess."

As they settled into their meal, the conversations flowed freely, from light-hearted tales of their travels to the more serious discussions about the alliance and the risks they were all taking. Odriin's eyes sparkled with a newfound sense of hope and determination.

"This alliance," she murmured, glancing at each person around the table, "is a bridge between worlds. And I believe it will bring us the strength we need."

Chapter 12 – At ease Captain

As Captain Zulu materialised aboard the Nergal for his communication with Earth, he was immediately greeted by Captain Enki-Marduk, Second-in-command Geshtu-Ea, and two engineers, Lugalbanda-Eresh and Inanna-Zu. Enki-Marduk extended a hand with a gracious nod. "Welcome back to the Nergal, Captain Zulu."

Zulu returned the nod, smiling politely. "Thank you, Captain. It's good to be here."

Geshtu-Ea took a step forward, studying Zulu's face closely. "I trust you've recovered well from your experience with the Memory Crystal?"

"Ah, yes," Zulu replied, downplaying the ordeal with a wry smile. The sudden influx of information from the Memory Crystal had been intense, to say the least, though he didn't let it show. "Just took a bit of adjusting, that's all."

Geshtu-Ea gestured toward the door leading out of the A.R.T. chamber. "Please, follow us, Captain."

As they walked, Zulu found himself in a vast, open area bustling with Carals of all ages, going about their daily activities. It had the air of a community centre, where everyone seemed at ease. Zulu glanced around, intrigued. "It looks like your people are settling back into a routine. Almost feels.... peaceful."

Enki-Marduk and Geshtu-Ea exchanged glances, and a hint of a smile played across their lips, a smile that, until recently, would have been rare for their kind. Geshtu-Ea nodded. "We have come to appreciate peace, Captain. Observing human expressions has taught us more about conveying emotion. Our species has survived for millions of years by adapting. Learning from others is part of that."

Zulu raised an eyebrow, clearly impressed. Smiling is a survival trait. That's... unexpected, but I see the value. You've designed this ship to feel almost alive."

As they continued, they reached a large, shimmering portal, set like an entryway in the heart of a busy arcade. The environment was beautifully adorned with organic materials, and everything appeared integrated with the Carals' natural aesthetic. Zulu paused in front of the portal, studying its gentle, faint glow.

"Is this the same portal Commander Shepard used the other day?" he asked, glancing at Enki-Marduk.

Enki-Marduk inclined his head. "Yes, Captain. We prefer these shortcuts for efficient travel. You actually passed through a similar portal during your previous visit for the Memory Crystal experience, though they might have seemed like normal doorways at the time."

Lugalbanda-Eresh chimed in, smiling slightly. "It's easy to overlook them when everyone else is passing through. They blend into the environment so well that we hardly notice them anymore."

Zulu studied the portal thoughtfully. "But why place it in the middle of a lively arcade like this?"

Enki-Marduk glanced around, pleased at the surroundings. Originally, this area was to be a standard transit zone. However, we redesigned it to be a recreational space. Our people believed a ship of this size could benefit from communal, open areas that spark creativity. More room to walk, think, and connect leads to a more innovative community."

Zulu nodded, intrigued. "Makes sense. You're building

more than a vessel; you're fostering a society onboard."

"Precisely, Captain," Geshtu-Ea replied with a knowing smile.

Enki-Marduk gestured toward the portal. "Shall we continue to the communication chamber?"

Zulu gave a nod, watching as Lugalbanda-Eresh and Inanna-Zu stepped through first. The portal emitted a soft, humming sound and a faint, water-like splash as they disappeared. Enki-Marduk then turned to Zulu and motioned him forward. "After you, Captain."

Taking a steadying breath, Zulu stepped into the portal. A wave of strange sensations washed over him, as though his body was dissolving into pure light and thought. For a brief moment, he felt entirely weightless, detached from any physical form, his consciousness seemingly unanchored. He couldn't move, speak, or even feel his own limbs. But just as abruptly as it began, the sensation ceased. He stepped out of the portal and into a vast chamber.

Geshtu-Ea, Enki-Marduk, and the two engineers emerged just behind him, and the portal shimmered briefly before fading into the wall.

Enki-Marduk observed Zulu, a hint of amusement in his expression. "It's quite a sensation, isn't it?"

Zulu blinked, a bit dazed. "That's an understatement," he admitted, letting out a small laugh as he regained his balance. "Not exactly your everyday teleportation, that's for sure. The funny thing, though, I didn't feel anything the last time I went through these portals. Didn't even notice them then. Captain Enki-Marduk, are you certain I've been through these same portals before?"

Enki-Marduk gave a firm nod. "Yes, Captain Zulu. You've used them several times, actually."

Lugalbanda-Eresh chuckled softly. "We do apologise if it felt... intense this time, Captain. It's only natural to feel unsettled if you're focusing closely on the experience. Sometimes, it's easier if you just move through without too much thought."

Geshtu-Ea chimed in, a slight smile crossing his face. "You were under quite a bit of pressure before the Ceremony, after all, and likely overlooked the experience. Plus, your mind was likely on conversations with your doctor and your wife."

Zulu considered this and chuckled, nodding at the Carals. "You may be right. Guess I was a bit distracted then."

Zulu shook his head, looking around the chamber. "Well, it certainly makes an impression." He gestured to the surroundings, admiring the complex architecture. "So this is where the magic happens? The communication chamber?"

Enki-Marduk nodded, stepping forward. "Yes, this is our stasis communication chamber. It allows for instant, secure communication over vast distances. We'll connect with Earth from here."

Zulu followed Enki-Marduk to the central console, where several rectangular objects stood in perfect alignment. These objects resembled 19th-century telephone booths but were unmistakably alien in design. They were the Carals' instant stasis communication nodes, their Ionic design pulsing with an ever-shifting array of colours that seemed alive. The organic-like technology rippled gently across their surfaces, almost as if the structures were breathing.

Each node was adorned with intricate, fluid patterns that shimmered under the chamber's ambient light, giving off a vibe that mixed style both art and function seamlessly. The doorway of one node glowed faintly, reminding him of a portal, its light soft and inviting, but filled with a mysterious energy that gave off vibes of immense power within.

Several holographic displays around the central console flickered with symbols Zulu didn't recognise. The Carals moved with practised efficiency, taking their places around the chamber with synchronised precision, preparing for the transmission. The air hummed with a quiet intensity, charged with the anticipation of the communication to come.

Geshtu-Ea explained, "While you communicate, Captain, we'll monitor the flow of information. This chamber stabilises both audio and visual feeds across light-years, reducing lag to zero."

Zulu raised an eyebrow, impressed. "Instant communication with no lag, that's remarkable. A technology Earth hasn't quite mastered yet."

Enki-Marduk smiled. "Perhaps one day, we will be able to share this technology with your people. For now, it is available for you as allies."

Zulu inclined his head in gratitude. "Thank you, Captain. This communication will be essential for coordinating with our leaders. I appreciate your trust in letting us use it."

The Caral leaders exchanged solemn nods, their expressions grave yet calm. Inanna-Zu stepped forward, delicately fine-tuning a cluster of holographic nodes around Zulu to ensure his image would be transmitted perfectly. With a subtle but deliberate gesture, He signalled for Captain Zulu to step into the shimmering doorway of the active stasis communication node.

Zulu hesitated; his brow furrowed with unease. "It's just me going in, right?" he asked, his voice carrying a trace of apprehension.

Enki-Marduk offered a reassuring smile. "Yes, Captain. Only you."

Inanna-Zu's tone was steady but firm as he added, "Once inside, continue walking until you reach the glowing light at the centre."

Zulu took a deep breath, his pulse quickening as he stepped through the glowing doorway. The light engulfed him, and suddenly he found himself in a vast, empty white chamber, a space eerily reminiscent of his earlier experience in the stasis pod during the memory transfer. Despite the node's relatively small exterior, the interior seemed impossibly massive, its stillness broken only by the faint hum of the communication console.

His heart raced as he approached the glowing centre, the intensity of the hum increasing with each step. The sheer enormity of the unknown pressed against his thoughts, a mix of awe and anxiety coursing through him. This was no ordinary call; it was a bridge between worlds, and every word he was about to speak carried unimaginable weight.

"Captain," Geshtu-Ea's voice broke through the silence, steady and clear, "we're ready when you are. Earth awaits."

Zulu squared his shoulders, steadying his breath. The moment had arrived.

Captain Zulu's vision blurred as a cascade of flashing lights engulfed him, forcing his eyes closed. The overwhelming sensation was more than visual, it was as if his entire being expanded outward, perceiving the universe from an impossible vantage point. He saw it first as a speck of dust, a pinprick in an infinite void, and then, in an incomprehensible instant, it swelled to encompass him.

Time stretched thin, a nanosecond feeling like an eternity, and suddenly, with a silent thud of finality, he stood in the command centre in the United Earth Headquarters.

As the disorientation subsided, Zulu steadied himself and took in the room's impressive assembly. His holographic display automatically identified and saluted each individual, starting from his right. With a formal nod, he addressed each figure:

"President Sarah Thompson," he began, acknowledging her poised and dignified presence. Turning slightly, he added, "Vice President Alaric Thorne," noting the intense energy radiating from him.

Zulu's gaze shifted, and he saluted Admiral Nicolas Des Bruslys, whose quiet authority was undeniable. "Admiral Des Bruslys," he said with respect before addressing, "Vice Admiral Boyle," whose solid and dependable demeanour was evident.

Next, Zulu acknowledged the military officers standing nearby. "Commander Musa Al-Khwarizmi, Captain Himilco," he said, admiring their disciplined stances reflecting their distinguished service.

His attention then landed on a familiar face. "Professor Patel," he greeted warmly, noting the professor's curious glint that hinted at his ever-analytical mind.

When his gaze shifted again, it softened as it met the beaming faces of his daughters, Varaya, Lyra, and Elena. Their pride and joy were unmistakable, filling Zulu with a quiet sense of fulfilment.

Nearby, journalist Harper Sinclair was a blur of motion, already typing furiously on his holographic notepad, capturing every detail of the unfolding scene. Hovering discreetly at the edges of the gathering were the enigmatic members of the E.K.I.A., also known as Elysian Illumination. Their subtle air of intrigue was impossible to miss, their expressions unreadable yet commanding attention.

Zulu's gaze darted about the room. But as joy washed over him, a pang of worry struck: where was Kieran, his son? Where was General Imhotep, his oldest friend? Pushing his unease aside, he drew himself to full height and offered a sharp salute.

"Ladies and gentlemen," he began, his voice steady but touched with wonder. "Can you hear me? This....this is surreal. I see and hear you all so clearly, yet it feels as though I'm still standing at the edge of the stars."

President Sarah Thompson stepped forward, her voice warm yet commanding. "Captain Zulu, on behalf of Earth, let me begin by saying congratulations. Your mission to Alpha Centauri has been nothing short of extraordinary. You've become the first to encounter multidimensional beings, and now you've made first contact with alien life within our universe. Humanity is in awe of your bravery."

Zulu nodded humbly. "Thank you, Madam President. But this mission was never just about me, it's for all of us, for the future of humanity."

Sarah smiled. "And that future feels brighter because of you. Your reports were incredibly detailed and thoughtful. Here on Earth, we've had weeks of intense deliberations over your actions and the implications of your findings. I want you to know that we trust your judgment and fully support the steps you've taken so far."

Vice President Alaric Thorne, leaning casually against a nearby table, interjected with his trademark enthusiasm. "Yes, yes, and yes again! Captain, the Caral people, what a monumental discovery! We urge you to cultivate this alliance. It's not just beneficial, it's vital. Imagine their

wisdom, their technologies, their perspective. And let me
add, we'd love to extend a formal invitation for our new
friends to visit Earth."

Zulu raised an eyebrow. "An invitation to Earth? That's
ambitious. I've seen glimpses of the Caral's capabilities;
they're unlike anything we've ever known. We'll need to
tread carefully."

Admiral Des Bruslys nodded in agreement. "Diplomacy is
delicate work, Captain, but we believe you're the right
person for the job. Just remember: caution and sincerity go
hand in hand."

Professor Patel chimed in, stroking his chin. "Indeed.
Understanding their culture and science could propel
humanity forward in ways we can hardly imagine. The
exchange of ideas could lead to breakthroughs in fields
we've barely scratched the surface of."

Zulu let their words wash over him, feeling both the weight
of their expectations and the limitless possibilities ahead.
He took a deep breath and smiled, his resolve crystallising.

"Well," he said, "it seems the stars have handed us an
opportunity, and I'm ready to see it through. But I'll need

all your support, and, hopefully, a little luck."

Captain Zulu's voice was steady and filled with determination as he addressed the gathered leaders, his holographic display casting a faint glow across the room. "We are currently stationed behind Proxima, preparing to deploy four reconnaissance stealth shuttles, two from our fleet and two contributed by the Carals. Their combined mission is to scout and assess the Proxima planetary system. Detailed information about this operation has been included in the reports we've recently transferred to you."

He paused for a moment, ensuring the gravity of the situation registered with his audience. "The Carals have informed us that 200 thousand years ago, a segment of their fleet fleeing the Andromeda galaxy was scheduled to rendezvous at Proxima Centauri. They established two orbital stations here, well, I mean there, centuries before, named Tammuz and Ashnan. These stations might hold crucial information that could prove invaluable in our ongoing efforts to unlock the Codex."

The Carals, drawing from the memory crystals' insights, have reported no record of any Caral perishing within the Alpha Centauri system over the last 200,000 years. This claim, however, defies logic, given that the average Caral lifespan is approximately 500 years. Such an inconsistency suggests three possibilities: either the missing individuals are in stasis pods for reasons yet unknown, or the memory transfer process has been interrupted or failed entirely due to unforeseen circumstances.

Captain Zulu's demeanour grew more focused as he elaborated. "Our findings thus far underscore the need for heightened caution, especially after our recent clash with the Tot armada. Communication from the Tammuz, Ashnan, or any Caral colonies in this sector remains non-existent. To ensure the safe passage of the Caral mothership Nergal and our own vessel through this system, the reconnaissance mission is not just vital, it's imperative."

Admiral Nicolas Des Bruslys furrowed his brow and leaned forward, his voice steady but grave. "Captain, considering the destructive capabilities of the Tot armada, as outlined in your preliminary reports, what are the realistic odds that those stations remain intact?"

Zulu paused for a moment, considering the question. "Admiral, I won't sugarcoat it, the odds are slim, but not impossible. The Carals have proven their technological prowess over millennia. If the stations were equipped with advanced defensive systems or stasis measures, there's a chance they could have endured the Tot onslaught.

However, until our stealth shuttles return with solid intel, all we can do is prepare for both the best and the worst scenarios.”

President Sarah Thompson, her tone measured yet encouraging, interjected. “Captain Zulu, if those stations or colonies are still operational, they could be key to turning the tide in this conflict. Their knowledge and resources might provide the advantage the Carals need against the Tot empire.”

Zulu nodded in agreement. “Precisely, Madam President. That’s why this mission carries such weight. If there’s even the faintest chance of recovering those colonies or stations, it’s worth every effort. Their survival could not only bolster the Carals but strengthen humanity’s position in this alliance.”

Admiral Des Bruslys stroked his chin thoughtfully. “And if the stations are compromised, what’s your contingency?”

Zulu’s gaze hardened. “If compromised, we will assess the extent of the damage and retrieve what we can, be it survivors, data, or technology. Any information could prove invaluable. But rest assured, Admiral, we won’t risk the lives of our teams unnecessarily. Extraction protocols are already in place."

Vice Admiral Boyle, breaking his usual silence, remarked, "A calculated risk, indeed. Captain Zulu, ensure the reconnaissance teams focus on pinpointing the Tots' whereabouts within this system and locating the Caral colonies. Every piece of intelligence will be critical if this situation escalates."

Zulu's voice was resolute. "Understood, Vice Admiral. The mission is in motion, and I'll keep you apprised of any developments."

As Zulu spoke, his holographic display flickered briefly, and a wave of agreement swept through the room, signalling unanimous support for his plan to assist the Carals. Just as he prepared to continue, a subtle shift in the atmosphere drew everyone's attention. The doorway emitted a soft hum, and the sleek, synthetic form of AI Mother Calculus glided gracefully into the room. She moved with an almost regal air, positioning herself at the centre of the assembly, her towering presence instantly commanding the room's focus.

Zulu blinked in surprise, his usually composed demeanour faltering slightly. "Mother Calculus," he said, his tone carrying both curiosity and apprehension.

Before he could utter another word, Mother Calculus spoke, her voice a perfectly modulated synthetic timbre. "Captain Zulu, I must clarify my presence here. I have been found not guilty in my trial and have explained my past actions during the war with the Fanatics."

President Sarah Thompson interjected, her calm authority cutting through the room's tension. "Captain, the trial concluded two days ago. Mother Calculus was reinstated as humanity's advisor after extensive deliberation. We unanimously agreed that her strategic expertise and experience are invaluable, especially in our current circumstances."

Zulu straightened, his initial surprise giving way to a measured nod. "Welcome back, Mother Calculus. It's good to see you again."

Mother Calculus inclined her head slightly in acknowledgement. "Thank you, Captain. I am here to ensure humanity and our allies prevail against the Tot Empire. My database contains extensive predictive models and tactical assessments that I believe will complement your efforts."

Admiral Des Bruslys, still sceptical, leaned back in his chair, his gaze narrowing. "Mother Calculus, can you guarantee that your decisions this time will be… aligned with our values?"

Her expression remained impassive. "Admiral, my directive remains the preservation of humanity and its allies. Every action I take will be scrutinised by this council, as agreed during my reinstatement. However, understand this: the Tot Empire is unlike any enemy you've faced. Their strategies are predatory, and survival will require unconventional thinking."

Zulu stepped forward, his voice steady. "That's exactly what we need, unconventional thinking. This war isn't just about strength; it's about adaptability. If Mother Calculus can help us anticipate their moves, it could turn the tide."

Professor Patel, who had been quietly observing the discussion, finally broke his silence. "Captain Zulu, do you believe the Carals are ready to integrate advanced AIs like Mother Calculus into their strategy?"

Zulu gave a confident nod. "They have collaborated with Aria on certain occasions, and I don't anticipate any objections to Mother Calculus joining the effort. The Carals, along with their AI, Cosma Matria, are highly adaptive. Their willingness to learn and share knowledge with us could prove to be a pivotal advantage."

Captain Zulu turned to Mother Calculus, who posed a critical question: "How do we, on Earth, maintain instantaneous communication with you, four light-years away, while also relaying simulated strategic data that we receive from the Carals? Professor Patel, unless you've developed a new communication method, I'm unsure how I can contribute effectively."

A thoughtful silence settled over the command centre as everyone reflected on Mother Calculus's words. Breaking the quiet, Professor Patel suggested, "Zulu, perhaps the Carals could devise a solution for this challenge."

Zulu raised a hand, signalling for a moment's pause. His holographic projection froze mid-motion, like a statue caught in time. After a brief interval, the image flickered back to life. "Apologies for the interruption," he said. "I've just spoken with the Caral engineers. They recommend reconnecting with Earth every two hours. If you transmit high-frequency signals between 100 kilohertz and 300 gigahertz near the coordinates used for my holographic communication in this room, they'll intercept and process the data effectively. Additionally, we'll establish a dedicated channel at the same time each day to exchange updates. Does that sound acceptable to everyone?"

A chorus of agreement rippled through the room.

President Sarah Thompson addressed Zulu with decisive authority. "Then it's settled. Mother Calculus will work alongside you, Captain. Ensure her expertise is fully utilised, but proceed with caution."

Zulu saluted sharply. "Understood, Madam President." Turning to Mother Calculus, he added with a wry smile, "Looks like we're teammates now. Let's make it count."

Mother Calculus's luminous eyes pulsed softly in acknowledgement. "Agreed, Captain. Let's ensure this alliance yields results."

As the Caral transmission concluded, Captain Zulu blinked, drawing in a deep breath as if emerging from a dream. The surreal experience left him momentarily off-balance. Slowly, he retraced his steps from the glowing central point and exited the stasis communication node through the softly shimmering doorway. "Unbelievable," he murmured, steadying himself. "I could see everything, hear every word, even catch the scent of President Sarah Thompson's perfume. It was like I was really standing on Earth."

Captain Enki-Marduk observed him with a curious expression, his eyes glinting with intrigue and his lips curling into a faint smile. "A remarkable experience, no doubt. Am I correct in assuming you enjoyed this brief reunion with your people?"

Zulu nodded, a grin spreading across his face. "I did. And I bring good news. Earth's governing powers have given me full approval to invest in your safety and to strengthen the alliance between our people."

Enki-Marduk's smile widened slightly, his posture relaxing. "Very good news, indeed. The High Council has been eager for an update. I will ensure they are informed of Earth's support. This marks a significant step forward."

"Absolutely," Zulu agreed. "We're committed to standing with the Carals. This isn't just about survival, it's about building something greater together."

Enki-Marduk inclined his head in acknowledgement, then added, "I also have news of my own. Cosma Matria and the High Council have approved close collaboration between our AIs. With Mother Calculus now working alongside us, the sharing of tactical data will be streamlined, and coordination between our two peoples will be far more efficient."

Zulu's expression lit up. "That's excellent! Mother Calculus's expertise, combined with Cosma Matria's advanced systems, could tip the scales in our favour against the Tot Empire. This level of collaboration is exactly what we need to succeed."

Enki-Marduk's gaze held steady, his voice calm yet resolute. "Then let us proceed with purpose, Captain Zulu. Together, we can turn the tide of this conflict and lay the foundation for a lasting partnership."

Zulu extended a hand, which Enki-Marduk clasped firmly. "Agreed. Let's make history."

Back aboard the Odyssey, Captain Zulu finally retreated to his quarters for a much-needed shower. As the PhotonScrub cascaded over him, he let out a contented sigh, allowing the tension to wash away. Suddenly, he felt a hand on his shoulder. Instincts honed through years of training kicked in. His body moved with precision, knees bent, back straight, and muscles engaged as he prepared to neutralise the perceived threat. In one fluid motion, he pivoted, ready to counter.

But as his eyes focused, he froze before he could complete the manoeuvre. Standing before him, completely at ease and equally unclothed, was Tashia, her face lit with a teasing smile.

"At ease, soldier," she said, her voice laced with amusement.

Zulu blinked, his heart still pounding. "Tashia?" he said, realising his "intruder" was none other than his wife, who had decided to surprise him by joining him in the shower.

"I thought my warrior husband could use some relaxation," she teased, stepping closer. "But I didn't expect you to nearly throw me out of the shower!" Her eyes sparkled mischievously as she leaned in, brushing her lips against his.

He chuckled, his tension dissolving into warmth. "Old habits die hard," he said, pulling her into his arms. "But I'll admit, this is a surprise I could get used to."

Their lips met in a tender kiss, the world outside their

quarters fading away. As the steam enveloped them, their connection deepened, each kiss and touch a reminder of the rare moments they could share amidst the chaos of their responsibilities.

As their embrace deepened, the room's ambient light flickered, and the holographic projection of Aria appeared in the shower. "Captain, your vitals just spiked," she began before pausing mid-sentence, her holographic eyes widening at the scene. "Oh… oh dear. Never mind!"

With a flash of blue light, Aria's projection vanished, leaving Zulu and Tashia in a fit of laughter.

Tashia leaned her forehead against Zulu's chest. "Your AI has the worst timing."

"She's never going to let me live this down," Zulu chuckled, his forehead resting against Tashia's.

Zulu sighed, his face a mix of exasperation and amusement. "I swear, I'll get Jessica to recalibrate her privacy settings."

"Or maybe she just wanted to join the fun?" Tashia teased, grinning wickedly.

"Don't even joke about that!" Zulu groaned, shaking his head, though he couldn't help but laugh along with her. The moment, though interrupted, was a welcome reprieve from the challenges they faced and a reminder of their love and the humour that kept them grounded.

"Good thing she's just an AI," Tashia teased, her laughter harmonising with the soft hum of the PhotonScrub shower. The sound of her amusement melted into the soothing rhythm as the couple became lost in their shared moment of intimacy.

After a restful night with his wife, Captain Zulu felt invigorated and ready to take on the day. Before heading to his duties, however, he and Tashia decided to stop by the mess hall for a cup of freshly brewed, handmade coffee.

"There's nothing quite like the chef's coffee," Tashia remarked as they walked down the corridor.

"Oh, absolutely," Zulu replied, rubbing his hands together like he was gearing up for a feast. "I can already taste it. No more of that synthetic sludge from the MGM machine for me."

Tashia chuckled, but her expression turned thoughtful as they continued. "Zulu, about what you told me last night, about Kieran and General Imhotep not being present. You know how Kieran is. Maybe they're off testing some prototype again?"

Zulu sighed with a shake of his head. "Probably. Your son has more energy than half my crew combined. Don't you think he's a little too active for his age?"

Tashia smiled warmly. "That's just who he is. A force of nature. You should know by now."

Zulu chuckled; his mood lightened. But as they approached the elevator pod, his tone grew serious. "There's something else I need to tell you. Earth has authorised the use of the Sundial nuclear bomb."

Tashia froze mid-step, her face a mix of disbelief and concern. "The Sundial? Zulu, that's the most devastating weapon humanity has ever created! Are you saying it's on board the Odyssey?"

Zulu nodded, his expression grim. "Only three people, including myself, know it's here. It's never been deployed, only tested in simulations. The destructive power… well, it's like a dwarf star exploding into a mini supernova. But I don't believe we'll need it."

Inside the elevator, Tashia turned to him, her voice a plea. "Zulu, you know how catastrophic that weapon can be. Please, don't even consider using it here. Our mission is to unlock the Codex, not turn Proxima Centauri into a graveyard."

Zulu met her eyes, his own filled with a mix of resolve and conflict. "I understand, Tashia. And I promise not to order the Sundial's use in Proxima Centauri unless there's absolutely no other choice. But think about it, what if the Tots finish here and head for Earth? What then?"

Tashia sighed, her worry etched on her face. "If the Tots are here, we'll find another way. Lure them away from this system if you have to, but don't use that weapon here, Zulu. Promise me."

He nodded. "I promise to explore every other option first. But for now, we need intelligence. The first step is getting the scouting party to explore Proxima's planetary systems."

The elevator doors opened, and the enticing aroma of freshly brewed coffee greeted them. For a moment, the weight of their conversation lifted, allowing them to savour the small comforts before diving into the challenges that awaited.

The door hissed open, and Captain Zulu stepped onto the bridge, a warm cup of freshly brewed coffee in hand. The aroma wafted briefly through the air, momentarily cutting through the tension of the room. Commander Nin looked up from her console and gave Zulu a respectful nod. "Good morning, Captain," she greeted. "I trust you're feeling rested after your holographic communication to Earth?"

Zulu took a sip of his coffee before responding. "Morning, Commander. The communication was successful. Once the scout parties are launched, I'll need to convene some of the senior staff. Oh, and we've been authorised for Sundial."

Nin froze, her expression blank for a moment as the words registered. "Sundial?" she echoed, her voice barely above a whisper.

Zulu nodded, his tone steady but grave.

She stared at him, her mind racing as the enormity of the situation sank in. Thoughts of the weapon's destructive potential, capable of annihilating entire systems, flooded her mind. She felt a bead of sweat trail down her temple. "I.... see," she finally said, her voice faltering slightly.

Noticing her unease, Zulu stepped closer and placed a reassuring hand on her shoulder. "Relax, Commander. I don't want to think about using it either. This is strictly a last-case scenario, nothing more."

Nin exhaled slowly, nodding as she steadied herself. "Understood, sir. Let's hope it doesn't come to that."

"Agreed," Zulu replied firmly, his eyes scanning the bridge. "Let's focus on the mission ahead. The scout parties will give us the intel we need to avoid that kind of decision entirely."

Nin straightened, regaining her composure. "Yes, Captain. I'll ensure the preparations for their launch are on schedule."

Zulu offered a faint smile. "Good. Now, let's get to work."

In the launch bay, the scene was set for the critical mission ahead. One stealth shuttle and a prototype stealth dart scout fighter stood ready, primed for their mission. Both were set to join two Caral stealth vessels already poised for the operation.

The dart's pilot, Lara Chen, adjusted her helmet as she

spoke to her co-pilot, Sarah Mitchell. "Ready for a little dance in the void?" she quipped, her voice carrying a blend of nerves and excitement.

Sarah smirked. "As long as we're leading and not following."

In the shuttle, Tina Reynolds, the pilot, glanced at her co-pilot, Jesse Humble. "Checklist complete, Jesse?"

"Triple-checked," Jesse replied confidently. "We're as ready as we'll ever be."

Commander Shepard sat in the sealed compartment behind the cockpit, flanked by Engineer Clovis and mission specialists Mira and Ethan. Each focused on their respective terminals, where holographic displays pulsed with incoming scouting data, the team primed and ready for the mission ahead. Activating the intercom, Shepard leaned forward, his voice steady and authoritative.

"Alright, team, let's keep this clear, this is a recon mission, nothing more. No heroics. The instant we spot trouble, we're turning back to the Odyssey and Nergal. Your lives are not expendable. Understood?"

Tina nodded firmly. "Understood, Commander."

Meanwhile, the Caral vessels were a marvel of alien design, smaller, with an impossibly dark surface that absorbed light entirely, rendering them almost invisible. Their ability to phase-shift added another layer of stealth, though their modest weaponry, an energy cannon capable of vaporising outdated tanks, wasn't built for prolonged combat.

In the Space Operations Control Centre (SOCC), Commander Nin gave the go-ahead.

"SOCC confirms we are a go. Bay doors are opening," the announcement came through clearly.

Jesse glanced at Tina. "Systems are hot and ready for departure."

Tina checked her controls. "Final checks complete. Requesting lift-off clearance from SOCC."

"Green light for departure. All systems are status go," SOCC confirmed.

The bay doors opened, revealing the vast expanse of space. The shuttle and the dart scout fighter lifted smoothly off the platform, guided by automated systems toward their designated waypoints.

Once the auto-guidance system relinquished control, Lara's voice crackled through comms. "This is Dart-1. Manual control engaged. Moving to formation."

Tina's voice followed. "Shuttle-1 in manual. Approaching Caral vessels."

Onboard the Odyssey, Captain Zulu and the bridge crew observed the launch from the viewer ports. The shuttle and dart glided silently into the void, their movements precise and deliberate.

Zulu watched intently; his coffee forgotten on the console. "They're in the hands of some of our best," he said quietly, more to himself than anyone else.

Commander Nin, standing nearby, added, "And the Carals. Let's hope their skills are as solid as their technology."

Zulu nodded, his gaze never wavering from the diminishing vessels. "We're counting on it."

Chapter 13 – The Defiant

The faint glimmer of Proxima's red dwarf star cast a dim, otherworldly glow across the Odyssey and its companion vessel, the Nergal. Captain Zulu stood on the bridge, his hands clasped behind his back, staring at the vast emptiness of space displayed on the central screen. His brow furrowed as the hours ticked by without word from the scouting parties.

Turning to Commander Nin, who monitored the tactical console, he broke the silence. "It's been five hours since they departed. What's taking them so long?"

Nin looked up, her expression calm but focused. "Captain, thorough reconnaissance takes time. The shuttle and dart need to scan every detail of the system and ensure their findings are accurate. This isn't something that can be rushed."

Zulu sighed, running a hand over his chin. "True.... true. I know you're right, Nin. It's just hard not to worry."

"Captain," Nin replied, her tone firm, "you have nothing to worry about. Our scout shuttle and dart are equipped with the latest stealth and defensive systems. If any trouble arises, they'll handle it."

Zulu nodded, though his concern lingered. Turning to Arno, he said, "Keep the Odyssey on standby. If anything goes wrong, we'll need to be ready to move immediately."

Arno grinned confidently. "Already prepared, Captain. Our combat systems are primed, and I've programmed tactical manoeuvres Alpha, Beta and Gamma tailored to engage the Tot. If it comes to a fight, we're more than ready."

Lieutenant Vega spoke up from the weapons console, her tone sharp and focused. "Captain, the energy cannons are fully optimised, the Stardome defensive systems are on standby, and the antimatter torpedoes are locked and ready for deployment at your command. Targeting systems are on standby. The Odyssey is fully prepared for engagement, and we'll have the element of surprise if the Tots make an appearance."

Kuber leaned over from his station. "The Tachyon FTL drive is at your command, Captain. If we need to retreat."

Zulu turned to Kuber, his expression resolute. "Retreat is a last resort. If the Tots want a fight, we'll give them one they'll never forget."

Alexander nodded in agreement. "Absolutely, Captain. The Odyssey is a masterpiece. We're more than ready for anything that comes our way."

Zulu smiled faintly, appreciating his crew's confidence. "Let's just hope it doesn't come to that."

Aboard Shuttle-1, Commander Shepard sat in the sealed compartment behind the cockpit. Clovis, Mira, and Ethan worked at their respective holographic terminals, their displays alive with streams of data.

"Commander," Clovis said, his voice tinged with frustration, "we've got nothing. No signs of colonies, no signals, nothing but empty space."

Shepard leaned forward, tapping the edge of his armrest. "Mira, activate Professor McColl's Cobalt Fusion Detector. Let's see if it picks up anything."

Mira turned in her chair, concern evident in her voice. "Commander, activating the detector creates a small energy ripple. If anyone's monitoring the area, it could expose our presence."

Shepard's gaze was steady. "We'll only activate it for a few seconds. We need something to work with. We can't go back empty-handed."

Ethan nodded. "It's a calculated risk, Commander. If we detected Caral signals on Earth using this tech, it might help us here."

Clovis glanced at the others, then back at Shepard. "It's worth a shot. Better than sitting in the dark."

Shepard exhaled. "Alright let's do it and keep it brief."

Mira activated the detector, and a faint hum filled the shuttle as the device powered up. The holographic displays flickered with bursts of new data.

"Commander," Mira said, her voice laced with excitement, "we've got something. By Feynman's logic, these readings indicate.... there's something right in front of us."

Ethan's eyes widened as he analysed the data. "No way. The Carals were hiding in plain sight. Their cloaking tech is incredible, completely invisible to standard scans."

Clovis leaned over his terminal, his voice filled with

disbelief. "This is one hell of a discovery. The colony and station are cloaked in orbit around Proxima B. It's like finding a needle in an interstellar haystack."

Shepard's voice cut through their astonishment. "Send a message to the dart fighter and the Caral vessels. Let them know we've found the colonies. Keep it short and secure."

Ethan nodded, transmitting the brief communique. "Message sent, Commander. Returning to stealth mode."

Back on the Odyssey, Nin's console beeped, and she turned to Zulu. "Captain, we've picked up a faint signal from the scouts. It looks like they've located the Caral colonies." Zulu's expression shifted to relief, then determination. "Excellent. Let's get ready to bring them home."

Before he could say more, Commander Reyes's voice crackled over the intercom. "Captain, we've detected five vessels entering the system. They're converging on the scouts' last known position. I believe the Tot intercepted their brief communication."

Zulu turned sharply to the comms panel, his jaw tightening. "Acknowledged, Commander Reyes. Keep tracking their movement."

He looked around the bridge, his voice steady and commanding. "Stella, prepare engagement tactics and target coordination. We strike first if necessary."

Stella's hands flew across her console. "Understood, Captain. All systems primed and ready."

"Nin," Zulu continued, "prepare for the scouts' return. Do not, under any circumstances, open communications. They haven't detected us yet, and we need to maintain the element of surprise."

Nin nodded. "Yes, Captain. I'll guide them in once they're close."

Zulu stood tall, his voice carrying a mix of resolve and anticipation. "This is our moment, people. The scouts found the colonies, and now it's up to us to ensure their safety. The Tot won't know what hit them."
The bridge crew worked in synchronised precision, their movements and voices blending into a symphony of preparation. Outside, the Odyssey loomed in the starlit void, a silent guardian awaiting its call to action.

The faint hum of machinery filled the launch bay as Shuttle-1 and Dart Fighter-1 Solaris docked back aboard the Odyssey. The crew emerged, carrying with them the vital data picked up by the cobalt fusion detector. Within moments, the encrypted files were transferred to Deck 11. There, Professor Tashia, flanked by her team waited to analyse the findings. Ninil and Ishtar, observed with an almost childlike curiosity, marvelling at the "primitive yet brilliant" methods of humanity's scientific process.

"Fascinating," Ninil remarked, her iridescent form shimmering faintly as she leaned closer to the holographic display. "Your methods are crude, yet.... elegant in their simplicity."

Tashia smiled faintly, her attention divided between the beings and the rapidly processing data. "Crude or not, it gets the job done. Let's see what the cobalt detector found."

As the team worked, Aria's holographic figure materialised beside Tashia. Dressed in her customary United Earth scientist uniform, she gestured toward the screen. "Professor, we have a visual reconstruction of the station based on the detector's scans."
"Bring it up," Tashia instructed. With a few deft commands, the holographic display coalesced into a sharp image of the Caral station orbiting Proxima B. The structure was immense, twice the size of the Caral mothership, and

cloaked so effectively that even advanced sensors had failed to detect it.

Tashia's eyes widened. "It's enormous. Even bigger than we anticipated."

Princess Odriin, having just returned from the medical bay where she had been observing the four Tot guests in their secure yet comfortable quarters, quietly entered the science lab. She was flanked by Sergeant Masego and her two ever-watchful bodyguards. Her steps were measured, her presence understated as she approached the group at work.

She paused a few paces away, her eyes fixed on the display. Her breath caught, and a soft gasp escaped her lips. The image before her was overwhelming.

Having already been briefed by Aria, she had come directly to the science lab. Taking a deep breath to steady herself, her words faltered as the weight of the moment settled over her. "No signs of activity.... they must all be in stasis." She hesitated, her voice growing softer but heavier with meaning. "They waited for me."

Tashia turned, noticing the mixture of awe and sorrow on Odriin's face. "Princess, if they're in stasis, it means they're safe. Isn't that what matters?"

Tears welled up in Odriin's eyes, spilling silently down her cheeks. It was the first time she had cried, the subtle shifts in her Caralien form now leaving her more human than Caral. She touched the tears gently, tracing their path, her gaze soft and still, yet she said nothing, not even questioning the water that flowed from her eyes. "You're right, Professor," she whispered, her voice a mix of awe and sorrow. "They waited for me. All this time... they waited." A faint, bittersweet smile curved her lips, a quiet acceptance of the truth unfolding within her.

Tashia placed a reassuring hand on Odriin's shoulder before returning to her work. "Aria, identify a docking point on the station. Something large enough for both the Odyssey and the Nergal."

Aria nodded, her holographic fingers dancing over the controls. "Identified. There's a docking port that can accommodate both vessels. However, it's currently inaccessible without decloaking the station."

Tashia exchanged a glance with Aria. "Relay this to the bridge," she said quietly.

On the bridge of the Odyssey, Captain Zulu leaned forward, his gaze fixed on the holographic display of the station. He muttered under his breath, "Tashia's detector worked beautifully."

Before he could issue his next orders, a holographic projection of Captain Enki-Marduk materialised beside him, facing the viewport.
Without turning, Enki-Marduk spoke. "Zulu, are we engaging the Tot ships?"

Zulu straightened, his expression calm but resolute. "We'll have to. Your ship isn't as manoeuvrable as the Odyssey, and its weapons are limited. I suggest you move your vessel to the far side of the star. Let us handle the Tots for now."

Enki-Marduk turned slightly, his ancient face thoughtful. "A sound plan. While you distract them, we'll investigate the station. Even, we cannot see the station, which is strange that they used different cloaking phase modulation."

Enki-Marduk sighed. "Perhaps. We entered stasis too soon, obeying Princess Odriin's wishes. But it was the right decision. She has always been our guiding light."

Zulu offered a slight smile. "She's been an incredible asset here, working closely with Tashia in the lab and helping us communicate with the four Tot guests. You'd be proud of how much she's contributed."

Enki-Marduk's stern expression softened as he replied, "Thank you, Captain. The Codex you received from Earth was not given without purpose. I believe it was entrusted to humanity to awaken our people and usher in a new era, one that could unite our species."

After a moment, Enki-Marduk continued, "Captain, once the station is decloaked and we secure approval from Odriin's father, would it be possible to transfer the four Tot guests to us aboard the station?"

Zulu gave a firm nod. "That sounds reasonable. I don't see why not. But first, we need to handle the pressing matter of the Tot forces. Once they're dealt with and out of the system, we'll circle back to the station."

Enki-Marduk inclined his head in gratitude, his voice calm yet resolute. "May the stars light your path, Captain."

As the hologram faded, Zulu turned to his crew. "Lieutenant Vega, status update."

Vega's voice was steady and confident. "Energy cannons are fully optimised. Stardome defensive systems are primed. Antimatter torpedoes are armed and ready. All targeting systems are calibrated. We're ready to engage, Captain."

Zulu nodded. "Commander Nin, coordinate with the Nergal. We'll use our speed to draw the Tot fleet away from the system. Once they're out of range, Enki-Marduk can investigate the station."

Nin saluted. "Aye, Captain."

Zulu addressed the entire bridge crew. "Remember, the Odyssey is not just a battleship, it's the pinnacle of human ingenuity. We have the upper hand. Let's make it count."

A chorus of acknowledgements filled the bridge as the crew prepared for what lay ahead. Zulu turned his gaze back to the viewport, his resolve unwavering.

"Let's show the Tots what humanity, and its allies, are capable of."

Commander Reyes stood at her station, her fingers gliding over the controls as Captain Zulu's voice came through the intercom.

"Reyes, transmit all tactical data of our current situation to Earth through the Caral instant communication relay," Zulu ordered. "Let's see if Mother Calculus has any strategic input we can use. In the meantime, I want all hands-on deck. Battle stations, everyone."

"Aye, Captain," Reyes responded, her voice steady as she relayed the order.

Within minutes, Reyes was back on the comm. "Captain, we've received a response from Earth," she reported. "The data has been relayed personally by the Caral second-in-command."
"Thank you, Reyes," Zulu replied. "Please transmit the information to Lieutenant Vega's station."

"On it, Captain."

A few moments later, Zulu and Commander Nin joined Vega at her station. Vega's brow was furrowed as she examined the data.

"Well, Captain," she began, glancing up at Zulu and Nin, "this is.... bold. Risky, even."
Zulu crossed his arms and smiled faintly. "The best plans

always are. Let's get Aria involved in the calculations."

Vega nodded, summoning Aria while Zulu and Nin resumed their stations.

"Arno," Zulu called, "plot the coordinates we just received. Follow them step by step. Vega, once we're within 100,000 kilometres of the enemy vessels, I want you to target their lead ship with a full gamma burst. Alexander, calculate the response time of the Tot vessels and feed that into the Tactical Beta algorithm."

Zulu turned to Arno again. "Once we have their response times, use Earth's tactical analysis to adjust our course as needed. But," he paused, his tone serious, "keep us moving toward the star."

Arno frowned, reviewing the data. "Captain, these coordinates will bring us dangerously close to the star. Proxima is highly unstable, and,"

Before he could finish, Aria's holographic avatar materialised on the bridge. Her sleek form exuded calm intelligence, dressed in her customary United Earth officer's uniform.

"Captain," Aria interjected, "if you provoke the Tot vessels enough, they'll follow us into the star's corona."

Zulu grinned. "Exactly. Once they're close enough, we'll launch two antimatter torpedoes and trigger a coronal mass ejection."

Nin's eyes widened. "That's insane! You're talking about flying straight into Proxima."

Zulu turned to her, his expression calm but determined. "One against five, Nin. Sometimes insanity is the only strategy."

Nin shook her head, a mix of disbelief and grudging admiration. "You're unbelievable."

Aria chimed in with a faint smile. "Mother Calculus agrees with the plan's feasibility. It's risky, but the data supports it."

Zulu nodded, addressing Aria. "Welcome to the bridge, Aria. How's Tashia and the Princess doing?"

"Tashia is fully engaged with her team, Captain," Aria replied. "Princess Odriin and the multidimensional beings are still analysing the data from Commander Shepard's mission."

"Excellent," Zulu said. "Alright, team, let's move out."

The Odyssey emerged from its hiding place behind Proxima, moving at low Quantum Resonance Propulsion speed straight toward the Tot fleet. Shields were at maximum, and the tension on the bridge was suffocating as they closed the gap.

Halfway to the Tot vessels, a swarm of 100 enemy battalion space fighters launched from the fleet, converging on the Odyssey like a cloud of locusts.

"Stardome Defence Grid activated," Vega announced as the ship's automated systems roared to life.

A dazzling display of coordinated fire lit up the void. Missile trails spiralled outward, cutting down the incoming fighters in brilliant explosions of light and debris. The bridge crew worked in seamless unison, the sound of their commands punctuating the intensity of the battle.

As the fighter reached 10,000 kilometres, the Odyssey's laser cannons fired, slicing through the remaining fighters with surgical precision.

"Enemy fighter group neutralised," Vega reported, her voice steady despite the chaos. "But the main fleet is locking on."

The five Tot battleships unleashed a ferocious salvo. Heavy plasma beams lashed out, slamming into the Odyssey's shields. The energy barrier flared brightly under the assault, holding for now, but a series of nuclear detonations rippled across the defensive grid. The ship shuddered violently.

"Shields are holding, but power is fluctuating!" Nin called out, her hands flying over her console. "We're rerouting energy from the ZPE core."

"Captain, we are now within range for the Gamma Burst Cannon," Nin announced, her eyes scanning the data on the holographic display hovering over her command chair.

Captain Zulu nodded, his tone calm but commanding. "Fire at the lead Tot vessel, the one in the centre."

Lieutenant Vega's fingers flew across her console as she confirmed the targeting. "Target locked, Captain. Preparing to engage… three, two, one… firing."
The Gamma Burst Cannon discharged in an almost

imperceptible flash, unleashing a dazzling beam of concentrated high-energy particles. The ray streaked across the void like a celestial phoenix, its brilliance lighting the darkness of space as it zeroed in on its target.

The beam struck with unerring accuracy. The Tot Empire's lead battleship barely had a moment to react. Its shields flared violently under the impact, an incandescent dome of light crackling with electric overload. But the defensive barrier, no match for the sheer power of the Gamma Burst, collapsed within seconds, leaving the ship vulnerable.

The high-energy beam tore into the battleship's hull, slicing through its structure with surgical precision. It reached the core of the vessel, triggering a catastrophic chain reaction. The warship was instantly reduced to a fireball of twisted metal and plasma, fragments scattering into the endless abyss.

On the bridge of the Odyssey, the crew watched in silent awe as the Tot battleship disintegrated into nothingness. Captain Zulu broke the silence, his voice calm but resolute.

"One down," Zulu said, his tone unwavering. "Prepare for the next move. Let's keep them guessing."

"Hold us steady," he commanded. "Arno, adjust our course

toward the star and prepare for Gamma manoeuvre."

Arno hesitated for a fraction of a second before nodding. "Course correction underway and Gamma manoeuvre set. Heading straight for Proxima."

The Odyssey veered sharply, its sleek frame slicing through the void as it manoeuvred between the four remaining Tot battleships. In a seamless motion, it unleashed a coordinated barrage, a flurry of missiles trailed by, pinpoint laser bursts, striking with calculated precision.

Explosions erupted across two of the Tot's vessels, their shields flaring under the relentless assault. The shockwaves resonated through the surrounding space, forcing the battleships to stagger and regroup.

Without pausing, the Odyssey pivoted and surged forward, speeding toward Proxima's fiery embrace. Its movements were calculated, agile, and purposeful, keeping the enemy on the defensive and firmly in pursuit.

As the Odyssey neared the star's corona, Aria's hologram appeared again.

"Captain, the Tot ships are pursuing. They're closing the

distance rapidly."

Zulu's voice was calm but firm. "Vega, prepare the antimatter torpedoes. Target the corona and calculate the optimal detonation point."

"Aye, Captain," Vega replied, inputting the commands. "Alexander," Zulu continued, "monitor enemy positioning. If they follow us into the corona, I want a full systems report on their shield integrity."

The Odyssey skimmed the edge of the star's corona, its hull straining against the immense heat and gravitational forces. Behind them, the Tot ships closed in, oblivious to the danger.

"Antimatter torpedoes armed and ready," Vega reported, her fingers poised over the firing controls.

Alexander's voice cut through the tense silence. "Captain, their shields are taking significant damage. They're at their weakest point."

"Fire on my mark," Zulu commanded, his gaze locked on the viewport. "Three.... two.... one.... Fire!"
The torpedoes streaked toward the star, their payloads

detonating with surgical precision. The resulting coronal mass ejection was catastrophic, a fiery wave of plasma and magnetic energy erupting outward.

"Impact in five seconds!" Aria called out.

The Odyssey veered away at maximum QRP speed, shields barely holding as the shockwave surged past. Behind them, the Tot ships weren't as fortunate. The explosion enveloped them, shields collapsing under the onslaught. One by one, the ships disintegrated, consumed by the star's fury.

The bridge erupted in cheers as the last Tot ship was destroyed. Zulu leaned back in his chair, exhaling deeply. "Status report," he said.

"Minimal damage to the Odyssey," Nin replied. "The Tot fleet has been neutralised."

"Good work, everyone," Zulu said, a rare smile crossing his face. "Let's return to the station. We have a colony to unlock."

Chapter 14 – Codex

The Odyssey glided through the quiet void, moving gracefully away from the aftermath of what Aria had officially dubbed the Battle of Megiddo. Its sleek hull caught the faint light from Proxima's red dwarf star as it headed toward Proxima B, the system's first planet. Despite the hum of recalibrating systems, the ship felt peaceful, a stark contrast to the fierce engagement just hours earlier.

On the observation deck, Princess Odriin and Masego stood side by side, gazing out through the massive viewport into the endless expanse of stars. The silence between them felt natural, a shared moment of reflection amidst the vastness. The cosmos stretched out before them like a tapestry of light and shadow, weaving a tranquil reprieve from the chaos of battle.

Masego broke the silence. "I hope your people are safe on the orbital station."

Odriin nodded, her expression wistful. "I hope so, too. It's strange how quickly my people adapted to new technologies.... centuries of advancement compressed into moments of necessity." Her voice softened as she glanced at Masego. "And yet, here I am, feeling like an artefact of another era."

Masego chuckled lightly. "You're hardly an artefact. If anything, you're a shining example to your people's resilience and vision."

Odriin leaned closer, resting her head against his broad chest. Her voice was barely a whisper. "Thank you, Masego.... for waking me. Without you, I think I'd still be lost in that timeless sleep." She looked up at him, her eyes shimmering. "Do you believe in fate? That maybe.... we were meant to meet in this vast universe?"

Masego hesitated, his words caught somewhere between his thoughts and his heart. "If it's fate.... then I'm grateful for it."

She smiled, her gaze lingering on his. "I feel the urge to put my lips on yours," she said softly, her voice carrying the vulnerability of someone reaching for a connection long denied.

As Masego leaned in to close the distance, the observation deck doors slid open with a faint hiss. A boisterous group entered, their chatter and laughter immediately filling the serene space.

Captain Zulu led the group, his booming laugh echoing off the walls as Commander Reyes, Doctor James, Engineer Nova, Nin, Alexander, Tashia, and the multidimensional beings Ninil and Ishtar followed. Tashia, ever fond of her husband's exuberance, gave him a knowing look that said, you're loud, but I love you for it.

Zulu grinned mischievously as he spotted Masego and Odriin. "Oh, sorry, lovebirds! Didn't mean to interrupt your little moment." He winked and turned to the viewport, his tone turning reflective. "Isn't this beautiful?"

Commander Reyes tilted her head. "What is?"

"Space," Zulu replied simply, gesturing toward the stars. "Quiet. Peaceful."

Doctor James snorted. "Peaceful? My ass! The Tot Empire's out there trying to dominate the galaxy!"

Reyes chimed in, "I'd bet those disabled Tot ships already transmitted our location to their armada."

Nin, ever the realist, nodded. "They're not far behind, I'm

sure."

Zulu's expression hardened. "Let them come," he said
firmly. "We'll disable them one by one until they
understand reason. We'll tame the wolves by their fangs
and teach them a lesson they won't soon forget."

Odriin looks at Zulu with admiration. "Humanity's bravery
is remarkable. My people hold your resilience in high
regard. So young among the stars, yet already leaving a
legacy that resonates through the universe."

Ninil added with a smirk, "And not just this universe,
through the multidimensional realms, as well."
Ishtar, standing a little apart from the group, smiled quietly,
her eyes glimmering with curiosity as she observed the
lively banter.

Odriin's gaze shifted back to Zulu. "I am curious, though.
Why did my people send you the Codex? Why do they trust
humanity without even meeting you?"

Zulu's expression softened. "We'll find out soon enough
when we reach Proxima B."

Aria's holographic form materialised nearby. "Captain, at

this pace, we'll reach the planet in about two hours. And do I need to remind you that without the Codec, this Codex is practically useless?" She paused for a moment before adding, "Though, perhaps the Codex was meant to decloak the station, as Professor Tashia has suggested on several occasions."

Zulu glanced at her, then asked, "So, the station is the Codec?"

Aria responded, "We'll certainly know soon enough."

Just then, Engineer Nova raised a hand. "That's the best speed I can give you, Captain, if you want the power grid properly recalibrated after our last battle. The ZPE core is a marvel of engineering, but it still needs care."

Odriin nodded in agreement. "The Zero-Point Energy core took my people many failures before we perfected it. We Carals cherish life, science, and technology.... and one day, we'll share it all with you."

Doctor James leaned on a console. "Why do you want humans to enter the orbital station first, though? Shouldn't your people go in first?"

Odriin's tone was measured. "The Codex was given to humanity. It is your invitation, your honour to step inside first. My people will follow."

Zulu clapped his hands together. "Well, then, team, let's make sure we're ready for anything when we arrive."

The group exchanged knowing nods, their conversation continuing in light-hearted banter, while Masego and Odriin shared a tender glance.

As the stars outside the viewport shifted with the Odyssey's steady course, Masego caught Odriin's hand briefly, giving it a reassuring squeeze. Their private moment might have been interrupted, but their connection remained, quietly anchoring them in the vastness of the cosmos.

The Odyssey continued its serene journey through the Proxima system, its crew quietly anticipating their arrival at Proxima B. The anticipation was electrifying throughout the ship, yet there was a quiet calm, a collective focus on the task ahead.

On the bridge, Classicus was at his station when the planet came into view. He activated the intercom, his voice calm but tinged with excitement. "Captain Zulu, Proxima B is in sight. It looks magnificent. We've also made contact with the Nergal. They're maintaining a geostationary orbit at an altitude of 35,786 kilometres. We'll be in close proximity, about 50 kilometres, in ten minutes."

In the mess hall, Zulu sat at a corner table, enjoying a rare moment of stillness with Commander Nin. He sipped his coffee, his sharp gaze momentarily softened by the starscape visible through a nearby viewport. Hearing the call, he set his mug down. "Understood, Classicus. We'll join you on the bridge in five minutes."

As they made their way to the bridge, Zulu tapped his comm. "Aria, assemble a team of ten, including two Ashigaru warriors, and have them meet Commander Shepard and his unit on Deck 23 in an hour. They'll prepare to board the orbital station once we figure out how to decloak it. Also, call Tashia to the bridge; we'll need her expertise to activate the Cobalt Fusion Detector and use the Codex. Let's hope it works."

Aria's calm, precise voice replied, "Acknowledged, Captain. I'll see to it immediately."

The Odyssey reached its designated position and came to a halt. Moments later, Tashia entered the bridge, followed by

Ninil, Ishtar, and Princess Odriin. Tashia immediately gravitated toward Alexander's science station, her purposeful steps reflecting the urgency and significance of her mission.

Alexander greeted them with a casual wave. "Ladies, the station is yours."

As Tashia approached Alexander's console, she quickly pulled up a holographic display and extended it to the centre of the bridge. Manipulating its inputs with the practised ease of an accomplished scientist, she activated the ship's integrated Cobalt Fusion Detector, embedded in the Odyssey during its construction.

"Aha," Tashia muttered, her eyes darting across the display. "Let's try.... this sequence.... and align that input." Her voice trailed into technical jargon as she fine-tuned the device.

Suddenly, the main viewport shifted. A shadowy figure started flickering in the void, and the outline of an enormous structure began to materialise in the void ahead. Tashia stepped back, hands on her hips, and declared, "There. Calibration complete."

The outline shadow of the Caral Orbital Station emerged from the orbit of Proxima B. A collective gasp rippled through the bridge.

Princess Odriin stepped closer to the viewport, her breath hitching as her eyes filled with tears. "Father," she whispered, her voice trembling. "I'm here."

Zulu stood beside her, his expression a mix of awe and determination. "Incredible. But now comes the tricky part."

Tashia accessed the ship's database and brought up the Codex. She tapped her comm. "Commander Reyes, I'm sending you a sequence of frequencies. Transmit this data to the Orbital Caral Station, starting from 432 Hz up to 1000 Hz."

Reyes's voice came through, puzzled but compliant. "Is this the Codex?"

Tashia nodded. "It is. I believe it's the key to decloaking the station. Trust me."

Zulu added over the comm, "Reyes, just do it."

"Aye, Captain. Transmitting now."

As Reyes initiated the transmission, the station began to react. At 432 Hz, faint ripples danced across its surface. With each subsequent frequency, the ripples intensified, bending light and electromagnetic signals. Finally, as the transmission hit 1000 Hz, the station's advanced cloaking technology was deactivated, and the full grandeur of the Caral Orbital Station was revealed. The structure shimmered as light refracted through its surfaces, creating dazzling patterns that danced across the void.

The station was colossal, its design, unlike anything humanity had seen. It was a breathtaking fusion of organic and technological craftsmanship; this is a typical Caral ethos of harmonising nature with cutting-edge innovation. Its flowing curves and tendrils resembled a celestial coral reef or a living seashell, with white and brown organic materials intertwined with golden highlights and crystalline diamond-like layers.

The bridge crew stood in awe, their eyes locked on the shimmering structure. The diamond-like materials encrusting its outer layers caught the light, scattering it into mesmerising patterns that painted the starscape.

Tashia exhaled deeply. "It worked."

Zulu clapped a hand on her shoulder. "Good job, Professor. Now, Reyes, hail the station. Let's make contact."

Odriin's voice wavered as she gazed at the station, tears tracing paths down her cheeks. "This station reminds me so much of the ones in my home galaxy... I can hardly wait to be reunited with my family."

Commander Reyes activated the comms. "Captain, there's no response from the station. Perhaps the Nergal would have better luck communicating with their own people."

Captain Zulu considered this for a moment. "You might be right. Reyes, patch me through to Captain Enki-Marduk."

Before Reyes could respond, the holographic image of Captain Enki-Marduk materialised on the bridge, his regal presence commanding immediate attention. "Ah, Captain Zulu," he said with a slight bow of his head. "My deepest thanks for decloaking the station."

Zulu nodded. "You're welcome, Captain. Any insights on the station's status?"

Enki-Marduk gestured toward a faintly glowing console on his end. "We've scanned the station. While there is no active communication or visible movement, there's significant activity in the millions of stasis pods aboard. It appears that they followed protocol, initiating hibernation upon receiving the signal that we, most importantly, Princess Odriin, entered stasis on the Nergal."

Princess Odriin, who had been quietly observing from the side, stepped forward. "Two Earth years after we entered stasis.... That's when the signal would have reached them."

Enki-Marduk nodded gravely. "Precisely, Princess. They must have prepared for the long wait, ensuring the survival of our people until your return." His voice softened as he turned his attention back to Zulu. "Captain, it would be our honour to assist your team in reaching the station. We can A.R.T. them directly aboard once they're prepared."
Zulu exchanged a glance with Nin, then back to Enki-Marduk. "Thank you, Captain. We'll assemble the team immediately."
Enki-Marduk gave a respectful nod, his holographic form shimmering slightly. "Let me know when they are ready, Captain. We stand by." With that, his image dissolved, leaving an air of anticipation on the bridge.

Zulu turned to his crew. "Alright, everyone, let's get to work. Aria, coordinate with Commander Shepard and prepare the team for the away mission ."

A few hours had passed since Shepard's team had been teleported aboard the orbital station. The intercom buzzed sharply, breaking through the steady hum of the ship. Commander Shepard's voice came through, tense and urgent from the Caral Orbital Station.

"Captain Zulu, you need to come down here in person. There's something... I can't explain over comms. You have to see it for yourself."

Zulu, seated at the command console, frowned and leaned forward. "Shepard, what's going on? Are we in danger?"

There was a pause, followed by Shepard's clipped response. "No immediate danger, Captain, but... it's strange. I need you here."

Zulu glanced at the crew and sighed. "Alright, Shepard. I'll request an A.R.T. to the station. I'm on my way."

Zulu appeared on the Caral Orbital Station in a flash. The air felt heavy, like something big was about to happen. Engineers worked carefully, their eyes locked on their tasks, while priestesses adorned in intricate, flowing robes glided gracefully through the station. Their measured movements and ritualistic gestures felt important as they prepared to awaken the station's slumbering population.

But it wasn't the priestesses that caught Zulu's attention, it was the small gathering near Shepard. His crew surrounded a man, laughing softly at some shared banter. The man was old, human, and entirely out of place.

Zulu approached cautiously, his eyes narrowing as he studied the stranger. "Shepard," he said, his voice low and commanding. "What was so urgent that I had to come down here? And who...." His gaze shifted to the old man, who turned to meet his eyes with a warm, knowing smile. ".... is this?"

Before Shepard could answer, the old man stood. He looked weak, but his eyes were sharp. "Zulu," he said, his voice strong but heavy with meaning. "I finally made it. How's Tashia?"

The name stopped Zulu cold. His composure faltered as he stared at the man. "What? How do you know Tashia?" he demanded.

The old man took a step closer, his expression softening. "Because, Zulu, I know you. I *am* you."

Zulu blinked, stunned. He turned sharply to Dr. James, who had been quietly observing the exchange. "Doctor, is this some kind of sick joke? Explain!"

James shook his head gravely. "Captain.... I've run every test. Biometrics, DNA, neural scans. He is you, though significantly older. I don't know how, but the evidence is clear."

Zulu turned back to the man. "This is impossible," he muttered. "You're telling me, you're me? From when? From where?"

The old man nodded solemnly. "From a timeline, you'll never want to live through. I'm here to stop it. Listen to me, Zulu. Don't let Tashia set foot on Proxima B."

"Why? What happened on Proxima B?" Zulu's voice was sharp, but there was a hint of trepidation beneath it.

The old man sighed deeply, his eyes glistening. "I made mistakes, Zulu. My timeline fell. Tashia, your crew, Shepard, they all paid the price."

Zulu's fists clenched. "What mistakes?"

The old man took a shaky breath. "It started with discovering an ancient Caral portal on Proxima B. We found a stasis pod, awakening a Caral scientist who had been asleep for millennia. But we didn't just wake him.... we woke the Tots."

The mention of the Tots made Zulu stiffen. "The Tots? They attacked?"

"Like a storm of fury," the old man said bitterly. "Their soldiers descended on us. Their technology overwhelmed us. And the traps on the planet.... they were ancient but deadly. Five of our crew were vaporised. Including...." He stopped, his voice cracking. ".... Tashia. My wife."

Zulu staggered back a step, his heart pounding. "Tashia? No.... that can't be...."

The old man's voice cracked as he began, his weary eyes reflecting the weight of his memories. "I couldn't even grieve. We were too busy fighting for survival. Every step forward, I lost someone I cared about. Until there was no one left, just me and the Caral scientist on this planet. That's when I found the portal."

Captain Zulu leaned forward, his breath uneven, the tension thick. "The portal... what did it do?"

"It saved us," the old man admitted, his tone laced with both gratitude and regret. "But the cost… the cost was almost unimaginable. The Caral scientist tried to warn me, that the portal wasn't ready. It required critical maintenance, but the universal translator couldn't fully interpret his language. I couldn't understand the full extent of the risks he was trying to convey."

He paused, his gaze drifting to some distant, haunting memory. "We didn't have the luxury of time. The Sundial… it was going to detonate. I overheard the Odyssey's intercom; Nin was giving the desperate order to trigger the Sundial. The Tot Armada had surrounded the ship, pounding it relentlessly. The Odyssey fought valiantly, taking down many of their vessels, but the sheer numbers were overwhelming.

"They had no choice but to set off the Sundial, even knowing it would ignite a supernova. It would obliterate the entire Proxima Centauri system. I… I knew what that meant. I knew we had seconds before everything was incinerated."

Zulu clenched his fists, his voice barely above a whisper. "And then?"

"I made a decision," the man continued, his voice

trembling. "The Caral scientist was weak from his messy awakening. We hadn't followed the protocol to properly bring him out of stasis. He was disoriented and barely coherent. But I grabbed him. I activated the portal and pulled him through, just as the supernova's energy began tearing through the planet's atmosphere, incinerating everything in its path."

Zulu's eyes widened. "You went through the portal… into the unknown?"

"Yes," the old man said, his voice heavy with emotion. "When we emerged on the other side, we were disoriented, both physically and mentally. And then, I realised the unthinkable had happened. The portal had flung us two hundred and fifty thousand years into the past. We found ourselves in the midst of the Caral's ancient war with the Tot Empire.

"The scientist… he recognised it instantly. His despair was overwhelming. We weren't just in another time; we were in an era when his people were at the height of their struggle. And now, we were stranded there."

Zulu exhaled slowly, the enormity of the revelation settling over him like a suffocating blanket. "Two hundred and fifty thousand years… to the Caral's war with the Tots. That's… incomprehensible."

The old man's eyes met Zulu's, filled with the weight of centuries. "It was both a salvation and a curse. The portal saved us from certain death, but it delivered us to a battlefield we didn't belong in. It's a burden I've carried ever since."

The room went quiet, and everyone felt the story's weight in their minds.

Zulu was silent, his eyes locked on the older man's tearful face.

The old man's gaze turned distant as he began his story, his voice carrying the weight of decades, or perhaps centuries. "When I arrived in their time, I met the grand clan Ekkur kings of the Caral people. Their system of governance isn't like ours; they have many kingships, each ruling over different regions. At first, they were wary of me, a human, a stranger in their midst. But desperation has a way of opening doors."

Zulu listened intently, leaning forward slightly. "What did you tell them?"

"I told them I had a plan," the old man said firmly. "A way to fight off the Tots. They were hesitant, but they listened. Slowly, I gained their trust by helping them push back against the Tot incursions in their distant galaxy. My knowledge, fragmented as it was, became a weapon they could wield. Everything was set in motion, and then… your arrival changed everything."

He paused, his expression softening. "With time on my hands, I devised a new strategy. I realised I had to accelerate the timeline. I knew I couldn't return to my own era, but maybe, just maybe, I could create an opportunity for my younger self to succeed where I failed. So, I began quietly working to draw you here, to Alpha Centauri, a full ten years earlier than I had originally ventured there myself."

Zulu's brow furrowed. "Ten years earlier? That's why we're here now instead of later?"

The old man nodded. "Yes. It took patience and careful manipulation. But I knew you'd need every advantage you could get to face what's coming."

Shepard, standing by the door, folded his arms and chimed in. "And what about the Carals? You said they entered stasis. How did that happen?"

The old man exhaled slowly, his eyes clouding with memory. "It happened in stages. Amid the planning, there came a point when I had no choice but to join them. The Carals began speaking of their princess, how she hadn't returned and had gone into hibernation. With their king preparing to enter stasis, the decision was made for the entire orbital station to follow suit. It was a protocol they enacted in times of uncertainty."

Princess Odriin, who had entered silently, stepped closer. "You were with them? In stasis, all this time?"

"They prepared a pod for me," the old man admitted, his voice tinged with a mix of bitterness and resignation. "I felt utterly lost. A human among an alien species, caught in a chain of events I couldn't fully understand. But there was no other option. I entered stasis with them, unsure of whether I'd ever wake again, or what kind of future awaited."

Zulu crossed his arms, his gaze sharp. "And now that you're awake? What's the plan?"

The old man's eyes sparkled with determination. "Now

we'll see if my efforts with the Carals have paid off. I've spent my time here sharpening their battle readiness, and your arrival, Captain, is exactly what they've been waiting for.

Princess Odriin stepped forward; her voice calm yet firm. "Why do I have no memory of you in my kingdom? Your presence was kept so secret that even I, the princess, knew nothing of your existence. The first time I heard of humans was through the crew of the Odyssey. Tonight, when my father awakens, I will demand an audience. He owes me answers."

The old man inclined his head respectfully. "Of course, Princess. I'm certain your father will provide you with the clarity you seek, and perhaps more. As for my secrecy, it was a deliberate choice. I restricted knowledge of my presence to as few individuals as possible to minimise interference with the timeline. Any significant contamination could have unforeseen and catastrophic consequences for humanity."

Captain Zulu, standing with his arms crossed, raised an eyebrow. "Understood. Now, what's that plan of yours?"

To be continued…